I0703862

GENERATION WITCH:

AWAKENING

Nanci M. Pattenden

Generation Witch: Rebirth

Copyright © 2025 Nanci M. Pattenden

All rights reserved. No part of this book may be used or reproduced by any means, graphic, electronic, or mechanical, including photocopying, recording, taping or by any information storage retrieval system without the written permission of the publisher except in the case of brief quotations embodied in critical articles and reviews.

This is a work of fiction. All characters, names, incidents, organizations, and dialogue in this novel are either the products of the author's imagination or are used fictitiously.

Published by Purrfect Press
Ontario, Canada
www.purrfectpress.com

The views expressed in this work are solely those of the author and do not necessarily reflect the views of the publisher, and the publisher hereby disclaims any responsibility for them.

ISBN: 978-1-998860-02-9 (print)
ISBN: 978-1-998860-03-6 (e-book)

1 2 3 4 5 6 7 8 9 0

Generation Witch

Rebirth (Book 1)

Awakening (Book 2)

Detective Hodgins Victorian Murder Mysteries

Body in the Harbour

Death on Duchess Street

Corpses for Christmas

Books 1 to 3 Collection

Homicide on the Homestead

United in Holy Deadlock

Abduction of Life

D.E.M.ON. Tales Series

Assassin Eco-Corpses

Bobcat Got Your Tongue?

A Craptacular Understatement

Double Dog Dare Ya

Even Equines Don't Like Liver

Frozen Foes and Dominoes

Growing Up Grim

Hoodoo in the Loo

The Improbable Goog Pursuit

Junk in the Trunk

ACKNOWLEDGMENTS

As always, a great, big thank you to my editor, MJ Moores of Infinite Pathways, and Christopher Watts, my graphics guru.

THANK YOU

ONE

*I*t had only been a couple of months, but I couldn't shake the blues. Ever since Cooper left for Nova Scotia to help settle his gramps, recuperating from a heart attack, I'd felt lost.

I needed time to heal after we'd taken care of Uncle Montgomery. *Taken care of. That sounds so final, gangster-like.* He wasn't dead. At least I didn't think so. Besides, he'd killed my mother and grandmother, and come after me and the rest of my family. None of us really knew where he went. He simply vanished, with the help of the spirts of Mother and Granny. *Maybe they pulled him into their realm?*

Shortly after my twenty-first birthday, Great Aunt Priscilla and her daughter Susan returned to Dorking, England. Cousin Drew stayed longer to help with my witchy re-education. Our lessons now happened via video chat.

I kept my promise to Melissa, a.k.a. Missy, my childhood friend who recently returned to Ontario from Cairo. We'd become good friends over the last few months. She taught me a lot about the old Egyptian ways and superstition, but it only scraped the surface. Some of it seemed to align with magick. In return, I told her everything I knew about crystals. We were both interested in runes and other types of symbology, and learned those together.

With her new knowledge, her boss at the private museum near Peterborough let her have the lead on a fae exhibit, to be revealed a week before Hallowe'en, or Samhain, for those celebrating the old ways. She also expressed an interest in witchcraft and dabbled a little with minor spells. Dabbled responsibly. She promised not to try anything without my supervision. She turned out to be a quick learner.

Needing to earn a living, I took over Granny's potion business. Most of it was basic herbology, with a little spell or two worked in. Due to the unexpected inheritance, I didn't actually need to work; just wanted something to do. Several of Mother's old clients approached me about resurrecting her fortune telling business. I had great success with the séance last June, and the few clients I'd taken on seemed satisfied. Drew's fiancé, Randy, an over-the-top, but legit fortune teller, guided me via video calls. They'd set their wedding for Yule. Cooper would be my plus one. We both looked forward to spending Yule and Christmas in England.

An alert buzzed on my phone. A few seconds later, Nenka spoke from behind me.

"It's time, dear."

I jumped, spilling my coffee.

At least once a day since inheriting Granny's house, the little six-inch wood gnome snuck up on me, sending my heart racing. I think she enjoyed startling me. One of these days, I was certain my heart would give out. But I loved her. Nenka, her husband Tinkus, and son Nimagg, were my extended family.

"I'll never get used to you appearing out of nowhere like that. If you were a cat, I'd put a bell on you."

Her eyes twinkled. "Are you ready for your next lesson?"

While Drew helped me with the witchy side of things, Nenka taught me about the plants in Granny's garden. She also took care of them, fortunately. To say I had a black thumb was an understatement. More like a black hand. Both of them. Even plants that were almost indestructible withered under my loving care.

For the past month, we dealt with love potions, because that's what the majority of clients asked for. Pretty soon, people would want cold and flu remedies. So many folks these days were getting away from the store-bought stuff. We had a few joint lessons with Drew because a spell had to be included while mixing the potions, but I had the spell part down pat, more or less. Today, we were mixing up a batch of medicinal potions.

Several of my clients overlapped, wanting a reading and a potion. I had a group from the seniors-only residence who'd dubbed themselves the Grey-haired Grannies. About half of them still had their natural hair colour, and a few weren't anyone's grandmother, but they didn't care. They were the most energetic group of ladies of any age I'd seen in a long time.

One of them had rheumatoid arthritis, and nothing her doctor prescribed helped with the pain. She found some relief from one of Granny's medicines and was due in a couple of hours for a fresh batch. Granny had given her a couple of bottles shortly before passing late last spring, and the last bottle was almost empty. I hadn't made it before and was nervous.

"Ready when you are, Nenka. I've already laid out the recipe book, tools, and bottles on the work bench. Just need to gather the ingredients."

"Yes, I noticed. Pick up the basket and join me in the garden." She headed into the sunporch and waited for me to open the back door.

"Don't take this the wrong way, but would you like me to have a little door cut so you can come and go easily?"

"You mean a doggie door?" She shook her head, frowning. "No, dear. I don't believe I'd enjoy crawling out like an animal."

"No, no. A proper door, like in the tree. Complete with a locking latch on the inside."

Nenka laughed. "What is it you young people say? Yanking your chain? I don't need any extra doors. Thank you anyway."

"Yanking my chain. Good one." I picked up the basket and opened the door, following Nenka into the garden.

She pulled a piece of paper from her apron pocket. I'd written out the ingredient list yesterday and left it on the worktable in the basement. "We need fresh ginger, one garlic bulb, and some willow bark. There's already thyme drying in the workshop, and you've lots of cinnamon sticks. Why don't you ask the willow for some of her bark? About a cup should do."

I went to the garden shed and grabbed a box of fertilizer, specially made for trees. Long ago, I'd learned that you never took anything from a tree without asking permission from it and leaving a gift. People who didn't know better would leave crystals and other shiny things. Pretty, but useless. You have to leave something the tree can use. Fertilizer was always a good go-to.

Granny's property contained almost every sort of plant needed for potions and spells. She had a spiral of herbs that rose in height as you made your way along the circular path. I generally fell off it at least once a week. Tucked away in the far corner was what I always called the death garden. Every plant in it was deadly, if you consumed enough of it.

Most people knew about the poppy giving us opium and getting Botox from the hibiscus. Both are good for pain relief in the correct dose. Granny had also planted the foul-smelling henbane for bladder conditions and COPD, foxglove for digitalis, and sweet clover for warfarin. In small amounts, they're used in traditional medicine. So far, I hadn't needed anything from it. To tell the truth, those plants scared me. And the thought of using them? Terrifying.

I went over to the willow and parted the hanging branches. This is where I had my ceremony when I turned twenty-one in July. It had always been my special place growing up, and it held a doorway for the gnomes. I'd made a promise to Nenka to add more decorations to it, but so far hadn't gotten around to it. *Soon.*

Placing one hand on the trunk, I asked for permission to take one of its branches. The tree responded by gently rustling its leaves. After sprinkling a generous amount of fertilizer, I carefully cut one of the older branches. I'd strip the bark in the workshop. Nenka joined me under the canopy of the willow, dragging the basket filled with ingredients.

"I'll meet you in the workshop and we can begin." She left the basket for me to carry in and opened the tiny door in the tree trunk. "Don't dawdle."

I put the box of fertilizer and snippers back in the shed and went inside. Every time I pushed the near-invisible button on the wainscotting in the front hall, I got goosebumps. The hidden doorway into the basement whooshed open. It felt like stepping into another world. I turned on the light, removed my shoes and socks, then padded down the wooden stairs. Bare feet weren't mandatory, but the earth felt soothing. It also made it easier to ground. I placed the basket on the worktable. Nenka climbed up the staircase I'd had built for her. Even though she was somewhere around a hundred, she was still young for a gnome. Nenka climbed up onto the bench, then the tabletop, and down again regularly, and that had taken an unexpected toll on her knees. *At least that's one promise I kept.*

I opened the well-used medicinal recipe book to the page Granny titled *For Cora*. She had two recipes for arthritis. Cora's was extra strength, since her pain was so strong. Nenka read off the ingredients and amounts. I chopped and ground, reciting the spell that enhanced the potion. When the chunks of ginger and garlic broke down, their combined scents created an odd fragrance. Both gave off a pungent odour, but the ginger countered with a spicy, citrusy scent. Once prepared, I took three dark brown bottles from the shelf, slapped a label on them, and wrote Cora's name. Below that, two runes, the last part of the spell.

"Thank you, Nenka. I know you're doing a little more work with me than you had to with Granny, but I'll get there."

"I don't mind. Makes me feel useful."

The doorbell rang. Granny had the foresight to have the wiring extended to a speaker in the basement. The hidden space was basically soundproof, mainly to keep sounds in, not out. I quickly filled the bottles, put the cork stopper in, and raced upstairs, not bothering with my shoes.

Two of the Grannies stood on the porch. Cora, and her friend and chauffeur, Mary-Beth.

"Come in, ladies. Would you like a coffee or tea?"

They stepped inside. "No time. It's Lose Your Shirt Day. Won't tell you what we call poker night. Bus will be arriving soon to take us to the Great Blue Heron Casino." Cora eyed the bottles. "Got my order ready?"

"Yes. Finished it a few minutes ago. Give me a sec and I'll get a bag."

"You come into the twenty-first century yet, or is it still cash only?"

When I came back, I carried my brand new Square Reader. "Twenty-first century. I picked it up yesterday. You get the honour of christening it, so you can keep your cash for something more frivolous."

Cora paid and they hurried out to the car, not wanting to be late for the bus.

"Good luck." I waved as they drove off.

My phone dinged the same time I closed the door. *Cooper!*

"Hey, Coop. What's up? How's your Gramps?"

"Restless. We finished the extension to Dad's house and got Gramps moved out of the guest room and into his own private space. Now we have to get the rest of his things out of storage. Wanted to let you know I'll be back on Saturday. Would you mind printing up a sign for the bookstore? It'll be open for business on Monday. Gramps already spread the word to your crowd that I'm taking over. He's had several emails for requests, both books and special items. I've helped him fill them and couriered most of the items, witch express." Cooper laughed.

Cooper's family were helpers, or *cuideachaidh* in Gaelic. When witches needed an item they couldn't locate, they reached out to his people. Sometimes a location spell wasn't enough if searching for something too personal. *Maybe one day I'll understand how they work. Don't really care. Cooper's coming back.* Even though we only met after my granny died a few months ago, we'd become close. I'd resisted the electricity between us, what with having my hands full avoiding my great uncle's attempts to eliminate me. An uncle I knew nothing about, and baby brother my Auntie P. thought long dead.

We chatted for almost an hour, then he had to help his dad retrieve Gramps' things from storage. I missed Mr. Barker, but his heart attack finally convinced him to move to Nova Scotia with his son and daughter-in-law. Growing up without grandparents, he always felt like my grandfather. He'd sold the antique book shop to Cooper at a greatly reduced family rate, and reluctantly boarded the plane. Cooper went back with him to help his dad renovate. After a long month and a half of texting, calls and video chats, I could let my feelings for him develop. My life was finally becoming normal. I thought about Elspeth's reading of my palm in England. Normal for a witch who somehow had to restore her family's dwindling powers.

I made up the sign Cooper requested and headed to town to post it. He'd given me a spare key so I could pop in occasionally, make sure nothing went amiss, and pick up messages from the store phone. He took care of the emails. I'd spent some time cleaning up the apartment over the store, since I knew Cooper would move in, eventually.

On the way, I picked up a few non-perishable groceries so he wouldn't have to bother with that for the first few days. While recuperating, Mr. Barker was forbidden from using the stairs, so Cooper and his father had turned the back room into a bedroom. The area hadn't been touched since the move, so one weekend Missy helped me rearrange the furniture back to how it had been. The bed got shoved against the far wall. Cooper could deal with that.

Before leaving, I texted Missy to find out if she wanted to hear about a book I recently discovered.

Found an old book on runes. Want to see it?

Duh! Yes. Free now?

On my way.

With one last look around the store, I squeezed into my little lava-orange Smart Car and headed towards Peterborough. The museum Missy worked at was a little off the beaten path. Most of the visitors were school groups. Even though it was privately run, everyone was welcome. They still needed to spread the word to the general population to let people know the place existed.

Less than an hour later, I drove up their gravel driveway. The scenery along the way was spectacular. Most of the leaves were already turning beautiful shades of red, orange, and yellow. The perfect spot to practice some of my spells and commune with nature. Going back to my earliest memories, I had an affinity with trees. When I walked to the entrance, a blue jay screamed at me. Probably the same one that screeched every time I arrived. The sound of my car likely alerted Missy, who stood waiting for me.

She stepped onto the porch and closed the door. "I'm so glad you texted. I kinda tried a spell on my own yesterday and, well, it didn't go exactly as planned."

"Oh, no. I warned you about that. You haven't had enough training. Even I need Drew or her mom when I try certain spells. Please tell me you didn't blow anything up or start a fire."

"No. Nothing like that. There's this guy."

I smiled. "Ah. You did a love spell. What happened?"

"Not really sure. He's suddenly infatuated with someone else. Someone he didn't even like. They have, or at least had, a mutual dislike. Now she's royally pissed at all the attention and he doesn't even notice me any more. Please tell me you can help fix it."

"I need to know everything you did. Exactly. Word for word. You probably said something that wasn't specific enough. Do you have your spell book with you?"

"Yes. It's locked in my desk."

Fifteen minutes later, we huddled in the corner of the basement, away from prying eyes and ears. Missy showed me the spell she recited.

"Here's the problem. Like I thought, you weren't specific enough. He flipped for the first person he saw, and unfortunately, it wasn't you. There should be a way to reverse it, but I don't know it offhand." I checked the time. "Drew will know. We can video call her. She'll still be at her shop. I'm certain she can help. Then we can go over the rune book I found."

After a twenty-minute discussion, we had the reversal spell, along with a few details on Drew's wedding plans, including the latest picture of her dress.

"Thanks, cuz. I'll call you later and we can have a proper chat."

Missy peered over my shoulder. "Thank you, Drew. I promise not to try stuff on my own again until I'm better trained."

"You'd better not have your fingers crossed behind your back." Drew smiled. "Let me know how it comes out. Gotta go. Customer just came in."

I put my phone down and turned to Missy. "Unfortunately, we can't do this right now. We need a few items, and I don't carry herbs around with me. Can you come to my place tonight? We can fix it then."

She frowned. "Guess I can wait a few more hours. I'll come over when we close. I'll even pick up pizza."

"Perfect. I'll have everything ready. Now, let's have a look at this book. Strange, I'd never seen it at the bookstore before. It mysteriously appeared on the shelf. I suppose it's possible Mr. Barker ordered it before his heart attack, but there haven't been any shipments and I've gone through the shelves numerous times since he left. Must have overlooked it."

Missy grinned. "I doubt that. I bet it was sent because you need it." She mimicked waving a wand.

We spent all of Missy's lunch hour going through the runes in the book. Her boss had to go to a meeting, so we managed another hour with only a couple of interruptions from the only other employee in the museum.

Once I arrived home, I grabbed everything Drew mentioned to reverse the ill-worded spell and set up on the dining room table. Even though Missy seemed keen on learning about spells, there was no way she'd ever find out about the hidden workshop in the basement. That was family only. Cooper and his grandfather hadn't even been allowed in, despite knowing the true nature of my family.

It would be a couple of hours before my friend arrived, so I grabbed a romance novel and headed to the living room. When I crossed to the sofa, I swayed with a wave of nausea and lightheadedness. I reached out and grabbed the tall cabinet, where I displayed several crystals, to steady myself. *What the heck?*

It had been years since I was sick, and I hadn't been exposed to anyone with an illness. Out of the corner of my eye, something flashed. I turned to look, but there was nothing. And the dizziness stopped. *Weird.*

Four chapters in, another flash caught my peripheral vision. This time, nothing affected me. *Coincidence.* Halfway through the novel, the doorbell rang. The waft of melted cheese and pepperoni hit me before the door opened. Missy held a super-sized box from Score Pizza.

TWO

"Um, I don't think we can eat all that." I took the box and put it in the kitchen, Missy following close behind.

"It's a bribe. Can I stay over tonight? By the time we get finished, it'll be late. It's already dark and you know how steep the ditches are along Highway 7A. All I need is one deer to dart out, and I'm six feet down, probably with a broken axel."

"Sure. Plenty of room. You not working tomorrow?"

"No such luck. I'll be out of your hair bright and early." She made a face. "Well, maybe not bright."

We dug into the pizza, then made our way into the living room. Another dizzy spell struck.

"Hey, you okay?" Missy grabbed my arm when I faltered. "You got a strobe or something set up?"

"No. Why?" *Did she see a flash?*

"Could have sworn a red light flashed a few times. Must have been tail lights from a passing car."

"Yeah. Probably." *Not likely. The trees hide the property from the road. The only opening is the driveway, almost a hundred feet from the house.*

Fixing the poorly thought out spell Missy performed only took ten minutes. It wouldn't make the guy she liked become interested in her, but the mutual dislike between him and the other woman would return.

"Done. Do you want me to help you with a better spell?"

Missy shook her head. "No. I think I'll join one of those dating apps. I'd rather have someone like me for me, and not because of a spell."

"Better plan. I've got something to show you." I'd also found a book on wiccan symbols when at Mr. Barker's bookstore, cleverly called Antique Books. *Cooper's store, not Mr. Barkers.* I placed it on the coffee table while we ate. It was a basic book, kind of a beginner's guide to wiccan symbols. Missy already knew some. Well, three. The pentagram, triquetra, and the faerie star. She just didn't know the meaning behind them.

"Did you bring a notebook? Something other than your spell book."

Missy pulled a small spiral book from her bag, along with a pen. The book had an ankh on the cover, the matching pen had a small one for a topper. Not surprising, since her family moved to Cairo about fifteen years ago for her father's work.

"I came prepared. I've got stacks of notebooks with Egyptian stuff on them. The sphinx, pyramids, photos of King Tut's burial mask. You name it. If it's Egyptian, I've probably got a book with a picture of it on the cover."

"That's perfect. I think we should go over the meanings behind the symbols in depth this evening. Let's start with something basic, like the pentagram. People often confuse it with a pentacle. The pentagram is the five-pointed star. When you draw a circle around it, it becomes a pentacle. The five points represent the elements: Spirit, Air, Earth, Water, and Fire. The circle around it connects them all."

She wrote while I talked. I didn't need to look at the book for that one. Bit by bit, we worked through the first couple of chapters. She'd already memorized some of the symbols. Several times she glanced around the room, but said nothing. She must have seen the same flashes I did. At least they didn't bring on any more nausea or dizziness. That only seemed to happen when I got near the cabinet.

By eleven thirty, Missy yawned for the third time. "Sorry. It's been a long day."

"And you need to get up early. I'll show you where you can bed down. It's Granny's old room. You'll love the view from the balcony. It overlooks the garden. The garden lights make it seem magickal."

She hadn't stopped home to pack, so I gave her one of my nightgowns, then went back down to investigate the mysterious red flashes. When I approached the cabinet, the dizziness hit. *This isn't normal. Oh, God! Has Uncle Monty returned?*

Careful examination of the contents revealed nothing. I turned off the lights and stood in front, waiting for another flash. Nothing. Twenty minutes passed. Still nothing. I turned to leave and another flash went off. Nausea. *What the…?*

One by one, I removed items from the cabinet and examined them. Everything seemed normal. Regular crystals, doing nothing. The only thing red in there was the egg-shaped ruby crystal that Uncle Montgomery used to try to weaken me.

Hmm. Auntie P. warned me not to use the egg. Why? It wasn't flashing, but when I reached for it, I could feel something. Power? Energy? Evil? *Nope. Not touching it.*

After putting everything back on their shelves, I headed for bed. First thing in the morning, a call to Susan or Auntie P. would be necessary. What was it about that crystal egg? I started to get into bed, but something stopped me. A nagging feeling that I needed protection. My wooden box of assorted crystals sat tucked into the corner of my closet. I needed black tourmaline. After choosing a small stone, I closed the lid, then opened it again and took out a couple of pieces of clear quartz and one raw quartz cluster. The tourmaline went under my pillow to absorb any negativity that might make its way towards me. I put the cut quartz and raw cluster on the window sill. Even though the moon wasn't quite full, it was good enough to charge the crystals. I had a feeling I'd be needing them soon to help answer the questions running through my mind. *Why hadn't Auntie P. given me more information on the ruby? "Don't use it" wasn't much to go on. Why can't I use it? Why did it emit energy? And why did it flash and make me ill?*

Sleep came fast, but didn't linger. I woke up at 3:33 a.m. Half the devil's number. *Did that mean anything?* The house was quiet, but felt disturbed. I got up, grabbed the quartz cluster off the sill and put it under the pillow with the tourmaline. A swoop of pterodactyls flew around in my stomach. Something was up. Pterodactyls were my go-to feeling that something wicked this way comes. The house needed smudging. I quickly tiptoed down to the workroom, but Nenka beat me.

"Something's not right." The diminutive gnome wrung her hands, a nervous habit.

"You feel it too? I think the house needs to be smudged." I automatically reached for a sage bundle, but Nenka stopped me.

"No. The sage is for healing. You need to protect the house. Cedar." She pointed to a bundle further down the drying line strung across the room.

"Thanks. I got this. Go back to bed."

Nenka stayed put until I lit the cedar. Inhaling the woodsy scent, I walked the perimeter of the basement, then gave her a tiny bundle for their domain. Fanning the smoke with my hand, I went from room to room, floor to floor. When I got to Granny's old room, I slowly opened the door. Missy seemed to be sleeping soundly. I tiptoed around the room, then continued, even doing the rarely used third floor. Once the entire house had been done, I put the rest of the bundle in a bowl on my dresser and let it burn itself out.

The flying dinos settled down and let me sleep. I woke two hours later and heard water crashing in the shower. Missy was up. I dressed and went to the kitchen to start breakfast. Frozen waffles and bacon. She walked in as I took the bacon off the stove. I pressed the lever on the toaster for the waffles.

"Morning, Missy. Sleep well?"

"Yes. Thanks again for letting me stay. You didn't need to make breakfast."

I picked up the empty waffle box. "Frozen food. My specialty. Coffee? I have several to-go cups so you can take it with you."

She sifted through the selection of coffee and tea pods. "I'll try this one." She put the Mexico Dark Roast in the Keurig and leaned on the counter. "I had the weirdest dream. Someone walking around my room smoking."

Not wanting to alarm her, I said nothing about my smudging. "Yeah, that is weird."

After she left, I called Auntie P. "You told me not to use the egg but didn't explain why. I swear I haven't touched it except to place it on the shelf and occasionally dust it. Why is it suddenly emitting an energy, making me dizzy and ill?"

"That crystal egg must be infused with something dark. Could be magick. Could be something dreadful. It will be virtually impossible to reverse it without knowing the exact spell. If we try to cleanse it, we could make it worse."

Not what I wanted to hear. I'd felt the full force of the power within it. The crystal egg literally sucked the breath out of me when Uncle Monty used it against me. The memory occasionally gave me nightmares. *Was that another effect of the egg?* Instinctively, I reached for my throat.

"There must be something we can do. A way to block it? Anything? Put it in a special case surrounded by salt?"

Auntie P. laughed. "That only works in movies and TV shows. It's much more complicated than that. If it was simple, all cursed items could easily be contained. No. Somehow, we need to find what's controlling it."

Schist! Without Monty, practically impossible.

We had to do something before it got worse. "Do you think circling with salt or brimstone would slow it down? It helped when we poofed Uncle Monty."

Auntie P. took a deep breath. "Well, I don't suppose it would do any harm. I'll contact Susan and some of the elders. Maybe we can think of something. We've been more like a coven, unofficially, since you found the lost caves. We never stayed isolated like your family, but we kept to ourselves half of the time. You know, I don't even remember why our ancestors disbanded the coven. It happened two generations before me. I don't think there's anyone still living who would know."

"Thanks, Auntie. Meanwhile, I'll get some brimstone and try to avoid the area. Maybe I'll bury it."

She waved her arms frantically. "No, no, no. If you bury it without cleansing it, the bad energy will seep into the soil. Avoid it when possible, and if the effects get worse, call me immediately, regardless of the time."

We disconnected, and I rushed down to the workroom to check the supplies for brimstone. Nothing. The small amount I'd bought was used to send Monty wherever it was he went to. Brimstone was another name for sulfur. Easy enough to obtain. Fertilizer companies used it, but since I wanted it for protection and not the garden, a wiccan store would be best. There'd be nothing added to it, and maybe they even sold it raw. *Freshly ground would be stronger.*

The drive to the closest wiccan supply store was short. Unfortunately, they were out of brimstone. The owner gave me the names of a couple of suppliers of rocks and crystals that might have it in stock. One was way out in the country, the other in the city. If I was going to get lost, I'd rather do it somewhere I could simply hop on the subway to make my way back. Before making the trip, a quick phone call was needed. Save me going down for nothing.

Luck was with me. I drove down Highway 404 to Finch and took the subway into the heart of Toronto. The man at the store thought my request odd.

"Peculiar thing for a young lady to be buying. Hope it's for fertilizer and not a bomb." His laughter turned to coughing. Smokers cough by the smell of him. The yellowing on his fingers and mustache indicated a very heavy smoker.

I glanced at the name on his shirt. "Good one, Fred. The only bomb I'll ever be making is a bug bomb for the garden. Seriously, though, I don't like using chemicals or mass-produced products in the garden. Sulfur is a natural element, even though it stinks."

While I was there, I looked through the store, picking up a few raw crystals and several polished gemstones that were hard to find, including a larimar. You never know when you're going to need something exotic. A half hour later, I had more than I went in for. When in a store that sells gems, like a crow, I can't resist all that's shiny and sparkly.

They also had a large supply of black obsidian. I had a few raw and polished pieces, but something told me to stock up. I selected two dozen smaller pieces. They would go into the basement with the brimstone.

When I got home, I put on my black tourmaline bracelet and stuffed my pockets with every stone in my collection that even remotely helped protect against negativity. There was no way to avoid getting close to the egg, and I needed to shield myself from the negative energy it emitted. Tourmaline, onyx, amethyst, obsidian, and a new purchase today, shungite. They needed to be smudged with some cedar. A small bundle went into one bowl, the obsidians in another beside it. While the smoke circled around the stone, I grabbed the mortar and pestle.

Once enough brimstone had been ground into a fine power, I poured it into a dish, picked up a pair of heavy work gloves to protect my skin from burning, then ran up and into the living room. The gemstones in my pockets jingled at every step.

Immediately after entering the living room, I felt it. This time, the effects were minimal. *Gemstones rock, pun intended!* I put on the gloves and drew a circle around the crystal with the crushed stone, still amazed at how the beautiful ruby crystal egg could cause so much harm. Satisfied with the thick layer of black powder, I took the obsidians and placed them in a circle around the brimstone. Double circle, double protection, fingers crossed. *Should I have said a spell? Too late now.*

The alert on my phone buzzed. *Shoot. Running late.* My thirty-minute reminder that one of my mother's regulars had an appointment. Mother had been dead for about eight years, and when her clients saw me at Granny's funeral and discovered I'd moved into her house, they practically fought one another for my time. I needed to juggle both Mother's and Granny's clientele. Some wanted readings, some potions. A few wanted both.

As an experiment, I held a séance for a few of Mother's clients three months ago. Some of the Grey Haired Grannies. They were chosen simply because I remembered their names. It went amazingly well, so I started accepting appointments. Today, it was Mrs. McGillicuddy, one of my earlier guinea pigs. Not only did her late husband come through along with their deceased dog, but my ancestor, Fiona, put in an appearance. Fiona was the reason we were successful in banishing Uncle Montgomery. *I wonder...*

THREE

Mrs. McGillicuddy liked to change things up. Sometimes it was a tarot reading, occasionally palmistry. Today was a crystal ball day. That was something still being learned, but she enjoyed watching me figure things out.

As usual, she arrived right on time. While she settled, I lit the patchouli incense and two candles, then dimmed the lights. After grounding, I sat in the chair opposite her at the large, round wooden dining table. The crystal ball sat on purple lace in front of me, covered with a piece of fabric, suitably printed with stars and galaxies.

"This is so exciting." Mrs. McGillicuddy treated every reading like her first. I couldn't believe she was in her nineties. She had more fun than me. *Maybe when Cooper gets back I could start having fun?*

"What would you like to know today? Love? Money? Health?" I removed the cloth and laid both hands on the crystal ball, waiting.

Mrs. McGillicuddy giggled. "Love. There's a new resident, and all the single ladies are clambering after him. He has the most beautiful head of silver hair."

Smiling, I nodded, closed my eyes, then concentrated on the question. There was no specific amount of time to concentrate. Sometimes it came quick, other times, not so fast. The crystal ball started to get warm. My cue to look for an answer. Removing my hands, I stared into the ball. Nothing happened at first, then a tiny wisp of pale green smoke appeared. Then another, this time pink. *Hmm, pink?*

I racked my brain for the colours listed in my book. Green could mean prosperity and harmony, but pink hadn't been listed. *Not everything is in a book. Pink quartz is for love. Maybe pink smoke is too.*

"Is something wrong, Marcy? You look puzzled."

"What? Sorry. Trying to process what I'm seeing. Harmony and love. Unfortunately, I can't tell you the name of your suitor. Maybe if you place a rose quartz under your pillow, you'll dream of him. It is the stone of love, after all. Maybe a little marjoram. A love dream pillow would be perfect. I can make one up for you if you'd like. No charge, and I'll deliver it this afternoon."

"That would be lovely, but won't it be lumpy with a stone in it?"

"You won't notice it at all. I have a small stone and the pillow will be stuffed with marjoram and lavender. The two floral scents will mix beautifully. I guarantee you a pleasant sleep. What I can't guarantee is this silver fox you have your eye on will be the one you dream about."

"Fiddlesticks." She paid for her reading and winked at me. "Whoever I dream about won't know what hit him. Can't be too picky at my age."

When she left, I made up the love pillow, then spelled it. Remembering Missy's botched spell, I made certain the wording was specific. In my early teens, I accidentally spelled myself to forget about my family being witches. Even forgot about the gnomes in Granny's house. After moving back to the house, my memories gradually broke free. I frequently felt Granny's presence and got the occasional whiff of her rosewater perfume. She may have had a ghostly hand in reversing the spell. Unless I remembered exactly what I said all those years ago, my memories may never be one hundred percent unlocked.

As I headed to my car to deliver the pillow, my phone buzzed. *Cooper!* My heart did a little dance.

> Flight booked. Landing 2:35 Sat.

> Can't wait. I'll pick you up. Making a delivery. Call you in a half hour?

> I'll be waiting.

I sped into town, barely keeping close to the speed limit. Fortunately, none of the York Regional Police cruisers were around. The senior's building was easy to find, and this was my first visit. Mrs. McGillicuddy hadn't returned yet, but a few of my other customers were in. Emily corralled me in the lobby and dragged me into the game room.

"We were just talking about you. Can you do another séance? Cora's never been to one. It was so exciting. I told everyone about how you received a message of your own. We'd like to book one, right this minute."

I shrugged. "Sure. Let me open the calendar on my phone and we'll find a day that works. How many of you? Won't affect the price, but I need to get the room arranged."

"How about Saturday evening?"

"Um, this Saturday? I have to pick someone up from the airport. We'll be catching up well into the evening."

"Sunday?"

"Sure. It's best to do them around midnight, but not mandatory. I know they don't like you out late, so ten? Earlier?"

"Gertie goes to bed early. Is nine all right?" Emily looked at her gang. "Nine OK?"

They all nodded.

I made the entry on my phone calendar. "Nine it is, this Sunday. Let me know how many chairs to set up." I looked up when Mrs. McGillicuddy entered the room.

"Alice, over here." Emily waved her hands. "We've booked the séance."

I stood to give her my chair. "Here's your dream pillow. Let me know how it works."

She took a whiff. "Oh, it smells wonderful. Thank you. When's the séance?"

"Sunday. I have a few things to take care of. I'll see you ladies in a couple of days."

When I got home, I called Cooper for his flight details and to let him know the cupboards were stocked in the store's apartment. Now that his gramps was settled in the new attachment to the house, they were going to dinner to celebrate, and wish Cooper good luck with the book store, so he couldn't talk long. We'd see each other in a few days, anyway.

I texted Drew to see if she could video chat. Twenty minutes later, her face appeared on my laptop.

"Hi, cuz. Mum told me some weird things have been happening. Her and Gran are with the elders trying to figure out how best to deal with the crystal."

"I've put a ring of crushed brimstone around it, then circled that with obsidian stones. Hasn't eliminated the effects, but it's definitely lessened. I'm avoiding the living room whenever I can. I was thinking about something."

Drew laughed. "That's never good. Please tell me you aren't planning something dangerous?"

"No. When I tried the séance for the first time, you remember how Fiona showed up?"

"Remember? I'll never forget. That was spectacular."

"Right? So, I thought maybe I could try to contact her again. See if she knows anything about the ruby egg."

Drew scrunched her face, mulling it over. "Well, it's possible. However, she won't know what it was spelled with. It is possible, occasionally, to cancel out a spell without knowing what it is, but that's very hard to do. And it usually only works with weak spells. Whatever evil was infused into the crystal egg is far from weak, and may not even be a spell."

"Don't say that! Maybe she has a way to contact Uncle Montgomery? Assuming he's dead. Hey, maybe she knows where we poofed him to."

"Don't even think about trying to contact him. He's dangerous."

"Never crossed my mind. Promise. He's totally psycho. Only Fiona. And fortunately, I have a séance booked for Sunday evening. The same ladies I used as guinea pigs, plus a few more. Fiona came through because she knew I was in danger. Maybe it'll happen again."

Drew smiled. "Those ladies were amazing. All the strange stuff that happened, and they weren't fazed at all."

"I hope I'm half that energetic when I get to their age. Just wanted to run it by you. About Fiona, that is. So, you think it's a good idea?"

"I didn't say that, but it's not the worse idea you've had."

"Good. Oh, Cooper's coming home Saturday afternoon. I'm picking him up at the airport. Any update on the wedding plans?"

We chatted about her and Randy's wedding for over an hour, then she had to get ready to go out with him. With the time difference between Ontario and England, it was prime date time over there. I warmed up some of the leftover pizza and had a late lunch.

✷✷✷

Saturday morning, I picked up milk, eggs, and bread for Cooper. After putting them in the apartment, I gave it a quick clean and made up the bed. I'd washed all the towels and bedding shortly after they left for Nova Scotia, early in August. The store and upstairs apartment were ready for Cooper to take over. I vacuumed the carpeting on the main floor and wiped down the counter, then went home for a shower before heading to Toronto Pearson International Airport.

The plane was delayed due to a tropical storm that came up from Florida. Fortunately, only the tail end hit land, causing only minor issues. Cooper appeared out of the crowd, pulling a massive wheeled suitcase. I rushed over and hugged him. The warmth and emotion almost bowled me over. Cooper wanted to be more than friends, and so did I.

"Welcome home." I pointed to his suitcase. "All your worldly possessions are in one case?"

"No. A few boxes being couriered. Dad sent them after he dropped me off. Should arrive in a day or two. Nothing critical. So, are you ready to start our whirlwind romance?"

"Funny. Who said anything about a romance, whirlwind or otherwise?"

"Well, Dad and Gramps seem to think we're supposed to be together. So does your family. Who are we to argue?"

I cocked an eyebrow. *I believe we're supposed to be together, too. Every time I saw Cooper I got goosebumps. And the sparks when we touched! But can't get too involved until I've fixed my family's power issues.* "We'll see. Come on. It's going to be a nightmare getting out of here."

Traffic settled down somewhat once we managed to get on Highway 400. Shortly after 5:30, I parked in the single space allotted the store. Cooper had keys to the back entrance. He took one off the key ring and handed it to me. "You keep the spare key to the store and add this one to it. In case of an emergency."

We headed up to the apartment so he could ditch the suitcase. "Nice. Not a speck of dust." He opened the cupboards and fridge. "All my favs. Thanks, Marcy. How about dinner? A thank you for looking after the store. We can have a proper date later." He waggled his eyebrows. "Unfortunately, Sunday I'll have to do an inventory. Gramps knew where everything was, but I don't. Can you help?"

"Sure. I have a booking for a séance, but it's in the evening." I gazed into his mysterious silver eyes. *Even if I had an appointment during the day, I'd cancel.*

Neither of us wanted anything fancy, so I drove us to Montana's for dinner. Instead of lingering afterwards, we went back to the store for a coffee. I couldn't help but wonder what it was both our families saw that convinced them Cooper and I were meant to be together.

My family came from a long line of independent women, never staying with their spouses. The way Auntie P. described it, the marriages were more like a mating between animals. The founder of our former coven fell in love, but none of her descendants did. Somehow, that bit of DNA vanished from our genes. Until me.

Cooper ignited a spark in me, literally, every time we touched hands. Not certain why I didn't feel it when we hugged at the airport. At first, Auntie didn't approve of me "mating" with a helper. After meeting Cooper, she changed her mind. *Why?*

Even though Cooper didn't have jet lag, the long day got to him. We said goodnight, and I headed home.

Twenty-five minutes later, I walked past the living room doorway and a wave of nausea struck. Not hard, but noticeable. *Hope Auntie P. and the elders can help.* I pushed the button to open the hidden doorway and went down to grab another bundle of cedar to take to my room. After a quick smudge, I made some notes for the séance, then crawled into bed.

Again, I woke at 3:33 a.m. Three nights in a row. *Does 3-3-3 have any significance?* I fell back asleep and had no issues or nightmares.

FOUR

When I went into the kitchen in the morning, I popped a Snickerdoodle in the Keurig and opened my laptop to research 3-3-3. Nothing bad popped up in the search results. Apparently, that specific time means the universe is communicating with me. That number, in general, means the angels are sending messages of encouragement. *Why can't they simply pop into a dream and actually give me the message?*

Relieved that no warning of doom headed my way, I drank my coffee and gobbled down some cold cereal. Someone cleared their throat. *My little gnome.*

"Morning, Nenka. Do you need something?" I didn't even bother turning around.

"Is something wrong? I can't go into the living room."

That got my attention. My spoon dropped into the cereal, splashing milk everywhere. I swung around in the chair. "What do you mean you can't go in? Is something blocking you?" *Is the ruby affecting her?*

"Nothing physical." She stood, wringing her apron in her hands. Not a good sign. "I have this feeling. There's something bad in there."

Schist. I should have warned her. "Have you noticed the ruby egg-shaped crystal in the display cabinet? The backlit one."

"Yes. It's very pretty. You brought that back after…" Nenka avoided mentioning that day.

"After I got rid of my great uncle. The crystal was his, and he infused it with some sort of evil. Seems the evil has awakened. Aunt Priscilla is looking into it. Are you telling me you physically can't enter the room?"

She shook her head. "No, but I can't bring myself to go in there."

How can I fix this? I've already bothered Auntie P. and Drew. The supernatural website! "Don't worry about it, even though I know you will. I'll beef up the protection around it. Is that the only place you don't feel comfortable?"

She nodded, letting up on the apron slightly.

"I promised Cooper I'd help him with the inventory today. I'll see what I can do about the egg before I go. Oh, I'm having a séance tonight. You wanna watch?"

That brought a smile to her lips. No one else should be able to see her, unless they were part of my family. Strangely, both Mr. Barker and Cooper could see her.

She scampered off to wherever she goes, and I headed to the workshop after finishing breakfast. *One of these days, I have to find the other fae door.* Five keys, four doors. Granny's room, the willow tree, in the workroom, and behind the tapestry. Where was that last one?

Not wanting to delay further, I dumped the rest of my cereal in the garbage and put my dirty dishes in the sink. No rush to wash a spoon, bowl, and cup. I started towards the hidden door, hesitating before pressing the release button. *Was the protection wearing off?* Two more steps took me to the living room doorway. Without entering, I could feel it. The dizziness hit hard enough to make me grab the door frame. I swallowed bile and took a step back. *Holy Heliodor. It is worse!*

Backtracking, I pushed the button and almost tripped in my rush to get downstairs. Fortunately, I'd bought plenty of brimstone in Toronto. At least I thought I had. If the egg-shaped crystal kept getting stronger every day, I'd soon run out. I grabbed another rock and crushed it up with the mortar and pestle, grabbed the gloves, then hurried back up and spread it around the crystal, directly on top of the existing ring. After a moment's hesitation, I scooped up a small amount and sprinkled it on the crystal.

Being this close made my head spin, but that lessened when the ends of the circle joined up. *How long will this last?*

Safely out of the room, I took my laptop out to the sunporch and logged into the witchy website. A quick search of the forum didn't give me any tips, but they had set a room up to deal with protection. I posted my query, asking how to contain the evil inside an item. I checked off the little box to receive an email and phone alert when someone replied, then drove into town to help Cooper.

Even though I had my own key to the shop and back door, I wouldn't use it except in case of an emergency. I parked my car behind the store and texted Cooper.

I'm here. Let me in.

Use your key and come upstairs.

I fished my keyring from my pocket and selected the one with the yellow rubber ring, then headed up.

Cooper sat at his table, still eating breakfast. "Got a late start. Didn't realize how tired I was. Coffee?"

I poured a cup and joined him. "Travel is always exhausting. So, where do we start?"

"Good morning to you, too." He grinned, his silver eyes twinkling.

"Sorry. Morning."

"What's wrong? No comments about me being lazy and sleeping in? Something is definitely up." He took my hand. "Tell me, please."

Where do I start? "I think Uncle Monty is still somehow after me. But how is that possible?"

Cooper scooted his chair around the table, taking both my hands in his. Jolts of electricity coursed up my arms, into my heart. *Why does he affect me so much?* I closed my eyes, concentrating on the feeling, trying to block it so I could talk.

"There's so much you don't know about what happened in Alberta. I brought back an egg. A crystal ruby one. Probably expensive. Montgomery used it against me, and if Mother and Granny hadn't helped, I think it would have killed me."

Cooper shook his head. "Whoa. What? Back up the boat. Your mother and grandmother helped? But they're both dead."

I smiled at the memory. "They came down from the heavens, like angels. We basically had Maiden, Mother, and Crone twice over. They… amplified our power. That's the only word I can think of to describe it. When we poofed him, the egg dropped to the ground, its power gone."

"Poofed?" Cooper made a face I'd never seen before. A combination of puzzlement and confusion.

"Don't ask, because I can't tell you. Not that I don't want to. I mean, it's not one of those 'I could tell you, but I'd have to kill you' things. I honestly don't know where he went. Don't even know if he's dead or alive. Did I ever tell you about my ancestor's boy-girl twins?"

He nodded.

"OK, so, the coven poofed the boy-twin away at Stonehenge. We've found no written record that says where he went. All I know is they had some sort of ceremony. Then, a lightning bolt came down, struck him, and poof, like in Alberta when we banished Uncle Montgomery. Gone. No clothing left behind, no burnt remains. No smell of burning flesh, fortunately. Just gone. Is he dead? If so, why no remains? Was the lightning actually a magickal bolt that transported him to another realm? Who knows?"

"OK. I'd say I understand, but I don't. Why do you think he's after you again?"

"The ruby egg is affecting me. It started Wednesday. Slight dizziness and nausea. I've placed protection around it, and it helped, but not enough. Auntie P. is looking into it. I had to strengthen the shield around it this morning. The feeling is so strong that Nenka won't even go into the living room. I keep the crystal in the display cabinet with several other gems, and have been entering the house through the sunporch so I don't have to pass the room. Unfortunately, I can't ask my clients to do that and I have several coming tonight."

Cooper scooched closer and wrapped his arms around me. Electricity broke through my wall and flowed through me. Different this time. Comforting.

"How can you do that?"

Cooper eased up. "Do what?"

"The moment you hugged me, I felt something."

He raised an eyebrow and grinned.

"No, not that. Sheesh. It made me feel better. Safer."

"Hmm. Dad told me every now and then, someone in my family can heal with a touch. It's rare, though. I believe it's similar to what your cousin Drew can do, but more. No one's been able to do that for generations. I know I've never done it before. Maybe it healed your emotions? I'm glad it made you feel safe."

"Me too. You'll have to talk to your family about it." *Is that why everyone thinks we belong together? Because we've both inherited something rare?*

"I'll ask my family if they've ever come across anything like an evil crystal egg. Doubt they'll know anything, but it doesn't hurt to ask. There's nothing more you can do right now, so how about we get started? Before we do the inventory, I want to collect Gramp's car. A friend of his stored it until I got back so it wasn't sitting outside for months, waiting to be broken into. You'll have to move your car to the lot by the community centre."

We spent the rest of the day inventorying the books. Cooper bought an on-line program designed solely for that purpose. Whenever a book was rung up, the software recorded it.

Hours passed with no alerts from the witchy-site. Either no one read my post, or no one had any suggestions. Nothing from Auntie either.

✳ ✳ ✳

Cooper had lunch and dinner delivered though one of the food apps so we didn't waste time away from the task. During dinner, Cooper yawned several times. He'd had a busy day, and I had an appointment. Once the dishes were washed and put away, I headed home to prepare for the séance. *Would Fiona come through again?*

As I walked through my garden, leaves rustled in the herb wheel. "Nenka? Is that you?"

More rustling, then she popped out from behind the cilantro. Her kerchief sat neatly in place, protecting her hair, but her crisp white apron was wrinkled and covered in dirt. Her leather clogs and gloves didn't look much better.

"You've been busy. Digging tunnels?"

Nenka looked down at her dress and apron. "Gracious. I'm a mess." She looked up at the sun. "It's getting late. Completely lost track of time."

"Are you avoiding the house?" *I know I wanted to.*

She blushed. "I've sent Nimagg to stay with his grandmother across the field."

For decades, Nenka's parents hadn't spoken to her. It wasn't generally acceptable for a wood gnome to marry a house gnome. When she married Tinkus over fifty years ago, her parents disowned her. When the issue with my uncle surfaced this past summer, they took in her son. They've been a proper family since.

"I don't blame you. If you and Tinkus want to join him, I'll understand. You need to stay safe, too."

"Nonsense. It's our job to take care of you. Tinkus has spread word to the other fae that something might be up. Everyone is on alert. If anything happens, word will spread among my kind. You wouldn't believe what type of fae are all around here."

I laughed. "If you said there were unicorns roaming the forests, I think I'd believe you. It's time to get ready for the séance, and you need to get cleaned up."

Nenka scampered off in the direction of the willow to the fae door in its trunk. I went in through the sunporch and began setting up.

Six women were coming, so I placed the chairs around the table, with a seventh at the head for me, then moved the rest out of the way. Candles went into candlesticks and incense sat on holders specially made for the long sticks so the ash wouldn't drop onto the furniture. Each holder had a unique design. My favourite was the one with the dragon head. I'd light them about ten minutes before the ladies arrived. Enough burning time to permeate around the room, but not so long they'd burn down before we finished. After

Alice McGillicuddy's reading the other day, I'd placed the crystal ball in the moonlight to recharge. Even when the moon wasn't visible, it still worked. The moon never left the sky, even when it rotated out of sight.

FIVE

The table was set up basically the same as before. The crystal ball sat on the purple lace tablecloth in front of me, covered with the fabric printed with stars and galaxies. To spruce it up, I placed a white lace tablecloth over the entire table. I'd purchased the fabric in the summer when I first tried this type of reading. Since then, I'd properly finished it off with a hem. No one noticed before, but a fraying tablecloth didn't look nice, or professional. The silver candelabra sat dead centre. I found it at an antique market and it matched the single candlesticks mother had. My phone dinged, the twenty-minute warning for my appointment. I stood back to survey the room. *Perfect.*

"Looks lovely, dear."

I jumped when Nenka spoke—as usual.

"I wish I'd seen the one you did in the summer. It must have been amazing when your ancestor came through."

Pictures of that event ran through my mind. Everyone else had seen what was happening before I did. A bright white light appeared behind my chair. *With luck, she'll be back tonight.*

"Don't expect too much, Nenka. I've only done this a few times. Drew sat with me the first time, and her entire family the second. Not certain I can do this on my own. Make yourself comfy." I lit the four sticks of eucalyptus incense. "I'll be back in a few minutes. Since this isn't a freebie, I want to look my best."

An antique embroidered doll chair sat in the corner of the dining room, stuffed with horsehair, apparently. A matching ottoman in front of it. Another purchase from the antique store. I smiled while she made herself comfortable, then raced upstairs to change into a long black skirt and white blouse borrowed from Granny's closet. Quite different from my summer attire of jeans and tee. Sweatshirts and plaid flannel shirts were my go-to in the winter. Most of Granny's clothing went to charity after the funeral, but a few items fit me. The skirt and blouse were perfect for readings. When time permitted, I'd sew my own blouse with some of the same fabric used to cover the crystal ball.

The doorbell rang. Before going down, I grabbed my black tourmaline bracelet to protect me when I passed by the living room and the creepy crystal egg.

Only one car sat in the driveway. A brand new Audi Q5. One of the Grey Haired Grannies had some money. Unfortunately, I didn't see who drove. A question for another day.

Once the ladies were settled around the table and the candles lit, it was time to start. First grounding, then closing a circle around us.

"Do any of you have a specific question or person you wish to contact?"

Harriett raised her hand. "Do you think you could contact my daughter? She passed at a young age. Her name was Lizzy."

"I'll try. You don't need to raise your hand. Just speak up."

Closing my eyes, I concentrated. "Lizzy, are you here? Your mother would like to speak with you."

The candles flickered. The spirits seemed to enjoy doing that. Good way to get my attention. I looked at Harriett, but saw no one near her. When Alice's husband came through last summer, he stood beside her, an Irish setter at his side. Maybe it didn't always work that way. The candles continued to flicker. Someone was here.

"Lizzy? Is that you?"

Nothing.

"I'm sorry, Harriett. Someone is here, but they aren't revealing themselves to me."

A blue feather floated down from the ceiling and landed beside Harriett. "It's her." Harriett picked up the feather. "This is from a blue jay. Her favourite bird. She's telling me she's all right. I'm certain of that."

Okay then. If she's happy, so am I. "Anyone else?"

"Well…" Cora looked embarrassed. "Can you see if Robert is around?"

"Whoa. Who's Robert?" Emily tapped Cora's shoulder. "Your husband was Charlie. Spill."

"He was my beau before Charlie. Didn't come back from the Great War."

All the ladies started chattering at once.

"Ladies, quiet, please. You can grill her later. I'd like to hear the story, too, but not now. What's his last name?"

"Harrison."

It took a few minutes for everyone to settle again.

"Robert Harrison, are you here?"

One of the candles blew out.

"Oh, my. That happened before, too." Alice reached across the table and tapped Cora's gnarled hand.

A mist formed behind Cora's chair. Then another.

Alice pointed. "I see something."

I watched the two mists take shape. Human-like, but no features. "This is odd. There are two spirits with you, Alice. Both Robert and Charlie. They're watching over you. Robert is glad you met Charlie. Their love for you drew them together."

The spirits faded.

Alice wiped a tear away. "They would have been good friends if they'd met. They were so alike."

I rose and re-lit the candle. "Anyone else?"

All heads shook. I reached out to the universe. "Is there anyone here who has a message?"

The flames on the candles flickered and grew tall. They danced and intertwined.

The ladies gasped.

"It's for you again, dear." Alice pointed behind me.

As I turned, I looked at Nenka. She remained in her chair, eyes wide. The same white light as before appeared. It grew brighter, then exploded. *Fiona!*

The ladies spoke at once.

"What was that?"

"Am I dead?"

Mary-Beth fainted.

I quickly released the circle and hurried over to help the ladies with Mary-Beth. She'd slumped in the chair, but didn't slide off. "I'll fetch a glass of water and a cold cloth." *I hope the people at the senior's home don't hear about this.*

When I returned to the dining room, the ladies weren't there. "Nenka?"

"Yes, dear?" She hurried in from across the hall.

"Where'd they go?"

"She came around and they helped her to the sofa."

Schist. I had no choice but to go in. "Were you able to go in? Is it any worse than before?"

"No. No better, no worse."

Taking a deep breath, I made my way into the living room. The nausea was minimal. Mary-Beth sat at the end of the sofa, one hand on her chest.

"Here, drink this." I handed her the glass of water. "How do you feel? Should I call a doctor?"

All the ladies spoke at once. "No!"

"So silly of me." Mary-Beth handed me the empty glass. She looked a little flushed.

"Put this cloth on your forehead. What happened? Have you been ill?"

"She's a great, big scaredy-cat." Cora sat beside her, holding the damp cloth on Mary-Beth's forehead.

"I'm fine, now." She started to stand, but fell back onto the seat cushion. "Someone help me, please."

I took her hands and pulled her up, not letting go until she seemed steady.

"That was fun. Can we do it again? Promise not to faint."

I walked the ladies to their cars and made them swear an oath that one of them would let me know if Mary-Beth got worse.

Returning to the dining room, I blew out the candles. The incense had almost burned out, so I let it go while I put everything away.

"Nenka. What did you think of the séance?"

"Why did you have the crystal ball out when you didn't use it?"

"Partly because it's pretty, partly because it's quartz and has an energy of its own. A little boost."

"That white light was scary. You seemed to know what it was. So did that one lady."

"My ancestor, Fiona. I had my fingers crossed she'd come through. I'll do this again on my own and see if she manifests. Last time, I had family help boost her energy. Not sure what will happen on my own. She seemed to need extra energy. Maybe if I call Drew on video chat, she can send me some. Hmm. Wonder if that even works? Too late to call her tonight. I'll send a text now and ask. I'm sure she'll answer when she gets up."

Nenka said goodnight and disappeared. *There has to be a fae door on the main floor somewhere.*

The incense finally burned down, so I went to bed. Clean up could wait until morning.

Exhausted, sleep came quick. Unfortunately, so did 3:33 a.m. Someone must really want to send me a message. *Fiona? Could it be her trying to come through?*

✳ ✳ ✳

When I woke, it was after eight. A notification showed up on my phone. Drew had replied. Doing the math in my head to confirm the time in England, I pressed the video icon. She'd either be finishing up an early lunch, or starting a late one. Drew answered immediately.

"Morning, Marcy."

"Afternoon, Drew. So, you think it might work?"

"Maybe. Mum agrees. It's entirely energy, and that basically flows through the air and ground. It won't be as strong as being there in person, but we should be able to send enough energy to allow Fiona to speak. Doubt she'll be able to materialize. She only did that when Mum and Gran were with us."

"Last night I performed another séance with the ladies. Fiona didn't show up exactly. The same light and flash, without materialization. But I woke in the wee hours feeling like someone tried to contact me. Hopefully, it was Fiona and not something nasty. I know it's a lot to ask, but if necessary, would any of you be able to fly over? You have your hands full with the wedding plans, so I hope it doesn't come to that."

"Fiona tried to come through? You definitely need more energy. I wonder… she might have been weakened by her previous visitations. You know we'll come if you need us. We're like the musketeers. One for all, and all that. Have you reached out to any of the witches in your area?"

I grimaced. "On my do-to list. Maybe Missy can help. She's been eager to learn more spell work, and she's into crystals, just like me."

Drew gave me one of her "get off your butt" looks. "Marcy. Don't put it off. You've been into that shop north of you several times. Talk to them. Maybe Cooper can give you some names. There must be plenty of witches in the area or the helper organization wouldn't have stationed one in Newmarket."

I laughed when Drew mention that. "Did you know they have an acronym for the organization? W.H.O. Witches Helper Organization. Their logo is a little owl with a wand."

"Cute. Please, promise me you'll contact someone soon. Don't wait until it's too late."

I nodded and crossed my heart. "I'm going to see Cooper this morning. It's his first day running the bookstore. I'll ask him for some names. Not sure what the policy is on giving out contact info. Maybe he can be a middleman and contact them for me."

"Good. A more experienced one would be best. Not to knock your friend Missy, but she's even greener than you. Between the two of you, I doubt you'd be able to do much. Gotta run. Mum's coming soon. I'm closing for the afternoon and we're going mother-of-the-bride dress shopping."

"Have fun."

We signed off, and I got dressed. After filling up on Snickerdoodle coffee and toast, I texted Cooper that I was on my way.

With Labour Day over and school starting, traffic had increased over the past week. Forgetting kids were back at school, I ended up in the middle of parents driving their younger ones to daycare. My usual twenty-minute drive into Newmarket took almost forty-five minutes, thanks to numerous school buses.

Now that Cooper had his gramps' old car, I had to park behind the community centre. Still warm, the wading pool hadn't been closed yet. A few stay-at-home mothers and fathers with kids too young for school enjoyed the nice weather, letting the little ones splash around. I watched for a few minutes, then texted Cooper.

Be there in one min.

Back door's unlocked.

I let myself in, locking the door behind me. Cooper was in the store with a new box of books. Kneeling beside him, I reached in and took out a handful.

"How'd you get a delivery so soon? You've only been back a few days."

"Ordered them last week. Don't you remember? I told you boxes were being shipped. A couple of Gramps' customers emailed hoping he could find what they needed. Several of the ladies don't enjoy travelling and traipsing all over the countryside to find them. They're not available online, and Gramps has contacts. One was a rush, so that was couriered when it came in. The others weren't in a rush, so we collected them over the summer and Dad sent the box along with the rest of my stuff. I'll be calling them to come pick them up."

"Speaking of your customers, I have a huge favour."

Cooper's silver eyes sparkled. "Anything for you."

The heat rose up my neck. "Um, thanks. Is there any chance you can put me in contact with some of your witchy clients? With Drew making plans for her wedding, I really can't expect her to drop everything and fly over if I can't deal with the ruby crystal."

He dropped a book. "Wait. Is it getting worse?"

I nodded. "I've had to put more protection around it. Auntie P. hasn't gotten back to me, so I guess she hasn't found anything useful. It looks like it's time to bring in the reserves. Only I don't have any. Maybe some of the local witches could help? Has to be someone well practiced."

"Of course. It wouldn't be ethical to simply give you their contact info, but if I make you a part-time employee here,—unpaid, of course,—you could call them and let them know their orders have arrived. Introduce yourself. Explain things. One of these books is for someone who arrived from Scotland last spring and also wants to meet others. She's about the same age as your great aunt."

Cooper sifted through the box and pulled out a book with a faded, cracked leather cover. "It's not in the best shape, but with a little care, it will last another hundred years. Only have her email, no phone number. Why don't you contact her?"

"Thank you." I leaned over, gave him a hug, and whispered in his ear. "Does this mean I get an employee discount?"

He wrapped his arms around me and squeezed. "You need to get a salary before I can give you a discount." He whispered in my ear. "Maybe an arrangement can be made?"

"In your dreams." Laughing, I pushed him away and turned him towards the box. "Sort."

Once the books were taken care of, Cooper began contacting his customers. Not all of them were witches. I opened my email app and settled on one of the comfy chairs in the little reading nook in the centre of the store. The opening of the email was easy. Basically "blah, blah, new part-timer, your book has arrived, yada, yada." The rest proved tricky. I backspaced more than I typed. A half hour later I finally hit send, then crossed my fingers. *Please reply.*

Since no appointments were scheduled for readings or potions, I stayed at the bookstore. Not many new customers came in, but a few regulars picked up their special orders. Still no reply to my email. Cooper finally flipped the sign to closed and turned off the lights.

"How about we pick up some food and head to your place? I'd like to see this egg. Fish and chips?"

"Haven't had that in ages. Why don't I go over and order while you finish closing up?"

Cooper agreed. "I'll find your car in the lot and park close. Too bad we have to take separate cars, unless you want me to stay over?" He waggled his eyebrows.

"You wish. See you in bit."

The chip shop was around the corner, on Main Street, and had a bit of a line up. Cooper joined me fifteen minutes later. Five more minutes passed before the order came out. Cooper paid and we walked to our cars. He'd found a spot right beside my little lava-orange Smart car.

When we arrived at my place, I led him through the garden and in through the sunporch. Nenka peeked in while we ate.

"Good evening, Cooper. So nice to see you again."

He had his mouth full, so he waved.

"She has perfect timing, doesn't she?" I laughed and stuffed a fry in my mouth, speaking between chews. "Just pop in to say hi, Nenka?" Probably not. She usually had a purpose.

"I heard voices." She turned to Cooper, worry lines marring her forehead. "Are you here to help with the crystal?"

"Not sure how much help I can be, but I definitely want to see it. I put Marcy in touch with a witch that seems to be on par with her aunt's abilities." Cooper looked at me. "Any word back yet?"

"Don't think so." I opened the email app on my phone. "Nothing. Maybe she didn't like that I reached out to her for help. She doesn't know me. Probably thinks I'm a total flake."

Cooper's phone dinged. He chuckled when he read the notification. "Speak of the devil. It's her. She emailed the store." He opened the email and read it. "Wants confirmation about you. I'll let her know you're not completely flakey." He laughed, then sent off a short reply. "Now, let me see this egg."

Nenka had already disappeared.

"Don't know how she does that. Come on. It's in the display cabinet."

When we got to the living room doorway, I hesitated. The nausea hit before I got halfway there. Not a good sign. My head started throbbing. "The protection isn't holding. You go in."

Cooper looked at me, distinct lines forming along his brow. "Are you okay?"

"Yes, provided I don't go any closer."

He paused. "You sure?"

"Yes. Go. Middle shelf."

He walked over to the cabinet and crouched down. "Is it supposed to glow?"

"No, but it's been sending brief flashes."

"It's not flashing. There's a constant glow coming from it. You need to get rid of it." Cooper stood, stumbling. "It's even affecting me."

Cooper hurried into the hall, reaching to grab me the moment my knees buckled.

"Marcy!"

SIX

He led me back into the kitchen and helped me onto a chair. I shook my head, trying to clear the ringing. "Did you hear that?"

"Hear what?"

I stood and headed to the sunporch. "A low hum. It's gone now."

Cooper opened the porch door, letting in the fresh air. "Come on. You need to get out of the house. Stay at the store tonight."

"NO! It's not going to win. Thank you, but I can't."

We sat on a bench outside, under the balcony attached to Granny's old room. Cooper took my hand. "You have no say in this. Don't think of it as losing. You need to recoup. The bed is still in the back room. You're going to stay there tonight. Do you feel up to going inside and collecting a change of clothes?"

All my life I'd accepted defeat, evident from my long list of jobs and brief stay at university. I wanted to make this work. If I went with Cooper, I'd be running away yet again.

"Thank you, but no." My phone dinged. I pulled it from my pocket and opened the email. "It's her. The Scottish lady. She wants to meet tomorrow."

"Perfect. She can pick up her book and chat with you. If you stay at the store, you won't have to drive in. You're too shaky to drive safely, so you're coming in my car. I'll bring you back after closing tomorrow, maybe."

I really didn't want to stay alone. Nenka and Tinkus would be here, but if anything happened, they wouldn't be able to do much. "Fine. One night."

The headache hadn't quite left, but at least my legs were steady. I quickly packed an overnight bag, grabbed a few crystals, then ran downstairs, calling for Nenka.

"There you are. I'm staying at the bookstore tonight. Will you be all right here alone?"

"Yes, we'll be fine. If anything happens, we'll go to my parents."

"Perfect." I looked around and spotted a pencil and notepad on the counter. "Here, if you go, can you leave me a note?" I put them on the floor.

"Yes, yes. Now go. Don't worry about us. It hasn't affected the underground yet. We're safe in the tunnels."

Since the headache still lingered at the base of my skull, I stopped long enough to take something for it, then threw the bottle into my bag. Cooper put his arm around my waist and walked me to his car. Seatbelt fastened, I closed my eyes. The ride seemed shorter than normal. I jolted when the car stopped.

"Enjoy the nap? Headache gone yet?" Cooper smiled at me and unfastened his seatbelt.

"Naps make me feel worse, but I'll survive. Headache's still there. At least it hasn't increased. Funny how it's still affecting me so far from the house. Before, the effects disappeared the moment I left the room."

"Come on. You need to get settled. Coffee?"

"Tea, please. Herbal."

After Cooper and his dad brought his gramps to Nova Scotia, I'd come in and stripped the bed they'd set up in the back room and the one in the upstairs apartment. When Cooper told me he was coming back soon, I'd only put fresh linens in the apartment. He made my tea while I made up the bed in the back. Much as I hated giving in and leaving home, I really didn't relish the thought of spending the night alone. At least the ruby crystal couldn't reach me in town. *Or could it? Still have the headache, despite the distance and Advil.*

Cooper joined me, carrying a silver tray with two full steaming mugs and a plate of butter tarts. With the room back more or less the way Mr. Barker had it before the heart attack, it created a cozy sitting area in the centre. He put the tray on the antique table, then raised the folded ends so we'd have more room. The wing-back chairs were stuffed with something softer than a cloud. The only thing missing was a fireplace.

"Maybe I'll get one of those electric fireplaces for this room." Cooper pointed to the west wall. "Under that window. What do you think?"

"Funny you should ask. I was thinking a fireplace would set the room off perfectly, too." My turn to point, this time at the contents on the tray. "I see you hit the Cottage and got some of their award-winning tarts. They're yummy. It's no wonder they have so many awards."

Cooper nodded. "Thought something sweet might give you sweet dreams."

"Or amp up my headache." Sweetness overload sometimes had that effect on me. "But I don't care." I reached over and grabbed one before he had a chance to remove everything from the tray. Between bites, I asked him to tell me about the Scottish witch I'd be meeting tomorrow.

Cooper munched on a tart while he thought. "Well, you know her name is Sorcha."

"Yes. I looked it up. It's Gaelic for radiant."

"I've only met her twice, but that fits. Haven't had lengthy conversations with her as she only came into the store a couple of times before Gramp's heart attack. Her brogue is very strong. Like I said earlier, she's probably about your aunt's age and came to witchcraft naturally through her family, so she's very experienced."

There wasn't much else he knew, so we chatted for about an hour. After he headed up to his apartment over the store, I pulled a notebook from my bag and listed a few questions. At the top of the list—how to reverse a spell without knowing what the spell was. I also needed to find other ways to contain the crystal, so it would no longer affect me or anyone else.

Cooper left me the last tart. I devoured it, then got ready for bed. Once again, I woke at 3:33. Someone really wanted me to know something. Hopefully, the message came from Fiona since it's supposed to be a positive message. Maybe Sorcha could help with that. Extra energy seemed necessary for my ancestor to materialize. Assuming she was willing and able to help me.

Cooper knocked on the door what seemed like a few minutes later. I picked up my phone. A couple of minutes before eight. *Morning already?* Only an hour until Sorcha arrives. *Guess I went back to sleep.* I got up and unlocked the door.

"Morning, sleepy head. I've been up for hours. Do you always sleep this late?"

I ran my fingers through my hair. "First off, eight in the morning is hardly late. Second, I've been waking up at 3:33 every day for almost a week. Didn't I mention it?"

"Nope. Do you want breakfast? I waited for you and I'm starving."

"Sure. Whatever you're having. I need to straighten up before Sorcha arrives."

Cooper picked up last night's dishes and put them on the tray. "I'll take care of these. You get dressed and make the bed, then come up."

At nine sharp, I received a text. The Scottish witch had arrived. I headed to the door, and the curly red hair was the first thing I saw. Her face lit up when she smiled. My gut told me this woman was going to be a good friend. I let her in and led her to the back room. A lavender-scented candle sat in the centre of the large table where

Drew and I went through the grimoire Mr. Barker borrowed for us last summer. Cooper came in a few minutes later carrying the silver tray, this time holding a teapot and two tea cups. *Why hadn't Mr. Barker taken all that with him when he moved? Has to be expensive.*

"Morning, Sorcha. I thought you ladies might enjoy some tea. One of Gramps' special blends." He put the tray on the antique fold-down table. "I'll leave you to it."

I poured the tea and picked up my notebook. "First, thank you for coming. I guess I should give you a bit of background. My family has a long history in England. Not really sure why my grandmother moved to Canada. She passed a few months ago. My mother died when I was in high school. Things were a little strained with her as I'd sworn off witchcraft a year earlier. That's when I moved in with Granny, but only until university. I maintained my love of crystals and threw a psychic wall around me to keep the voices out. What I hadn't realized until after Granny passed was I'd accidentally spelled myself to forget almost everything witchy. I reached out to Granny's sister, Priscilla, in England. With the help of my great aunt and her family, I'm remembering and re-learning."

Sorcha said nothing, simply listened, nodding occasionally. "And what is it you would like me to do?"

"This probably sounds weird, but my family is all female. Husbands don't linger. We only give birth to girls, with two exceptions. An ancestor referred to as the Ancient One. Her name is Fiona. She had boy-girl twins. The boy grew up evil and the coven somehow banished him. Apparently, Granny and Auntie P. had a little brother. They thought him dead, but he'd been shipped to

Canada when he was a child, and adopted. Long story short, he somehow learned dark magick and was responsible for both Mother's and Granny's deaths, and came after the rest of the family. When we banished him, he left behind a beautiful ruby egg-shaped crystal. He'd used it against me and almost won. The crystal is now affecting me and I don't know how to contain it. That's where you come in, I hope."

"*Crivvens!*" She sipped her tea. "How is this crystal affecting you?"

Crivvens? Will have to look that up later. "Headaches, nausea, dizziness. I've ground up brimstone and placed a circle around it, with an additional circle of black obsidian stones. Reinforced the brimstone once, but it's still getting through."

She must have noticed my raised eyebrow at the unusual word. "*Crivvens* is an exclamation of surprise or shock. And what is it you require of me?"

"Two things, one long term, the other short. Long term, I don't know any witches in the area and was hoping to find some new friends. Short term? That's the tricky one. I've had a few video chats with my aunt and cousins. The general consensus is he spelled the crystal egg with evil intent. Problem is, no one knows what spell. They're trying to figure out if there's a way to minimize it. Without the spell he used, we can't reverse it, as you no doubt know. Would you be willing to help with that?"

"*Crivvens,* when you need help, you certainly go big. I'm new to the area, so I don't know many of the locals. Yes, I'm happy to be your friend. Actually, I was going to ask Cooper if he'd contact his clients to see if any of them wish to meet up. But to reverse or minimizing an unknown spell, *ah dinnae ken*. I don't know, but I'll give it a think."

Sorcha stood.

"Thank you for coming, Sorcha. I look forward to speaking with you again. Oh, I also wanted to ask if you'd be willing to join me in a séance. Just the two of us, and maybe my cousin, on video. I'd like to contact Fiona. Last time, it took my entire family to give her enough energy to materialize."

She nodded "Certainly. Haven't been to a séance for ages. Let me know when. Maybe Cooper can arrange a meeting with several of us before the séance."

"That's a good idea. Nice ice breaker. It was lovely talking to you. My aunt will be so happy to hear I've met another witch."

"I'd like to meet her some time, especially if I'm going to help. Give her my email. Leave it up to her to decide if she'd like to chat."

"Thank you, I will."

I walked with her to the front of the store. Cooper had just flipped the sign to open and held the door for her. He turned to me the moment the door closed behind her.

"So, how was it?"

"She's very nice and is willing to try to help. Even said I could give her email to Auntie P. Maybe they can come up with something. She also suggested asking if you would be willing to reach out to more of your special customers to arrange a meetup. She doesn't know too many local witches, either."

Cooper laughed. "Should I change the sign out front to read Antique Books and friend matcher?"

"You know, that's not a bad idea. A friend app—not changing your sign. I'll have to ask Drew if such a thing exists for witches. I'm sure she would have mentioned if there was one. Wonder how hard it is to create an app?"

I stayed at the bookstore for a couple of hours, then left to prepare for an appointment with a client. She needed an herbal remedy that wasn't even started.

When I pulled into my driveway, the vibes hit. *Holy Heliodor!* The headache was almost as bad as the ones caused when Uncle Monty had been in my head. My vision blurred. Forgetting the appointment, I reversed out to the road, then texted Drew.

> Can't get near the house.

> What? Why?

> Ruby.

The headache subsided and my eyes focused. I tried again.

> The protection around crystal egg not working.

> Bugger. Where are U?

> In the car on the road. Oh, my God! Nenka and Tinkus!

> Your gnomes?

> It's been affecting Nenka. Sent son to her parents.

> This is why you need to meet locals.

> Shoot. I did. I'll call her.

> Keep me updated.

I scrolled through my contacts.

"Sorcha. It's Marcy. I need your help, please. Whatever's in that stone is stopping me from entering my property. I don't know what to do."

"I'm at the Garden Witch. Give me your address."

SEVEN

I knew it would take her about a half hour to get here, so I drove up the road. Nenka's parents lived nearby. Maybe my gnomes joined their son. Trying to be inconspicuous, I hopped the fence and entered the woods.

"Hello? Is anyone around? I'm looking for a family of gnomes. Hello?"

Nothing. Feeling like an idiot, I kept walking and calling. Finally, rustling off to my left. "Hello?"

A tiny creature, unfamiliar to me, peeked out from under a fern. *Some type of faerie?*

Kneeling, I waved. "Hi. Can you help me?

"You see me?"

"Yes. I'm a witch."

"Only witch around here is Francine."

"My grandmother. She died a few months ago. Do you know Nenka and Tinkus? There's a problem at my house, and I don't know if they're all right."

"Yes. They passed through here this morning."

"Thank you. If you see them, please tell them Marcy is trying to fix everything. They should stay with her parents. Can you remember all that?"

She frowned. "Course I can. I'm not stupid."

"Sorry. Didn't mean to offend you. Thank you very much."

The little faerie disappeared back under the fern, so I went back to Cooper's car and waited at the foot of my drive for Sorcha. She arrived ten minutes later with a young woman, probably in her twenties. She had the blackest hair I'd ever seen, makeup to match.

"Marcy, this is Helena. She was in the Garden Witch when you called. Since we both are looking to expand our circle of friends, I thought extra help would come in handy. I took the liberty of telling her what little I know about your evil crystal."

"Hi. Glad to get all the help I can. Too bad we have to meet this way. Um, can you feel anything? It hit me the moment I drove onto the property."

"One way to find out." Helena walked up my driveway and immediately turned back. "Wow. Super bad vibes."

Curious, Sorcha stepped past the fence. "*Crivvens*. I agree. Mingin vibes." She placed a hand over her mouth and backed out.

Mingin? Must mean bad. "Feeling nauseous? Has that effect on me, too. Along with headaches and dizziness. I surrounded the crystal with black obsidian and a lot of freshly ground brimstone. It's helping, but only a little."

Sorcha glanced at the bracelet on my wrist. "Black tourmaline? Not bad, but apparently not enough." She went back to her car and rooted through a bag. "You said you're still re-learning. How's your spell work?"

"Basic. Still need written spells. Can't wing it yet. I did a protection spell around the house months ago, but I don't remember it. Not sure if it reached to the edges of the property. When my cousin visited in the summer, she helped me ask the angels to protect the property. Must be why it usually subsides when I leave. Guessing the protection around my land is keeping it from leeching out?"

"We'll help. We had a long chat on the way over. This will only be short term. You'll need a stronger one set up permanently, to help the angel protection. There's one other thing you should know." Sorcha looked at Helena and raised an eyebrow.

The Goth witch rolled her eyes. "Fine. Full disclosure. I used to practice dark magick. Don't believe it's a coincidence I was in the store when you called Sorcha. I didn't need anything, but felt like the store was calling, ya know? I may be able to help diminish the effects."

Together, they came up with a spell to help contain the affects of the crystal egg and wrote out three copies in Sorcha's notebook. She tore the pages out and handed them to Helena and me.

We sat in a circle at the entrance to my driveway, barely off the road. The few cars that drove past slowed. One stopped and asked if we needed help. *Glad this isn't a major route.*

Each of us had a copy of the spell on the ground in front of us. Sorcha pulled the necessary ingredients from her over-sized bag. With white, yellow, and black candles in the centre of our circle, I lit the incense Sorcha brought. After asking Archangel Michael to protect us, we held hands and recited the spell in unison.

> "Elements of the sun, Elements of the day, please come this way.
>
> Powers of the Night and Day, I summon thee.
>
> I call upon thee to protect us and this property.
>
> As we light these candles, please protect us from any and all negative forces.
>
> Seen or unseen, all must be guarded, and light the most aligned path ahead.
>
> Please grant us safety from all energy that attempts to hold us back from our path,
>
> As we will, so mote it be."

We each lit one candle. The flames flickered. The wind picked up. Grey clouds formed directly above the property.

"It's fighting back." Sorcha squeezed my hand. "We must keep reciting the spell."

We sat on the ground, chanting over and over. The wind died off, and the clouds drifted away, but didn't completely leave.

"Let's see if it worked." Standing, I brushed the dirt off my behind and slowly approached the fence line. "Here goes nothing."

I took a step. Then another. "So far, so good." I walked a couple more feet. "No nausea, no headache. Don't feel dizzy. I think it worked."

"But for how long?" Helena blew out the candles. "This is only temporary. If you want, I can look into it. I still have all my books on the dark arts in storage. Never thought I'd need them again, but something must have been telling me they'd come in handy. If I had some idea what type of spell was put on the crystal, it would help narrow it down."

I leaned against the car. *Did I want to go through that again? No, but…* "Okay, um. The thing is, he used the egg against me in the summer. My great uncle was somehow responsible for the death of my mother and grandmother. When I confronted him, he held the egg towards me." My hand instinctively moved to my throat at the memory of something restricting my breathing. I gasped. "It radiated a force of some sort. Drained me of my energy."

Helena shook her head. "Egg? I thought it was a crystal."

"Sorry. It's a ruby crystal, shaped like an egg. About so high." I held my hands about four inches apart. "It's actually beautiful."

"Hmm." Sorcha found that detail interesting. "The shape might be significant. The colour, too. Red is frequently used for love, but it's also associated with power."

Another car approached and stopped.

"Schist. I have an appointment and I'm not ready."

"We'll leave you then. If you need anything, call." Sorcha hugged me. "Be well."

Helena held her hand out. "Give me your phone and I'll enter my number. Always glad to lend a hand."

We gathered up the candles and incense and said our goodbyes. I walked over to my client.

"Hi. Sorry abut that. Afraid the potion isn't ready, but I can whip it up while you watch. Follow me up the drive."

I unlocked the front door and stepped inside. Everything felt normal.

"Make yourself comfortable in the dining room. I'll bring the ingredients I need." I quick-stepped past the living room and waited until my client settled before pushing the release button. Using Nenka's garden basket, I gathered up everything I needed and joined my client.

She watched me grind the dried herbs and mix up a little spring water infused with ginger.

"This is interesting. I'd never watched Francine make them. She always had them ready when I arrived."

"Sorry for the wait. Had an emergency to take care of. Here you go. Ten percent discount for the bother."

"No bother at all. Thank you. I always stock up on this in the fall. Helps ward off the flu and colds."

"Let me know when you need more. Again, thanks for waiting."

When she left, I poured a glass of white wine and sat in the sunporch to text Drew. She sent a video request immediately. I pressed accept.

"How are you? Did you fix the problem? I see you're in the sunporch, so you obviously made it into the house." Drew had worry lines across her forehead.

"Stop fretting. You don't want to be all wrinkle-faced for your wedding."

"How can I not worry? You need to dispose of that crystal. How'd you mange to get past the effects?"

"I have two new witch friends. Sorcha, from the Highlands, she's about the same age as Aunt Priscilla, and Helena, transplant from England. Don't know where exactly. Around our age. She looks like a Goth and used to dabble in the dark arts. Swears she doesn't any more, but that might come in handy dealing with the egg."

I relayed everything that happened, including my search for Nenka and Tinkus.

"What? You met a faerie?" Drew laughed. "Only you. I'm glad you're expanding your circle of friends. Missy's nice, but she's not our kind. I don't mean that in a snobby way. You need non-witch friends, but this is a good example of why you need to meet more witches. I'm not asking you to join a coven, but you do need to know some witches well enough to ask for help when you need it."

"About that. I was thinking an app to meet local witches would be handy."

Drew shook her head. "Are you forgetting about the witchy website? One of the forums is for meet-ups. Go in and search your area. With all that was going on, I guess none of us thought to mention it. Not everyone signs up, but anyone listed is open to meeting newbies. Sorcha should know about it. Gran said you sent her Sorcha's email."

"Yes. Since they're about the same age and experience level, with you all still in England, I thought it would be easier if they could put their heads together. Both her and Helena said they're willing to help."

Drew's over-the-door bell dinged in the background.

"Guess you have a customer. I'll let you go. Just wanted you to know I'm okay. Say hi to Randy."

I wanted to look up a few things in some of the old books, so I headed down to the secret workroom, pausing at the living room door. I felt fine, so I went in to check on the egg. Before I realized what I was doing, I had it in my hands. It felt warm and vibrated. *What are you doing? Put it away. Now!* I shook my head to clear the fuzzy feeling and put it back. When I got down to the work table, I lit a small bundle of sage, inhaling the woodsy scent. *What the frig just happened?*

Cooper called as I flipped through the books Granny had stashed in the workroom. Shelves and shelves containing mostly old books on herbs, ancient healing, crystals, symbols, and, of course, spells. She'd been collecting them for at least fifty years. My guess would be some were her mother's. Aunt Priscilla mentioned a lot of the books she had were from their mother. They must have split them when Granny moved to Canada. *Have to ask Auntie why Granny moved from England.* I stuck a bay leaf in to mark my page and answered the phone.

"Hi, Coop. What's up?"

"Why don't you tell me?"

"Um, what?" *How did he know what happened?*

"A couple of your new friends stopped in. Why didn't you call me and let me know?"

Oh, that. Was he angry or concerned? "If I'd called you, what would you have done? Are you telling me you can do magick all of a sudden? First reaction was to call Drew. Then I remembered Sorcha. Helena was a surprise. Sorry I didn't call you after. I had a client. I'm fine." *For now.* "Really. Are you mad?"

He sighed. "No, just concerned. You did the right thing. How about I come over after work? You'll have to bring my car back, then we can pick up something and watch a movie or two in my apartment."

"Perfect. Don't suppose I can convince you to watch some old Hallowe'en movies? 'Tis the season, almost. Not in the mood for something soppy." Truth be told, chick flicks had never been my thing.

"After what you just went through, you want to be scared? How about a comedy?"

"Sure. We'll figure it out. Anything but romance." *Well, anything but a romance movie. Romance in general? Maybe.* "The movie *Halloweentown* is on Disney Plus. Haven't seen that in ages."

After the call, I went back to the book. There was so much I still needed to learn. Now that Drew was planning her wedding, our video lessons became less frequent. Totally understandable.

Finding nothing to help me, I put the book back and went up to the sunporch with my laptop and logged into the witchy-wide-web, our version of www. Drew mentioned the forums, which I'd never completely explored. Hadn't been on it much at all. One of the threads was dedicated to meet-ups, broken down by country. I clicked on Canada. It was divided by province, region, and city, listed alphabetically.

I scrolled down to the Y's, looking for York Region. *Bingo.* Each of the nine regions had a thread. The one for Newmarket didn't have many posts. The last comment was a couple of years ago. Sighing, I typed a post and clicked enter, then backed out one level to look at the posts in the York Region section not under a specific area. It had a few more recent posts, the newest being almost a year ago, and no one looking to meet newbies. I exited out and scrolled through my emails.

A sudden wave of nausea hit. *Schist.* Then the headache. My hands shook. I stood, planning to leave. Everything blurred and I fell to the floor.

EIGHT

"Marcy? Marcy? Please speak to me."

Cooper? But he's at the bookstore.

"Marcy, wake up."

I opened one eye, surprised that the sun wasn't shining brightly. "Cooper. Why are you here?" I looked around. "Am I in your car? How did you get here?"

"I took an Uber. We had a date, remember?"

"But that's not for hours." I looked out the car window. "It's almost dusk. What in holy heliodor is going on?"

"You didn't show up or answer your phone. I picked up dinner and came over. You didn't answer the door. It was locked, so I came around back. You were passed out in the porch. I couldn't wake you. Found the car keys in your pocket, carried you to my car, and started home. You began to rouse when I got on the road, so I pulled over. What happened? What do you remember?"

"You called. We made a date. Haven't forgotten that. I was in the workroom going through Granny's books, then I went to the sunporch to search the web for something." I racked my brain, trying to clear away the fog. "The protection didn't work. The effects were much worse this time." Tears ran down my cheeks. "What am I going to do? I can't stay in my own home. I can't even go in to remove the crystal egg. Maybe you can?"

He shrugged. "Maybe. Maybe not. When I came in to get you, I got a bit of a headache. Nothing like what you've been experiencing, but it seems to affect me, too. You're staying with me until we figure this out."

He held up his hands when I started to protest. "No argument. Tomorrow, I'll come back and pack a bag for you."

"Um." *Did I want him rooting through my clothes? My undie drawer? No.* "Maybe Sorcha or Helena can do it? Oh, wait. It affects them, too. I'll call Missy. She's not a witch. Shouldn't have any effect on her. She knows a little about it. I'll call her."

"Your phone is beside your laptop. I noticed it, but didn't think to grab it. I had to get you out of there."

"Kinda need it."

"You need to go to the hospital. You've got a large bump and gash on your forehead. I think it might need stitches. At least it's stopped bleeding."

I touched my forehead. "What in blazes is this?"

"Don't have a first aid kit in the car, so I improvised. Tissue and duct tape."

"Seriously? I need my stuff. I'm conscious. You can't force me to go to the hospital." I opened the car door.

Cooper reached over and stopped me. "Fine." He turned the car around and went back to my house.

When we approached my driveway, he slowed. "You shouldn't get too close."

"No, pull into the driveway. Maybe it's subsided. I'll know soon enough."

He drove past the fence and stopped. "Well?"

"Slight buzzing, no headache or nausea. Keep going. I'll tell you if you need to stop."

We made it all the way to the house with no heightened effects. "You grab my stuff off the porch and I'll run up and pack a bag."

Ten minutes later, I had enough clothing and stuff to last a week. If I needed more, Missy could help.

Cooper stood at the foot of the stairs, my laptop tucked under one arm, a take-out bag in the other. "Grabbed our dinner. I dropped it when I saw you. No harm, no foul. Needs re-heating. Ready?"

"Where's my phone?"

"In my pocket. Come on. I can feel something affecting me. There's no way you're going to tell me you can't feel it."

"Yes, I can feel it." I glanced into the living room. "Let's get out of here."

"First stop, emergency. No arguments."

"No arguments. What are we going to tell them? It's not like I can say a crystal egg did it."

Cooper smiled. "No, but we can tell them you were dizzy and fell. That's not a lie. The only egg they need to know about is the one forming on your head."

Waiting in the emergency room was agonizing. The nurse checking me in couldn't contain her amusement at the duct tape on my head. Even the doctor laughed. We were back at the bookstore shortly after midnight. Too late to call anyone in town, too early to call my family in England. My stomach growled. Cooper nuked the food while I put on coffee.

"There's something I didn't tell you. Please don't be too angry." I set the table, trying to sound casual.

The microwave dinged. Cooper doled out the Chinese food. "Anything important?"

"Kinda." Taking a deep breath, I spat the words out. "I picked up the ruby egg before going down to the workroom. Yeah, I know I wasn't supposed to, but I couldn't help it. It was like something compelled me. Only held it for five or ten seconds." *I think.*

Cooper glared at me, but remained silent.

"I swear I heard voices. Soft. Indistinguishable, but definitely words."

He sat at the table, rearranging the Ho Fun noodles with his chopsticks.

"Say something, Coop. Yell at me. I don't care."

"You felt *compelled?* Like it was trying to control you?" He didn't raise his head to look at me. All his attention focused on the noodles.

I sighed. "Yes. But it wasn't strong."

He put the chopsticks down and finally looked at me. "We have to get that thing out of the house. I called Dad this afternoon. He and Gramps are reaching out to their contacts to see if anyone knows of an artifact that might help negate the effects, or at least contain it.

There are people who collect haunted items. Maybe whatever they used to contain the items inhabited with demons and whatnot would work to mask the effects. They're all in the States, unfortunately, but Gramps knows some of them. He's going to get back to me the moment he knows anything."

Digging into my food, I talked between bites. "I can call Missy in the morning." I glanced at the time. "Well, later this morning. She should be able to drive over after work, but once she removes it, then what?"

"No point in calling her until we know how to contain it. Eat up, then get some sleep."

I'd barely fallen asleep when I woke again. Surprise, surprise, 3:33. What did she need to tell me? The séance to contact Fiona couldn't wait much longer. I fell into a deep sleep, and dreamed. I found myself in a dark room, similar to the one Uncle had taken me to. A man spoke to me. Not Uncle Monty. Different. The words were unfamiliar. Latin, possibly. Or Gaelic. An evil presence surrounded me. My skin tingled, and not in a good way.

"Who are you? What do you want?"

"Return them to me."

The dream ended abruptly. A fissure split my head. The same almost unbearable headache I got when my uncle released me from his dream prison. But this time it wasn't my uncle. I fell back to sleep after taking a couple of Advil. When I woke, I didn't feel rested and still had a lingering headache.

Someone moved around above me. Then the scent of bacon wafted through the vents.

I sat on the edge of the bed, waiting for the fissure to close. It took longer than before. Whoever or whatever it was, was stronger than Monty. Once I felt well enough to move, I dressed and headed up to Cooper's apartment for breakfast.

He smiled when I entered his kitchen. "Morning. Sleep well?" He'd already set the table.

Tell the truth or lie? "Not exactly. Still waking at 3:33. I need to contact Fiona."

"Who's Fiona?"

"You remember? My ancestor. Great, great, etc. grandmother. The one who helped get rid of Monty."

"Ah. Don't recall you mentioning her name before. You think she can help again?" He sounded unconcerned, but I really didn't know him well enough to know for certain. Also didn't feel comfortable reading his feelings.

I took my place at the table and he filled our plates with scrambled eggs and crispy bacon. "From what I can gather, triple three can mean the universe has a message. I can't think of anyone else except Fiona, who'd need to contact me. Even if it's not her, a séance may help bring the message through."

"You're not going back to the house to do it. Use the table in the back room where you're sleeping. It's big enough for eight or ten people to sit around. Whatever supplies you need, we can buy."

"Sounds good. I'll email Sorcha and Helena to see when they're available. Drew, Susan, and Auntie P. might want to join virtually. Even if they can't send much, or any, energy, with two extra witches present, it should be enough to let Fiona come through."

I dug into breakfast. "Mmm. Who knew you were such a wiz in the kitchen?"

After Cooper opened the store, I texted Drew to see when they'd be able to join the séance. She replied twenty minutes later with a couple of options. I texted Sorcha and Helena with the dates and times. Tonight at eight worked for everyone, even though it was one in the morning for my family. When it came to helping, time didn't matter.

I drove to the Garden Witch and bought candles, candle holders, and incense. Crystals weren't an issue because I always carried some with me, and had grabbed extra when I packed my bag.

I took the back roads home. Unfortunately, the rush hour traffic on the main roads hadn't cleared. Took longer, but I enjoyed the little bit of country outside town.

Once the table was set up, I joined Cooper in the store. He quickly ended his phone call, telling someone he'd call soon.

"That was Dad. Still nothing, but there's one person they haven't heard back from. You get everything you need?"

"All set." My phone dinged. "A video request from Susan." I accepted and propped the phone on the counter so Cooper could join.

"Hi, Susan. You remember Cooper?" I turned to him. "Drew's mom."

"Yes, I remember. Nice to see you, Susan. Wish it was under better circumstances."

"We've found a little information, but I don't know if it will help. One of the elders remembers something about an artifact associated with The Ancient One, but nothing specific. We're looking into it. I know it's not immediate help, but maybe you can find something in one of the old books Francine has."

"An artifact? No idea what type?"

"Sorry, no."

"Okay. I'll see what I can find out. I'm at the bookstore for the foreseeable future. Nothing seems to contain the effects of the crystal for very long. I'll explain later."

Susan nodded, but didn't ask questions. "I'll contact you for the séance. We're gathering at Mum's."

"See you then."

"Who's The Ancient One?"

The spark in Cooper's silver eyes faded. Was he upset? "Guess you were out of the loop. That's what they call Fiona. She's kinda revered by everyone."

"Oh. And Susan's mum is your great Aunt Priscilla, right?"

"You got it. And before you say anything, I promise I'll tell them about my little hospital visit. I'd rather do that when they're all together, so I only have to tell it once. Good thing my hair covers it."

He grinned, the spark returning. "You didn't want to get into it with them, did you?"

I puttered around the store, going through some of the books on the shelves. Unfortunately, there was nothing of help. I needed the books in the workroom.

"Hey, Coop. Can I borrow your car again? I want to check on Nenka and her family."

"Sure. Promise you won't go into your house?"

"Promise to drive right past. I'm not anxious to pass out again."

I wandered into the woods a little beyond my property line, hoping to encounter either Nenka or that little faerie.

"Hello."

Startled, I spun around. *Nenka.*

"How can you manage to sneak up on me in the woods? I'm so happy to see you. Are you all okay?"

"Yes. We're fine. I got your message. Have you come to tell me you've contained it?"

"No. It's so bad I can't even stay there. I'm bunking down in the back room at the bookstore. I've even met a couple of witches who are helping me. How are you getting along with your parents?"

"We're still trying to reconnect. They're old and don't want to pass without resolving our issues. They finally accepted Tinkus and are enjoying Nimagg's visits."

"I'm glad to hear it. I wish I'd been able to resolve things with my mother and Granny. At least we were still speaking, even though it was strained. I'd better get back. Just wanted to check on you."

Nenka stood by the fence, waving as I drove off.

With nothing specific to do until the séance, I puttered around the bookstore. There weren't many customers.

Drew video-called a half hour early to chat. Susan and Auntie P. were in the background, fussing with incense and candles.

"Have you found out anything about the artifact?" I couldn't help but wonder if it was significant.

"Nothing. Gran has a vague memory, but it hasn't come to her yet. Do you think it's important?"

Drew's mother, Susan, came up behind Drew. "Hi, Marcy. Sorry we haven't discovered anything. I'm glad you found some witches locally. I don't think we'll be able to conjure up enough energy through the internet to help Fiona, though."

"Yeah, I'm glad too. You being on the call is help enough."

Cooper popped his head in the door. "Sorcha's here."

"Good. Bring her back. Helena shouldn't be much longer." I turned back to Drew. "Gather the forces. We're about to begin."

NINE

A minute after Cooper showed Sorcha in, Helena arrived. I made introductions. Despite what people think, holding hands during a séance isn't a necessity. We simply sat around the table. It was strange trying one with two strangers. At least they had an idea what to expect. Not entirely certain Cooper's mind was receptive enough, but he declined to participate, so it didn't matter. I opened the circle and got started.

Once again, the bright white light appeared. I didn't even have a chance to do anything.

"*Crivvens!* In all my days, I've never seen such a thing."

Auntie P. smiled at the old Gaelic word. I had a feeling she'd make Sorcha a good friend.

I turned back to the white light. "Fiona, is that you?"

The candles flickered.

"You can take some of our energy, like you did before. We've all agreed."

My arm tingled.

Helena released a soft gasp.

Fiona gradually morphed from a white light into a simple human shape.

"Fiona. Can you help me like you helped with Montgomery? He had a ruby egg-shaped crystal he used against me. It's beginning to affect me. Nothing will contain it."

"The coven has the answer."

"What coven?" Our family wasn't part of a coven. Hadn't been for generations. *Is this the message someone's been trying to send me in the wee hours?*

Auntie P. leaned towards the computer. "Did she speak to you?"

"Yes. Sorry. Forgot you can't hear her." I turned to Sorcha and Helena. "When she came through before, they couldn't hear her unless we joined hands."

"I didn't hear anything either." Sorcha looked at Helena.

"Nope."

I couldn't join hands with my family, so I'd have to relay. At the first séance with the ladies, they didn't hear either. No point joining hands with Sorcha and Helena. They weren't family, so it likely wouldn't work. "Fiona, I don't understand."

"Use the ring." With that last cryptic comment, Fiona vanished.

I closed the circle, but left the candles and incense burning. No one moved as I told them what Fiona said.

Helena was the first to slump in her chair, then Sorcha. The experience was always draining.

Cooper knocked on the door and entered, balancing a tray. "Special blends of teas Gramps said helped restore energy." He set it on the small table by the wing chairs.

"How did you know we had finished?"

He winked. "Special skill." He backout out the door. "Enjoy."

One by one, I poured the tea and brought it to Sorcha and Helena, then poured one for myself, and sat with them.

"Okay. When I mentioned not being able to contain the ruby egg, Fiona said, and I quote, 'The coven has the answers.' Then she said, 'Use the ring.' That was all."

"I have a question." Drew waved her hand. "Did she comment when you said we have no coven?"

"Afraid not. So, Auntie. Any idea what this ring is she mentioned?"

"No, but it could be the artifact. Unfortunately, there's no one left from the days of our coven. My grandmother's generation was the last. I suppose the place to start would be the descendants of the last members. Might take me a day or two to track them all down. Some have moved away. You've met a few who've remained locally."

"Okay. I'll read through Granny's journal and see if she mentions it. It's late over there. Why don't you guys go to bed?"

They ended the call, leaving me with my new friends. *How much more will I tell them?*

"I'm not the most subtle person, so I'll simply come out and ask. Who's Fiona?" Helena finished her tea and got up to refill it.

"Fiona is my great, great, something, grandmother. Our family follows a Dianic way. Females only. The modern Dianic Wicca is loosely based on it. It pretty much died out centuries ago, with only a few covens following it. As you no doubt gathered, we don't belong to a coven any more, but to some extent, still follow the old ways. Weirdly, we only give birth to females, with two known exceptions. In both cases, the boy was evil. Fiona gave birth to the first, one of a set of boy-girl twins. My great grandmother had the second. Montgomery. He's responsible for whatever darkness is embedded into the ruby crystal."

Sorcha listened, absorbing everything. "So, someone in the old coven had this ring, and it's been long forgotten. Interesting. It will be difficult to track it down without a description. Antique rings frequently end up being sold. It could be half way around the world by now."

"Maybe Cooper can help? That's his job, after all." Helena was on her third cup of tea. "This is fantastic."

Sorcha stood. "I think it's time to go. I need to meditate at home to build up my strength. Let me know if you need anything else."

The two ladies left, and I went up to Cooper's apartment. "Don't suppose you could locate a ring for me?"

"I'll give it a go. What's it look like?"

"Beats me."

"Right. Where was it last seen?"

"Don't know."

"You're testing me, right?"

I shook my head. "No. Apparently, it's a family heirloom. A talisman of some sort, I believe. Auntie calls it an artifact. Apparently, it's needed to help me rid myself of whatever evil entity is affecting me. Don't even know if this ring is still in England."

I sat beside him on the sofa, chewing my bottom lip.

Cooper let out a sigh. "What? Since you're hesitating, I know it's not good."

"I need to go back to the house. There might be a clue in one of Granny's older journals."

"No way. No. No. No. It's too dangerous."

"I disagree. When we got my clothes and stuff, I barely felt it. Maybe being out of the house weakens it? Or maybe I need to be near it to activate it. I know exactly where the journals are. Quick trip in the back door, down to the workroom, grab them off the shelf, and back out. Less than five minutes."

Cooper shook his head.

"You know I'm going, with or without you. You have a store to run. Can't keep an eye on me twenty-four seven. If you don't go with me now, I'll sneak out when you're with a customer tomorrow. Or in the middle of the night."

His eyes narrowed. "I could lock you in the back room."

"But you won't. Come on. Five minutes inside, tops."

Cooper relented, letting out a deep sigh. "Fine. But I'm not letting you out of my sight."

"Not allowed in the workroom. Family only, and you're not." *Yet. Whoa. Where'd that thought come from?* "I'll leave the secret door open. If you hear me yell or fall, then, and only then, you can come down."

"Fine. Let's get it over with."

When we drove up to the house, nothing happened to me. Not even the slightest twinge. We went around to the sunporch and stepped inside. We stood at the large opening joining the sunporch to the kitchen, waiting. Listening.

Still nothing. Strange, but good.

Even though the gnomes were silent beings, the house felt unusually quiet and empty without them. At least they were safe over the hill at Nenka's family.

We crept down the hall, stopping beside the near-invisible button on the top edge of the wainscoting. The doorway to the living room where the ruby crystal resided beaconed to me. *Nope. Ignore it.* I pressed the button and the workroom entrance whooshed open.

Cooper did as promised and stayed at the top of the stairs. I gave in and let him stand on the landing rather than wait in the hall. He could see part of the workroom, but not a lot. If anything happened to me, he'd know right away. When I reached for Granny's journal, I caught a whiff of rosewater.

"Granny? Are you here?" I took the journal from the shelf.

A gentle breeze caressed my cheek, then a second book shifted on the shelf. As I pulled it down, my head spun.

Schist.

Cradling both books against my chest, I ran to the stairs. "Move, Coop. It's started."

He waited until I joined him at the top before leaving. I barely heard the click of the secret door when it shut behind us. Neither of us even thought about locking the outside door to the sunporch as we made our way to the car.

Yanking open the passenger door, I stumbled inside, still fussing with the seat belt when Cooper floored it and reversed down to the road. He stopped long enough for both of us to fasten up. My heart raced as I tried to catch my breath. Cooper didn't look the least bit winded. *Need to exercise more.*

"That was close. I told you it wasn't safe." He turned to me, still scolding me, but something was off.

"Cooper? I can barely see or hear you."

TEN

Am I dreaming? My body lay below me on the bed in the back room of the bookstore. Cooper fussed over me. *Out of body experience? Did I die?* Cooper wrung out a cloth and placed it on my forehead. *Not dead.* I could hear Drew talking. My laptop sat open on the drop-leaf table that Coop angled towards the bed. He video chatted with her.

"Has there been any change?" Drew's pretty face showed more signs of worry.

"Her temp has come down. I think her breathing is better. Has your gran come up with anything?"

She shook her head. "No. Gran and Mum are in the kitchen on another video call. Should be ending soon. They've called some of the elders in the area to a meeting. There's talk of resurrecting our coven. Two attacks so close together has everyone rattled. This is much worse than with Uncle Monty. And Elspeth still insists Marcy is somehow going to heal our leaching magick. She can't exactly do that if she's constantly being attacked."

I wished there was someway I could talk to Drew. Let her know I was okay. Well, as okay as someone in a coma could be.

Something tugged at my feet. Could the angels be pulling me into the afterlife? I tried to resist. My feet felt like they were being stretched, but there was no pain, just tingling. Did that mean I was being called down, not up? A form materialized beside me, then a second. Granny and Mother.

"Don't fight it. You're being returned to your body. It's not your time. Remember, we're always here to help you." Mother's voice was filled with concern as she reached out to stroke my cheek.

They faded out of sight.

I gave in to the feeling, watching my still form as my spirit lowered towards to it. A jolt of electricity ran the length of my body, then darkness.

When I woke, Cooper sat at the table where we'd done the séance, laptop open, talking with someone. My head spun when I tried to sit up. "Hey."

Cooper turned. "Marcy!" He ran over and helped me the rest of the way up. "We were so worried."

"Not dead yet. When did you call my family?"

"As soon as I got you back here. I took your cell and called Drew. We've had several video calls. Susan and Priscilla, too."

"Several? How long was I out?" My head still spun a little, and I had a brain-splitting headache. "Where's my Advil?"

"Upstairs. Hang on." Cooper moved the drop-leaf table beside my bed, then sat the laptop on it so I could talk to my family. Priscilla and Susan had joined Drew.

He hurried up and came back quickly with the entire bottle and a glass of water. "Here. Don't strain yourself. You've been out for two days. I've closed the store."

My head almost snapped off when I whipped it around to look at him. "Two days?" When my brain stopped spinning, I shook two gel-tabs from the bottle and downed them.

Noticing I was now in pjs and not my jeans and tee, I looked at Cooper. "Uh, who changed me?"

He held up his hands. "Not me, I swear. Helena came over. Both she and Sorcha have been in and out helping and chatting with your family."

"Don't trust that young one." Auntie P. practically sneered at the mention of Helena. "Too much darkness around her."

"Aunt Priscilla, I told you. She *used* to practice the dark arts. Emphasis on used to. She swears she doesn't any more, but her experience with it might help figure out what Monty did."

Priscilla scowled. "Still don't trust her." Her expression lightened. "I rather like Sorcha, though. She'll be a good influence on you."

"She's like an aunt. Have you found out anything about the artifact? I asked Cooper if he could use his helper skills to locate it."

"Yes, he mentioned that. Unfortunately, we still don't know what it looks like. Now that you're back with us, when you feel better, see if you can find anything in the journals. Cooper didn't feel comfortable looking through them."

"Not even to help save me?" I looked at Cooper, trying to appear hurt. Instead, I burst out laughing, grimacing as a short jolt of pain hit my right eye.

"My headache is much better." *Kinda* "I'll go through them later today." I glanced at the window, but Cooper had drawn the curtains. "Is it morning?"

"Afternoon. A little past one. I'm guessing you're hungry. When did you last go two hours, never mind two days, without eating something?"

"Never. And now that you mention it, lunch would be nice. Soup?"

Cooper bowed with a flourish. "Your wish is my command. You chat with your family. Are you feeling up to sitting at the table?"

"Think so. Thanks."

He left to prepare something for me, probably canned soup, and I moved to one of the wing-back chairs, dragging the little table and laptop with me.

"Tell me the truth, Auntie. Do you really sense something dark within Helena? Honestly? I trust her. I really do."

"Well, it's more like darkness is around her, like an aura. I'll admit, it's faint. How long ago did she stop practicing dark magick? If only recently, that would explain the aura."

"Don't know. Never actually asked her, but I will. Normally, I'd say it's none of my business, but if she's going to be helping us with something dark, I guess it is my business. Did you track down anyone from the old coven?"

"Yes. Bronwen. She turned ninety-five earlier this year. She was barely twenty when the coven disbanded. She has some memory of the artifact, but it's spotty. Not sure if it's a form of dementia or just old age. Unfortunately, Bronwen was having a bad day when I visited. She lives with her granddaughter, who promised to let me know when she's having a good day. One clue; she called it a vessel ring."

I shrugged. "What's a vessel ring?"

"Ever hear of a poison ring?"

I nodded.

"They're also called vessel rings. Not only were they used to hold poison, but they also held sacred relics of saints or loved ones."

"Relics?"

"Bits of bone, teeth, maybe hair."

"Eww. So our artifact is a poison ring?"

"Sounds like it. There are a few more people to check on. Susan and Drew have split the list with me. Most of them are young enough they wouldn't have any first-hand knowledge, only stories handed down. Bronwen is our best bet."

"Okay. Thanks Auntie. I'll go through Granny's journal later this afternoon. What's this I hear about you starting up the coven again?"

Drew, Susan, and Priscilla stared at the laptop, mouths open. Like they say in England, they looked gobsmacked.

Susan spoke first. "How on earth do you know that?"

"Must be another skill surfacing." Drew nudged her mother. "She must be a mind-reader."

"I wish." How was I going to explain this? "I believe I had an out-of-body experience before I came to. I saw Cooper putting a wet cloth on my head and heard you talking. Granny and Mother appeared and told me it wasn't my time. Voilà. Here I am."

Priscilla shook her head and turned to Susan. "That girl never ceases to amaze me. Yes, we've been discussing it."

Cooper returned with two empty bowls in one hand, pot in the other. "Soup's on."

"Smells delish." My stomach growled.

"You eat and rest. We'll talk again later." Drew and Susan waved as Priscilla ended the call.

"Table." Cooper motioned to the large table on the far side of the room. He put the bowls down, dug two paper towel-wrapped spoons from his pocket, and doled out the soup. "Figured chicken noodle was the best for a patient."

"Soup at la can. Perfect." I spotted Granny's journal and the other book sitting on the table. "You wouldn't look through the journal, but what about the other book? I don't even know what it is. Granny led me to it."

He rolled his eyes. "Of course she did. I flipped through it, but can't make heads nor tails out of it. Eat first, then, if you feel up to it, you can go through the journal."

"Agreed. Hey, why don't you let Sorcha and Helena know I've returned to the land of the living?"

"Eat first."

I saluted, then dug in, finishing two bowls-full before Cooper finished one. Not a single noodle remained in the pot.

Cooper took the dirty dishes up to his apartment, returning with two large pieces of cake. "Thought you deserved a treat. And before you ask, one of these is mine."

I pouted, but accepted the luscious, dark chocolate cake. "Mmm. Don't tell me you've learned to bake?"

"Much as I'd like to take credit, Sorcha brought it over yesterday. Not entirely convinced it's a regular cake and not spelled."

I took a bite. "Delicious." I reached for Granny's journal. "I'll start reading. You text Sorcha and Helena. Invite them over, if they're free. I feel perfectly fine."

Holding the book in one hand, fork in the other, I started going through the journal. Most of it spoke of spells she tried, and the results. A lot of scribbles and symbols accompanied them. I'd previously only read the part surrounding her twenty-first birthday ceremony.

"Helena is at work, but Sorcha is free. She's on her way." Cooper put my phone down and collected the now empty plates.

"Why don't you open up the store? I'll be fine."

"Not until Sorcha arrives. Tell me, how can you be in a coma for two days, then wake up alert and ready to go?"

"Good genes? Magick? You complaining?"

"Never." Cooper kissed my forehead and took the plates upstairs.

I sat at the table, staring as he walked away. My entire body tingled. No way I could concentrate until it wore off. *Come on, Marcy. Think of something else. The headache and nausea the ruby caused.* Closing my eyes, my mind went back to the house and the flashes from the ruby egg. The lightheadedness. Feeling like I wanted to puke. *Better.*

Ten minutes later, he let Sorcha in and went out front to open for the rest of the afternoon.

She shrugged out of her coat, letting it drop on the floor, and hugged me so hard I thought my head would pop off. "I'm so happy you're all right. I can't believe it. You don't look like you've been ill at all."

"Can't… breathe."

"Sorry." Sorcha released me and scooped up her coat, draping it over the chair Cooper vacated.

"I feel perfectly fine. Had a headache and spins at first, but they're gone. Cooper was on a video call with my family when I came too. You've made quite the impression on my great aunt, and that's hard to do."

"Probably helps that we're contemporaries." Sorcha glanced at the books on the table. "What're you reading? They look old."

I tapped the book I'd dropped when she hugged me. "This is one of Granny's journals. With any luck, she mentioned the artifact in it. Auntie said she found out it's probably a poison ring."

"If it was a witch's ring, more than likely it was used to hold something spelled rather than poison."

"Actually, she called it a vessel ring. Guess it probably has a few different names. They're still trying to track down descendants of the old coven, and I asked Cooper if he could locate it. Not holding my breath, since none of us knows what it looks like."

"And the other?" Sorcha pointed to the book on the table.

"Not sure. I was drawn to it by Granny when I went for the journal. Never got a chance to look through it. Cooper said he didn't understand it. Maybe you can?"

Sorcha picked it up. "I'll give it a go."

ELEVEN

We spent the next couple of hours in silence, reading. Sorcha pulled a notebook from her bag and made notes. Since she looked deep in thought, I decided to ask about it later. Granny's journal was interesting. The first half she seemed to be experimenting with new spells. *Did I grab the wrong journal?*

As we read through, it got more interesting. She wrote of other witches, granddaughters of the old coven. Finally, a comment about the artifact. Regrettably, there was no description of it. At least not yet. She mentioned custody. A few pages later, Bronwen's name jumped off the page. I picked up my phone and sent Auntie P. a text.

Granny mentioned Bronwen in her journal.

Good. What'd she say?

Not much. Something about custody.

Will ask her about that. Thanks.

Sorcha looked up. "Find something?"

"A hint, but a very small one. Auntie will ask Bronwen about it, when she finally has a lucid day. I noticed you've been making notes."

"This book has a section on heavy protection and containment. One of them might work around the crystal. We'll probably have to come up with a variation of our own, but this will give us a head start on what to do. Hopefully, Helena can find something in one of her dark magick books about spelling a crystal with evil. We can use that to try to create a counter-spell."

Right on cue, Helena entered the back room, carrying a couple of bags. I glanced at the time. "Wow. Didn't realize it was that late.

"I wanted to see how you are." She held up the bags. "Brought dinner. Cooper's closing up the store and will join us."

Helena put the bags on the table and pulled out containers from a local Greek restaurant. Cooper came in a few minutes later.

Still hungry from two days without food, I devoured more than my fair share. No one said anything.

Helena reached into her satchel and pulled out a book. "Found this on spelling items with evil intent. I think we'd better put up some protection before going through it."

Cooper left us to our task after clearing the table.

My mind backtracked to the day Drew and I went through the dark grimoire in this very room. Lots of candles, incense, and a thorough cedar smudge. Fortunately, Helena brought everything we needed.

Sorcha walked the perimeter of the room, smudging. I lit the incense. Helena lit the candles. She'd brought white, black and blue candles. The white for purity, black to absorb negative energy, and light blue for healing and to help uncover the truth.

Helena opened her book to a section she'd marked with a ribbon.

Before she read anything, I asked what had been on my mind since she put the book on the table. "Is it safe to read it? Last summer I went through a dark magick grimoire and the owner cautioned me not to read anything word for word."

"No need to be concerned about that. This is no different from going through any spell book you may have. I know the type of grimoire you're referring to. Those definitely require extra protection and you should never read them word for word unless you're casting." Helena flipped to another page she'd flagged. "This section has incantations for suppression and confinement. Not sure if they'll work in this case, as they're intended for people or animals."

Sorcha glanced at the open page. "Since we're dealing with a rock of sorts, there are no feelings to suppress, and we don't need to stop it from going anywhere." She looked up at and smiled. "Unless this crystal egg has legs that you haven't told us about."

"Not that I've noticed." We all laughed. "That's actually a scary thought. If the egg was hollow, it could contain something sentient. Fortunately, this one is very heavy. Feels solid."

Helena flipped through the pages. "Maybe if we combine parts of different spells and add our own words…?"

Sorcha agreed. "That's likely the only way we're going to find a usable solution." She turned to me. "Have you found anything of your uncle's that might help? Who has his possessions?"

That threw me. "Possessions? I don't know. Never thought about that. He may have had a will, but I haven't the foggiest notion where to look. The place he took me to when he invaded my mind was an abandoned house nearby.”

“Do you know where it is? We should look to see what he left behind.” Helena closed the book. “Why don’t we go now? It’s dark enough.”

I wasn’t crazy at the idea of skulking around an abandoned house, especially at night. I thought back to when Monty took me there in my dreams. The room looked well kept. And he had an altar of sorts with an enormous book on it. I could tell the location from the partially uncovered window and the view outside.

“Yes, I know how to find it. It’s only a few blocks from here. But won’t someone notice us? I mean, we’ll need light and the windows aren’t completely boarded up.”

Sorcha dismissed my concern with the flick of her hand. “Between the three of us, we can maintain an illusion long enough to have a good snoop. All anyone on the street will see is exactly what they expect to.”

“And I know an illumination spell that will light up an entire room. Comes in handy in the winter when the electric bill goes up and the sun sets. Wish I had one for heat.”

“What are we waiting for? I’ll let Cooper know where we’re going, to be on the safe side.”

I left my new friends to pack up their belongings and went out front to talk to Cooper. “Here’s the address.” I scribbled the location on a pad by the register. “Shouldn’t be more than an hour or two.”

Cooper frowned as he looked up from the laptop. "I don't like the idea of you going into an abandoned house. I should come with you."

"No. You finish with your accounts. If we do get in trouble, we'll need someone on the outside we can call. Two powerful witches will be with me. We'll be fine."

"We'll take good care of her." Sorcha joined me at the counter.

"See? I'll be as safe as if Auntie P. was with me."

"Fine. I know better than to try to change your mind. Call me when you get there and leave the line open. If anything happens, I'll know immediately."

"Sure, Coop. You worry like an old lady." A quick kiss, and we headed out the door. Three witches on a late night excursion.

"Wish I had someone like that watching out for me." Helena gave me a hip-bump as we walked. "If you get tired of him, send him my way. I have a few things he can help me with." She turned to Sorcha. "Too bad you didn't get to know his grandfather better. For an old guy, he was kinda dishy."

"I may be new to the area, but I had enough interactions to get to know him a little before he moved. He isn't dishy. Dashing describes him better." Sorcha sighed. "Must run in the family."

"Yes. I've met Coop's dad. They all have that same Depp look." I stopped and pointed. "We're here. How do we create the illusion?"

We waited as someone approached with their dog. Once they passed, Sorcha and Helena joined hands. "Follow our lead." I clasped Sorcha's outstretched hand. "Concentrate."

They recited something in either Latin or Gaelic. *Got to learn both one of these days.* A surge of energy reached the sidewalk, then dissipated. The building seemed to waiver briefly, then returned to normal.

"It's done. Should last long enough for us to have a good snoop." Sorcha released my hand. "Now, how do we get in?"

"Round the back, I expect. Wish we had cloaks of invisibility." A narrow path lead around the building. I took the lead. "From the view I got, his room was at the back, upstairs. Makes sense, as the neighbours wouldn't be able to notice anything."

We rounded the corner and entered a yard enclosed with a tall, thick cedar hedge. Someone had boarded all the windows up, but several planks were missing here and there. The back door also had planks across it, but on closer examination, hadn't been secured in place. One end was nailed into a two-by-four, noticeably newer than the blackened, rotting boards everywhere else. The new board had hinges.

I grabbed one of the boards and pulled. It opened like a regular door. Unfortunately, the original door behind it was locked.

Sorcha gently pushed me aside. "Let me see. I don't think it's really locked." She placed both hands on the door. "It's spelled. Should be easy enough to disarm." She said a few words and turned the handle. The door opened. "See? Basic locking spell. I guess he didn't expect anyone like us to find this place."

We filed in and Helena lit up the room. The kitchen. It was a little dusty, but looked like someone had used it not too long ago. *My tormentor?* A thin layer of dust barely coated the counter and table.

I called Cooper, turned the volume all the way up, then put the phone in my back pocket so he could hear everything. More importantly, he would be able to hear me if we ran into trouble.

Next, we headed into the living room. Helena extinguished the light in the kitchen and lit up the living room. "Takes energy to keep the room illuminated. We only need it in the room we're in."

Made sense. As long as I could see where I was going, I was happy. "There's the stairs."

Helena lit up the staircase and led the way, keeping the living room bright until we all started up. "Left or right?"

"Good question. Both rooms probably have windows facing the back. I wasn't in the room long enough to see where the door was. I'll check left, one of you check the other."

Just enough light filtered into the rooms to tell us which one Montgomery used. "Here." I stepped in. "This is the one. And it's still got all his stuff."

Helena extinguished the light in the hall and focused her energy on this room. We all gasped at once. In the centre, a large pentacle had been painted on the floor.

"Is… is that… blood?" I knelt down to get a better look. "He drew the pentacle in blood?"

TWELVE

Sorcha shivered. "This room is filled with energy, and not the good kind."

Helena stood in the doorway, afraid to enter. "I can feel it too. I'd better stay out. Somehow, the room can sense that I used to practice the dark arts. It's calling to me."

I hadn't asked before, but now was the time. "Um, how long ago did you stop the dark stuff?"

"Not long. I gave myself to the light at Ostara, about six months ago."

No wonder Auntie P. was concerned. "Okay. Better safe than sorry. As long as you can keep the lights on in here, I agree. Are you even safe in the house?" I heard a muffled voice from my pocket and pulled out my phone.

"What was that, Coop?"

"I don't think you should stay in there if it's affecting Helena. Please, get out."

"We found what we need. Won't be long. Promise." I put the phone back in my pocket. "Let's grab the book and leave."

"We need to cleanse the room first." Sorcha reached into the oversized bag she always carried and pulled out two bundles. "Cedar and sage." She lit them and smudged the room, then handed the smoking bundles to Helena. "I'll come back another day and take care of the entire house myself. Let's get the book for now."

It lay open on the altar, a ribbon hanging from the top. Sorcha put the ribbon in place, then closed the book. It had a lock on it and she spelled it before clicking it shut. "Don't want anyone to open the book without proper protection." She looked at me. "That includes you. I realize this is your family's property, but I don't want you futzing with it unsupervised."

I couldn't help but smile. "You don't know how true your suspicions are. I would definitely open it and go through it without telling anyone. Can I assume you're going to take it home and not leave it with me?"

"With your permission. I would like to try to cleanse it tonight. Because it's specifically for the dark arts, it's impossible to remove all the evil intent, but I may be able to minimize it. And the spell I put on the lock forbids anyone, including me, from opening it for 24 hours. I'm going to call your great aunt first thing in the morning to discuss it with her. I'll send her a text tonight so she can prepare, too."

Nodding, I pulled my phone out. "We're leaving the house now, Coop. Should be back in twenty minutes or so. I need to try to fix the vibe the house is giving off."

"Okay. I'll come down and meet you."

Sorcha and Helena did their thing with the house while I stood and watched. Temporary protection placed around the house would prevent more evil from entering, hopefully. Sorcha would make it permanent later.

More lessons with Drew were definitely needed, but she was going to be preoccupied pretty much until Christmas. Her Yule wedding would be a couple of days before. She and Randy were heading off during the reception, not returning until after New Year's Day. Susan and Auntie P. said they'd pick up the slack, but they were busy with the wedding preparations, too. *Maybe Sorcha could help with my lessons?*

By the time we finished and moved around to the front of the house, Cooper had arrived. He paced the sidewalk, his eyes never leaving the house. From the look on his face, he had to be worried, again. I joined him as my energy wasn't needed to remove the illusion.

"Did you find everything you were looking for?" Cooper held my hand as we walked. "The sound was muffled, but I could tell you were excited about something."

"Yep. Found Uncle Monty's spell book." I looked at Sorcha. "Or is it a grimoire?"

"Will have to have a closer look, but I believe it may be a mixture, starting as a basic spell book."

"Helena, how do you feel? Did the house have any lasting effects on you?" I didn't like the thought that something I initiated could harm someone. Especially someone outside the family. She didn't need to put herself in harm's way for me. Neither did Sorcha.

"So far, so good. I'll double or triple up on my protection when I get home. Don't feel any different."

We arrived back at the bookstore and said our good nights.

Cooper noticed I didn't come back with anything. "Thought you said you found his book. Where is it?"

"Sorcha is safe-keeping it. She wants to put as much protection around it as possible. She's also going to go back later to try to completely cleanse the house. I wish I could do the same type of spells they do. Even though Drew has been teaching me, I still feel like a kindergartener."

"Can't say I'm unhappy that you didn't bring the book back. I remember when Gramps got the loan of that grimoire for you and Drew. He didn't want you to know, but he had a few issues after returning it to his friend."

"What? What kind of issues?"

"Nothing major. Flickering lights, a weird smell. Few items moved. Fortunately, that didn't last long."

"Wish you'd told me. We could have fixed it before Drew went home." I yawned. "Think I've had my fill of fun for the night."

After I climbed into bed, I could hear Cooper moving around upstairs. *The vent! That's how he knew when to bring the tea after the séance.* Having someone worry about me gave me a warm feeling. I soon drifted off to sleep.

My eyes opened with a jolt. *What was that?* Positive someone touched me, I turned on the lamp by the bed. The room was empty, the door still shut. I picked up my phone to check the time. Surprise. It was 3:33. *Did Fiona still have a message for me?*

Wanting to try to contact her, I racked my brain to figure out how to do it myself. The crystal ball sat in the living room at home. I'd left it on the window sill to charge in the moon light. There was no hand mirror to use. *Water.* I tip-toed upstairs and grabbed a wooden salad bowl from Cooper's kitchen cupboard, then partially filled it with water. I had candles and crystals. The only other thing required was darkness.

Back downstairs, I placed the bowl on the drop-leaf table, then set an arc of candles around it. After they were lit, I turned out the light, then dropped a clear quartz crystal into the bowl. The bundle of cedar we'd used earlier still sat in a dish on the large table. I re-lit it, smudged, then grounded.

Staring into the water, I concentrated on Fiona, then let my mind go blank. My eyes needed to relax, much like looking at a 3D picture. After about ten minutes, visions ran through my mind, almost like I was dreaming.

It wasn't Fiona.

Instead, a strange creature appeared. My gut said it was whoever or whatever had been invading my mind. He was humanoid, his skin blackish-green. My assailant walked in a circle, exposing a short tail. *Is this what has been waking me, or was it Fiona trying to warn me? Couldn't be this creature. Triple three is supposed to be good.* An evil aura surrounded him, making me light-headed. His thoughts entered my mind. He wanted the ruby crystal egg and the book, and I swear he looked directly at me, clawed hands reaching out. The image appeared and disappeared in a flash. The entire event lasted only seconds.

I continued to stare into the water, but nothing more happened. I turned on the light and blew out the candles. The cedar was safe in the glass dish, so instead of extinguishing it, I let it burn out, then climbed back into bed and fell into a deep sleep.

I woke to someone shaking me and yelling. Half awake, my mind was foggy. I blinked several times, trying to focus.

"Cooper?" My voice sounded raspy.

"Marcy! Thank God. I've been shaking you for several minutes. I thought you were in another coma."

I tried to sit up, but didn't have the strength. Cooper helped me, gasping when the covers fell away.

"What happened to your neck?"

"My neck? What are you talking about?" Reaching up, my hand touched something sticky. "What the…?"

Cooper's gaze went behind me. The expression on his face was… scared? I turned, afraid of what I might see. My pillowcase was slashed and soaked in blood. I swooned, falling back. My head hit the wall, almost knocking me out.

"You need to go to the hospital."

Still foggy from the deep sleep, and possibly from the bash on the back of the head, I couldn't comprehend why. "I'm fine."

"You're not fine. I could barely wake you and you have gashes on your neck that are still bleeding. Don't you people have a—"

I cut him off. "Don't you dare say witchdoctor."

"No, I'd never. But aren't there witches with medical degrees?"

"Yes, but I haven't had any reason to seek one out. Growing up we never needed them. Nenka probably knows a poultice I can use.

Oh, Nenka! I'm not at home. Her family has gone to her parents' home until whatever this is, is fixed. How bad it is?"

"Pretty bad. At least the bleeding has almost stopped. Can you stand?"

With Cooper's aid, I got on my feet. "Little wobbly, but I can walk."

He helped me to the two-piece bathroom on the main floor and gently cleaned the blood off. My nightie was a write-off. I looked in the mirror. Three gashes ran half way around my neck. "Do you think I need stitches?"

"Yes."

"Sorcha?"

"I'll call her."

Less than a half hour later, she arrived. "Marcy, that needs to be seen to immediately."

"I don't know any doctor I can call. How do I explain this to a regular doc? Can you do anything?"

"Sorry, no medical training. I recall meeting a local witch who's in medical school. Maybe he can help?"

"Please, if you wouldn't mind calling him? All I need is stitches. I can get an herbal poultice if Cooper will drive me."

Sorcha found his number and made the call. "He can't get here before ten. Meanwhile, he said to wrap it with gauze to keep it clean."

I hugged her. "Thank you for coming. One of these days, I hope to be able to handle most things myself, but I'm glad to have you as a friend."

After Sorcha left, I asked Cooper to help me find Nenka. He agreed quicker than expected, even printing up a sign for the front door—*Family Emergency. Closed until one.*

We drove past my place, slowing until I found the spot where I'd parked before. "Here. Pull over here. A little past the fence."

Cooper grabbed my arm when I opened the door. "You need to keep that wound clean. No way you're traipsing through the woods. Nenka knows me. Wait in the car."

Ten minutes later he came back, Nenka following so close she almost rode his foot.

"She insisted on seeing you."

I opened the passenger door, and she climbed in with Cooper's help.

"Let me see."

Carefully, I unwrapped my neck, exposing my wounds.

"Oh, my. That is bad."

"There's an intern coming in a little while to stitch me up. He's a witch, so my explanation won't make me sound too crazy. I hoped you'd know a poultice I could use. Never had to mix up anything for something so serious."

"Yes, I know the plants you'll need."

Cooper opened the voice recording app on his phone, holding it so Nenka could talk into it. Almost everything she mentioned grew in the garden, but it wasn't safe to try to collect them. Fortunately, every ingredient was also a wild plant that grew locally. Nenka led Cooper through the woods so he could pick the herbs we needed. I hugged Nenka, thanking her repeatedly.

We arrived back at the bookstore a half hour before the intern.

Cooper washed the plants and did all the chopping and mixing. He placed the mixture in the fridge to allow it to gel up. The plan was to apply it on top of the stitches.

At ten sharp, someone knocked on the front door. Cooper let the intern in and led him upstairs. He remained silent while I explained what had happened.

"I can see why you didn't go to a traditional doctor. He'd probably admit you to an asylum. Where's this mixture you want to apply?"

Cooper removed the dish from the fridge. It had set nicely. As he explained what was in it, the doctor nodded his approval.

"Yes, that should do nicely. Now, I'm going to apply a topical numbing to your neck before stitching it up. It won't completely freeze your neck, so you'll feel the stitches. Mostly just pressure. Maybe a little pin prick. Then I'll apply your ointment and re-wrap. Change the dressing daily. The stitches will dissolve, so I won't need to come back unless you develop an infection." Less than ten minutes later, he was packing up his bag.

"Thank you, Doctor Barnstable. I'll make certain she takes it easy for the next week or so." Cooper winked at me. "Might be difficult."

"I can give you the name of a fully licensed wiccan physician in the area, in case you ever need one."

"Yes, please." I had a feeling I might. "I really appreciate you coming out on short notice. How much for the house call?"

"How about a copy of the recipe for that poultice? I'm still an intern, so I'll consider this a practical lesson. I've heard about your grandmother. If you've taken over her practice, I can send people your way for potions. Rumour has it she was very good."

"Better than very good. And yes, I've taken on a few of her clients. Still learning, but I have help."

Cooper walked with him to the door, and I headed down to my little apartment. Despite the intense need to crawl into bed, the sheets needed to be stripped and washed. Or tossed. Sucking up the pain, I managed to pull the sheets off by the time Cooper joined me. He remade my bed after helping me to the wing-back chair.

I slept until mid-afternoon. Waking refreshed for a change, I looked at the laptop. *Better called Auntie P. before she finds out.*

THIRTEEN

When I opened the video chat app, I noticed three missed calls. One from Drew, one from Susan, and one from Auntie P. *They already know.*

I didn't need to toss a coin to decide who to call first. The matriarch of the family. She answered immediately.

"Hi, Auntie. Were you sitting at the computer waiting for me to call? Have you been chatting with Sorcha?"

"Yes. She sent me a text last night to arrange a discussion about the book. We spoke shortly after you called. Sorcha wasn't tattling. We'd already arranged the call and I could tell something was up."

I gestured to my bandaged neck. "As you can see, I've been taken care of, so there's nothing to concern yourself with. Since I don't have to waste time telling you about my incident, what did you decide about Montgomery's book?"

"Nothing to concern myself about? Really, Marcy!"

"Sorry, I didn't mean anything, just that I'm fine. The medical student that Sorcha called gave me the name of a fully licensed wiccan doctor, in case I ever need one. Right now, I'm much more concerned about the book. Sorcha was going to try to cleanse it."

It took a few minutes for Auntie to settle her feelings. I'd upset her again. *Does the doc have a cure for foot-in-mouth disease?*

Auntie finally spoke. "Sorcha showed me the book. It's ancient. We don't believe we can cleanse it as the evil is completely embedded into it due to the dark magick spells in it being used for such a long time. I could feel its strength through the computer. It's centuries old and we should destroy it unless we can find a place to permanently hide it. That has to be done with great care."

"Understood. Before she closed it, she placed the ribbon to mark the spot Monty had left open. I didn't see what it said. Would it be of any help?"

"Yes. It reads like it may be the spell used to infuse the ruby. We don't know exactly what with, unfortunately. She's gone through some of the book and there doesn't seem to be a reversal. We're both trying to write up something. It may not be possible to rid the crystal of the intent, but we should be able to contain it. It might need to be destroyed."

My heart sunk. The ruby was stunning and would be a nice addition to my collection. "Oh, no. That's a shame. It's such a beautiful crystal. I really had hoped I could keep it."

"Don't get your heart set on it. First things first. We have to contain it somehow. That's priority one." Priscilla glanced over my shoulder and smiled.

When I turned, Cooper stood in the doorway with a tray. "You can come in. Smells like soup."

"You haven't eaten yet. Aren't you hungry?" He set the tray down. "Hi, Priscilla."

"Good afternoon, Cooper. I see you're having a hard time keeping my grandniece out of trouble." Fortunately, she smiled.

"What else is new? Don't suppose you could cast a cooperation spell on her?"

"Very funny, guys. What ever happened to being kind to injured people?" I pouted, then burst out laughing. "I know I tend to go head first without thinking." My hand instinctively went to my throat and my laughter stopped. Stretching the stitches wasn't a good idea. At least the numbing hadn't worn off yet. "This is a lesson learned. A huge lesson. But in my defense, I didn't do anything to cause it. Did I?"

"Well." Auntie P. hesitated. "If you hadn't brought that crystal home…"

"But how was I supposed to know anything would happen? And if I'd left it there? Then what?"

Cooper put his arm around me. "Someone else would have picked it up. A town employee, probably."

"Right. And he likely would've either trashed it where it might end up in the wrong hands. Or worse, brought it home to a child. Think what havoc that would bring. An innocent exposed to all that evil."

Auntie P. nodded. "Yes. Leaving it for someone to randomly pick it up wasn't an option. I would have brought it back here to Dorking, but without knowing what its power is, it could have caused major issues with the airplane. That book Montgomery left behind should tell us what he did.”

I could sense something was up with my aunt. “What’s wrong, Auntie? And don’t say nothing. I can tell.”

“It’s Helena. I’m concerned about her. Sorcha told me the house affected her and how Helena had to stay out of the room my brother used for his spells. Did you find out how long ago she left the dark arts behind?”

“Yes. Ostara.”

Her mouth actually dropped open, her eyes wide. Would have been funny except for the circumstances. “That’s barely six months. The evil that permeated in that room would have keened it in her aura. I realize you need help from people around you, but the darkness will seek her out and try to take over. If you insist on having her help, she needs to quadruple her personal protection, and you and Sorcha will have to double up, too.”

Cooper stood behind me, hands on both my shoulders. I reached up and placed a hand over one of his. “What about Cooper? He was affected, though only slightly. And my little gnome family. They’re still staying away from the house.”

“Cooper felt it? This is worse than I thought. Witchcraft usually does not affect helpers. Much as I hate to say it, Montgomery may have gone further than learning black magick. This sounds demonic.”

“Schist! A demon? Seriously? Now I have to try to find a demonologist?”

"Possibly. For the time being, symbols are a good place to start. Since you're staying at the bookstore, the building will have to be protected. If I recall correctly, it's brick, so you won't be able to carve into the walls."

Cooper leaned over my shoulder. "How about a wall hanger? Should be easy to find a sign maker."

Auntie nodded. "Yes, that will work. You'll need something over all doors and windows. The Egyptians, Turks, and Vikings had several symbols, some of which cross over into wicca. The ones that come to mind are the triquetra, evil eye, turtle, arrow, dragonfly, tree of life, and the Helm of Awe."

"Maybe Missy can help with that. She grew up in Cairo and studied Egyptology at the university. I've been teaching her spell craft, and she's more than willing to teach me all about Egyptian beliefs and curses."

"Be careful who you include. Everyone involved will likely be affected. Bringing in a non-witch isn't advisable."

"I can ask general questions. She's too green to have her help. Already had to call Drew to reverse something she did. The shop north of here sells several items with the evil eye. I can drive up and get a few things to hang around the store."

Cooper tapped my shoulder.

"Cooper can drive up." A headache niggled at the base of my neck. I closed my eyes to try to will it away. "I'm feeling a little tired. We'll chat later."

"You must get lost of rest so you can heal. I'll be in touch with Sorcha, and let you know if we find anything."

Much as I hated to lie to Auntie, there was no way I was going to tell her about the earlier headache, and I'd practically forgotten about the goose-egg on my forehead. The headache was probably an effect from bashing my head against the wall earlier. People do get plain ordinary headaches.

Cooper put up the *closed for family emergency* sign, made sure I was in bed, then drove north to pick up the items I'd written down. Several different items with the evil eye topped the list. Contrary to the name, the evil eye doesn't hex people. It protects against evil intentions directed at you. The tree of life would definitely be there as it was wiccan. Not sure about the rest, but he'd find what he could.

He returned forty-five minutes later and texted me to open the back door. When I opened it, Cooper balanced several bags in his arms. I grabbed the closest one and held the door open.

"Did you buy out the store?"

"Almost."

We put the bags on the large table in my make-shift apartment and he removed the contents. The first items he pulled out were two small bags. He opened one. "Evil eye rings, several sizes. Thought maybe Sorcha and Helena could wear them. Got several wall hangings, too. This one can go on the front door. Also, some pendants with the triquetra."

He reached in and pulled out a box, opening it so I could see when he turned it. He'd found a wire sculpture of a tree with crystals on the branches. "It's not exactly the tree of life, but the lady at the store assured me it will help. She was curious and asked why I needed so many items. She'd heard Sorcha and Helena talking after you called her. They were in the store, so she had an idea something big was going on. Hope you don't mind that I told her? She offered help if needed. I think she's a witch, too."

"The more the merrier. What else you got?"

Cooper pulled out a little turtle. "Thought this would look cute by the cash register." He reached in again. "And some little dragonflies. No arrows or Helm of Awe."

"And what's in that bag?" He'd pulled out two small bags earlier. One had the evil eyes and triquetras.

Cooper handed me the bag, and I peeked in. "Dragons? Auntie didn't say anything about those." He'd bought not one, but three tiny black dragon figurines.

He took one out. "I like dragons. Wouldn't that be cool if you could find a spell to bring them to life? The ultimate protection."

"They are cute. But protection? Sure, as a statue. But if they came to life they'd probably burn down the entire block."

"What about the other items? The arrow and Helm of Awe? Do you think we need them?"

I nodded. "Better to have too much than not enough. I'm sure we can find arrows somewhere. Maybe purchase a quiver at a sporting goods store? I looked up the Helm of Awe. Kinda looks like a snowflake. If you've a steady hand, a wood burning kit should do the trick. Wood is easy enough to buy. You can print out an image, trace it onto the wood, then burn it in."

"Yeah. I always wanted one of those kits. I'll do that later. Must be a hobby shop around."

"Probably. Michaels might sell them. I wouldn't mind going. Need to wrap a scarf around my neck first."

It took a little convincing, but Cooper finally relented. I didn't have a scarf with me, but Mr. Barker had left an ascot behind. Felt kinda weird wearing it, but fortunately it colour-matched my top. Between that and doing my jacket all the way up, the mummy wrapping around my neck didn't show. Good thing the day had brought a September chill.

We went straight to the back of the store and found everything Cooper needed to make a wall hanging with the Helm of Awe. They even had little kits with all the stuff needed to hang pictures. We wandered up and down the aisles and found an arrow with a twine rope for a hanger. Cooper grabbed a couple of those, intending to burn in some of the symbols.

As I was more or less house-bound until my neck healed, I needed something to do. The store had a jewellery supply section, so I stocked up on the required items, including an instruction book and several gemstone beads already drilled for threading.

By the time we got back, I was exhausted. Cooper ordered some chicken on one of those delivery apps. While waiting, he changed my wrappings.

"Getting low on the ointment. Tomorrow morning I'll drive out and see if I can find more of these plants. I sort of remember where they were, and no, you aren't coming."

"I'll call Missy and ask her about the Egyptian symbols. Her turn to teach, and she does love talking about their beliefs. It'll be easy to pump her for info without telling her why. Once it's over and done with, I'll give her the details. She won't be happy when she discovers we left her out of everything, but at least she'll be safe."

By the time we'd scattered Cooper's purchases from the Garden Witch around the place, the food delivery arrived. After we ate and cleaned up the kitchen, we both settled in my space to read up on our purchases. I had a book, but Cooper's kit had minimal instructions. Mostly safety. I curled up in one of the wing-back chairs and Cooper sat in the other, tablet in hand, watching how-to videos on woodworking.

A cozy evening. Something I could get used to.

FOURTEEN

Three days passed with little happening. Boredom set in. Missy busied herself at the museum, which was a good thing. Normally, either I'd visit her, or she'd visit me at least once a week. I still kept my temporary change of address a secret. I'd tell her soon. We had a video chat during her lunch one day, and she didn't seem surprised to see me at the bookstore.

Helena and Sorcha dropped in a few times to see how I was doing. Surprisingly, neither had any evil eye items, but Sorcha said she had a triquetra pendant she wore every time she read through Uncle's book.

I explained my aunt's concern to Helena about the evil seeking her out. She had no problem amping up her protection. She even accepted one of the eye rings and said she'd stop in at the Garden Witch to stock up. I didn't tell her that Auntie wanted me to keep her from helping. Her insight would come in handy, provided she was careful.

Since Sorcha had no family or coven here, she invited us to her home to celebrate Mabon. The small group I seemed to have assembled felt like family despite the short time we'd known each other. The celebration honoured the equinox change from the light half of the year to the dark half.

The meal was potluck. Sorcha made a roast beef stew, left simmering while I helped her decorate. Her front yard sported pumpkins of various sizes, uncarved, and her porch rail had been wrapped with an artificial leaf streamer. The leaves were a mixture of maple and oak in various shades of brown, orange, and red.

Inside, mini-pumpkins, pinecones, and gourds sat atop the fireplace mantle and windowsills. Several vases were filled with both dried and fresh flowers. Inhaling the aroma of homemade incense, I searched my mind to determine the ingredients. Frankincense, sandalwood, cinnamon, patchouli, and cloves.

While I helped Sorcha, Cooper arranged firewood in the backyard pit. That would be lit after dark. When everything was set, Coop and I headed home to clean up and change.

We returned a few hours later, freshly scrubbed, carrying our contribution to the meal. Earlier in the day, I'd baked two pies. One apple, one pumpkin. Since I was relatively new to baking, I used store-bought shells. My fingers were crossed that the pies tasted as good as they smelled.

Helena beat us to Sorcha's by a few minutes. She had made hot apple cider, which hung on a large wrought iron hook in the fireplace. Naturally, it simmered in a cauldron.

Missy appeared shortly after with freshly baked bread, still warm. Since nuts were part of the traditional Mabon celebration, Missy'd made two loaves of honey wheat bread, the tops sprinkled with crushed walnuts on one, almond slices on the other.

The oval pine table in the dining room had been set with simple white plates, and drinking glasses decorated with autumn leaves and pumpkins. The centrepiece was a silver candelabra holding white candles. Several dried leaves, pinecones, berries, and acorns surrounded the base.

We all took our seats and Sorcha said the blessing. "Lord and Lady, watch over us and bless us on this special day. Bless this food, this bounty of earth, and the new friends celebrating the day. We thank you. So mote it be."

We all repeated "so mote it be" then dug in.

By the time we finished, the sun had long since set. Completely gorged, we waddled out back to the fire pit. Sorcha lit it and, one by one, we said what we were grateful for. I was grateful for everyone sitting around the fire. Especially Cooper.

We lingered a few hours before breaking up the party. Sorcha had already arranged for Missy to stay over, so she wouldn't have to make the long drive home in the dark. Most of her route had no streetlights and a lot of deep ditches.

Sorcha refused our offer to help clean up, and practically pushed us out the front door. I almost dozed off in the car on the short ride home, so when I crawled into bed, I fell asleep instantly, with no weird dreams to disturb my rest.

By day four, I couldn't take it any longer. I snuck out while Cooper assisted a customer, leaving a note taped to the backroom door. Keys in hand, I "borrowed" his car and drove out to visit Nenka.

As soon as I climbed over the fence, the little faerie I'd first encountered appeared. "You're back. Nenka has been looking for you, anxious to find out if she can go home."

I crouched down closer to her level. "I had a little accident. Do you know where she is? I miss her and her family."

"I'll find her." The little faerie zipped away before I could thank her.

A few minutes later, Nenka appeared. This time I actually heard her coming, running through the layers of dead pine needles, crunching with each step.

"Marcy. I'm so happy to see you. Is the ointment working? I helped Cooper gather more plants."

"Yes, thank you. The medical student that assisted even asked for the recipe. So, how are you and your family? Are you getting along any better with your parents? It's the longest time you've spent with them for decades."

"Yes. It's almost like nothing ever happened. A little tension, but it's fine. Do you know when we can go home?"

"We're working on it. Might take a while yet. I thought I could pop into the house and check it out. Last time it was fine, initially. Took a few minutes before it kicked in. I've been away for what? A week? I should be able to slip in for several minutes without anything happening." My phone rang. *Cooper.*

"Aren't you going to answer that?"

"No. Not important."

"May I come back to the house with you?" Nenka looked worried, lines filling her tiny brow.

"If I say no, you'll cross the field and join me, right?"

She smiled.

"Okay, hop in the car." She slipped under the fence and I lifted her up.

I did a U-turn and went back to my place, idling at the foot of the driveway. The top of Nenka's head barely reached the arm rest. She stood, stretching her neck to look out.

"I don't feel anything, do you?"

Nenka shook her head. "Nothing."

Taking a deep breath, I drove up to the house. Still didn't feel any affects.

"I'd like to grab a few more of Granny's books. It's possible she may have mentioned the artifact, even though it seems to have been long forgotten by then. Her mother or grandmother may have spoken of it and Granny wrote it down." I snapped my fingers. "Her grandmother! There must be journals from both her mother and grandmother around. Maybe even previous generations. They wouldn't have simply tossed them out."

I reached over to open the passenger door. Instead of hopping out, Nenka sat twiddling her little thumbs.

"It'll be all right, Nenka. Everything seems safe. If either of us begins to feel even slightly off, we'll make a run for it. I've brought extra protection with me." I reached into my jacket pocket and pulled out a small obsidian. "Even have some protection for you.

Place this in your apron pocket. We shouldn't be in the house long enough for any ill effects, but this will absorb lingering negativity."

The diminutive gnome nodded, but still hesitated before sliding out the door.

We both looked around as we approached the sunporch, then entered the house.

I slipped through the secret door in the hallway and headed down. Nenka disappeared and popped out of the fae door in the workroom, a little bag over her shoulder. *Guess she needed a few things, too.*

About ten minutes later, it started. Dizziness at first. Nenka felt it as well.

"Marcy, we need to leave now."

"I need the rest of my crystals while I'm here. They're in my bedroom closet." I grabbed the oldest looking journals and raced upstairs. Some of them looked old enough to be Priscilla's mother's or grandmother's.

The nausea hit worse than before. As I reached for the wooden box on the floor of my closet, darkness ascended.

Once again, I found myself somewhere void of all light—no way to tell where I was or who with. Just like when Uncle Monty invaded my mind and took me away. *Is this presence using the abandoned house?*

"Hello? Where am I?"

Something moved behind me. I spun around but saw nothing. I could sense him, though. Not quite like when I picked up on regular people. Similar, but prickly. *Is this what a demon feels like? Pure evil?*

A deep, gravely voice came from the void. "Return my possessions."

Feeling a tiny bit brave and more than a little pissed off, my stubbornness came through. "If you mean the ruby crystal egg and the spell book, they were my uncle's. He's family. You're not. They're right where they belong."

A sharp pain filled my stomach. I dropped to my knees. Invisible icy fingers clutched my throat. His claws dug in as he squeezed tighter and tighter. I tried to pull them away, but there was nothing to grip. Something sticky coated my fingers. *My stitches broke!* I fell to my side and curled into a ball, trying to protect as much of my body as possible. Bit by bit, my breathing slowed.

I woke up back in the bookstore, once again floating above my outstretched body. Sorcha and an unknown man leaned over me. *Am I dead this time?* I listened as they spoke, hoping to find out what had happened.

"Is there anything you can do, Doctor Parker?" Cooper sat on the bed, holding my hand.

Must be the licensed wiccan doctor the intern recommended.

"For now, keep her comfortable. I've re-done the stitches. I believe a demon has possession of her. You may have to call in a priest. Unfortunately, this is something I have never had to deal with. Very few witches around here deal with the dark side of magick." The doctor picked up his medical bag. "You need to find a demonologist. I'll check in on her in a few days. Call me if she gets worse. There may be someone in the city who can help."

Cooper walked him to the door, leaving me with Sorcha. "Come on Marcy. Fight this." She placed several crystals around my still body and gently lifted my head to hang a pendant around my neck.

At least I wasn't dead. *Nenka!* What happened to my little wood gnome? I remembered she joined me in my bedroom when I went up for my gems. *Why haven't Granny and Mother come to me like before?* Somehow, I needed to contact them. I concentrated. *Nothing.* I called. *Nothing.*

Have they deserted me? Is it my time now?

Something tugged at my feet. *Am I trying to go back to my body?* I relaxed and went with the flow. Nope. Cooper was shaking his head. Turning my attention back to the real world, I resumed eavesdropping.

"Don't believe she's possessed. Why take control of her body and then have her lie in bed, in a coma?" Cooper sounded adamant about something.

Sorcha placed her hands on his shoulders, looking him straight in the eye. "There's no other way. I've done some research and found someone not too far. He needs to be called. Now."

"But a demonologist? Isn't there something *you* can do? I need to call Priscilla."

"Not until we've done everything we can. There's nothing she can do from England."

Cooper stared at my prone, still body for several minutes. "Fine. Call him. But I'm calling Priscilla to let her know exactly what's going on."

Watching them converse broke my heart. They had no idea if I would come out of it this time, or if they'd lost me for good. Somehow, I had to get back inside my body and wake up. Concentrating as hard as I could, I called on Archangel Michael for help. Again, something tugged at my feet, just like last time.

Please, let me return to my body. Relaxing, I let the feeling overcome me. The pull increased. Without warning, I zipped down with a jolt.

Thank you.

FIFTEEN

Cooper and Sorcha turned towards my moan. "Marcy?" Cooper ran across the room and sat beside me. "Marcy? Are you awake?"

One eye opened, then the other. "Hey."

"Hey yourself." He leaned down and kissed my forehead. "Thought we'd lost you. Again." Since he'd let his guard down, a rush of raw emotion flooded my mind. Relief, worry, and a little anger.

"Cooper, what's happening?" Auntie P.'s voice drifted over.

"Grab the laptop and bring it here, please." I wanted to see Priscilla. From the bit of conversation I'd heard, she didn't know about my latest trip into the void.

Cooper sat the laptop on the foot of the bed, then helped me sit up. I reached down and moved the computer onto my lap. "Hi, Aunt Priscilla. Cooper was calling to tell you I had a little, um, mishap." *How was I going to explain this? Mishap. What I did was stupid and dangerous.*

"I knew something was wrong. You didn't stay put, did you?" Her brow furrowed and her lips pinched. Even through cyberspace, it was apparent she was both upset and angry. Funny thing, I couldn't sense it the way I normally did. *Must be tired.*

"Guilty as charged. In my defense, it's pretty boring just sitting around for days on end. I snuck out and went to visit Nenka. But I took extra precautions. I had my black tourmaline bracelet on and said a prayer to the Greek goddess Soteria for safety and protection from harm. I even gave Nenka a crystal." I turned to Cooper. "How is she? I know the ruby egg has affected the gnomes, but I don't know to what extent. How did you find me?"

"Nenka. She pulled your cell from your pocket and called me. She's quite resourceful. Apparently, it doesn't affect her as much as you. A little headache and nausea. Immediately after I arrived, she went back to her family. I'll go find her later and let her know you're okay." Cooper patted his pocket. "Car keys stay with me at all times. What happened, exactly?"

"Not entirely sure. It's all a bit of a haze. It was similar to when Uncle Montgomery contacted me. I remember a black void and a gruff, growly voice. He wants his possessions. Guess the grimoire and ruby crystal egg? At least I wasn't possessed."

"Why did you go to the house in the first place? And alone? Without telling anyone or leaving at note at least?" The worry lines on Auntie's forehead smoothed out somewhat, as she could see I was reasonably okay, but she was still angry.

"Thought there might be something in one of Granny's other journals. We only had the one here, and I thought I could find more. Maybe some from older generations. Hoped they contain more information. Also needed the rest of my crystals." I turned to Cooper. "Did you bring them?"

"Wasn't going to, but Nenka insisted. Said you risked everything to get them. They're on the table."

Auntie P. shook her head. "You should have asked me. My sister didn't take our mother's journals when she moved to Canada. I have all the journals from our ancestors. Please, you have to start talking things out before acting. Obviously, the extra protection wasn't enough."

"Don't worry, Auntie. I've learned my lesson." I closed my eyes and took a deep breath. "My head's a little wonky. I need to lie down for a bit." My stomach growled. "Food wouldn't hurt either. I know you'll tell Susan and Drew, but make sure they understand I'm fine. Only a little leftover headache."

Cooper ended the call, gave Sorcha the computer, then turned to me. "Lay back. I'll make you some soup."

"Actually, I'd like something a little more solid."

"Don't push it. You haven't eaten much for a couple of days. Omelet?" Cooper went up to his apartment, leaving me alone with my new friend.

"Days? Again? Schist!" I looked up at Sorcha. "You've been quiet."

"Didn't want to interrupt. I've emailed the demonologist. He doesn't have a phone number on his website. I've asked him if he can do anything with the book to cleanse it. He may need to see the crystal. Is it all right if I ask him to go to your house to check on the ruby? Didn't want to mention him to your aunt until I get a reply."

"That's fine. I hope there isn't a demon in it. I know items can be possessed, but I've never heard of a crystal being inhabited. Don't suppose you had a chance to go through Granny's journals?"

Sorcha shook her head. "Not without your permission. I looked at the first page of each so I could put them in order."

"Great. How about you read to me while I rest? Didn't want to mention it to Coop, but my head is splitting. Can you get me a pill? Bottle's by my bed."

Once I was medicated and comfy, Sorcha picked up a journal. "This is the first one. She's quite young, so there may not be anything useful in it."

"Actually, that might be the best place to start. Priscilla said no one had mentioned the ring for generations."

Sorcha picked up the first journal and dragged one of the wing-backed chairs over to my bed. "I feel like I should be starting with once upon a time."

Instead of reading it word for word, she skimmed, giving me the highlights. "She talks about her lessons. Spells she's been trying. Sounds like she's a pre-teen. Too young to be included in anything with the adults. Do you know if your family was still in a coven when your grandmother was young?"

"No. Priscilla said it stopped with her grandmother. Or maybe it was her great gran? I'm sure they'd still have been in touch with the others, though. Anything else in there?"

She flipped through the pages. "No, just more spells. Let me try the next one."

Cooper returned with my food, the delicious scent arriving well before he appeared. "Do you want to try to eat at the table?"

"Yes." I threw back the covers and attempted to get up. "Little help here?" Something way less pleasant than the omelet assaulted my nose. "Wow. I need a shower. Why didn't you say something?"

Cooper raised an eyebrow and smiled. "I can help with that later."

"Nice try. Maybe draw me a bath? Soaking sounds good, and safer than standing."

He put the plate on the table and helped me over. "Do you want the bath after you eat?"

"Yes, food first. I need my belly full." I took a bite. "Mmm. Where did you learn to cook?"

"Mom made certain I could take care of myself. Didn't want me starving once my training was complete and I was assigned a location."

Sorcha relocated to the table and kept going through the journals while I ate. My plate was empty in record time, not a speck of egg left. Barely needed washing. Cooper took the teapot upstairs and returned with a fresh brew. Sorcha had stopped flipping pages, her lips moving silently while reading Granny's entry.

"Find something?"

"I think so. She wrote about a conversation she overheard. An argument about who got the ring next."

"Did she mention anyone?" I leaned over to look.

"No." Her Scottish brogue thickened as she flipped the next few pages. "That's all. The rest is spell work."

Cooper sat beside me. "It's a start. Maybe in one of the other journals she'll mention it again. For now, Marcy needs rest."

"No argument from me. You'd think being out for days I'd be refreshed, but instead, I'm exhausted."

"Probably because while you were out cold, your body was fighting whatever was affecting you." He helped me back to bed. "After you wake, I'll draw that bath you mentioned."

When I opened my eyes a few hours later, Sorcha was gone, and Granny's journals sat neatly on the table. I slowly rose. My headache was finally gone, and my head didn't spin.

"Cooper?"

Footfalls thudded on the stairs to his apartment above the store. Cooper burst into the room, breathing heavy. "Is everything all right?"

"Yeah. I wondered where you got to." It was nice to have someone so concerned about me. "Wouldn't mind that bath now." I waved a hand in front of my face. "And a change of clothes."

Cooper saluted. "Your wish is my command. One hot, steamy bath coming up." He headed back up, quietly this time, and I rooted through my stuff for something clean to wear. *Next task, laundry.*

I made it to the foot of the stairs and called him again. Even though I felt much better, I didn't want to risk a sudden dizzy spell halfway up. Coop put his arm around me and I almost swooned. Couldn't help but smile and lean into him.

By the time he helped me into the bathroom, the tub was almost full and the mirror coated with steam. That's when I noticed stuff floating in the water.

"Um, Cooper? What did you put in the bath water?"

"Rosewater, lemon balm, and lavender. I've been going through some of your books, looking for ideas on how to help you heal quicker, or at least feel better."

Wow. Gotta love a guy who goes the extra mile. Maybe I should take stock of everyone's insistence we belonged together. Being with Coop felt so natural, like we'd been a couple for ages.

"Thanks, Coop. I may soak for the rest of the day."

Half-hour later, the water started getting cold. So much for "the rest of the day." I felt better and didn't stink. The delicate scent of lemons, lavender and rosewater replaced the stench of days old B.O. The rosewater made me think of Granny. After I dried off and changed into clean clothes, I eased down the stairs to the store front. The closed sign hadn't been flipped to open.

"Why is the store closed?"

Cooper walked out from behind one of the stacks. "Been kinda busy trying to revive you. People have been leaving messages or sending emails looking for books, or some of the special items. Not going to go broke closing for a few days."

I walked over and unlocked the door, then flipped the sign. "I'm up. May as well let people in."

I'd barely taken two steps when the door opened.

"Afternoon. What can we help you with?"

"Just looking." She disappeared down one of the aisles.

"That's strange." Something was off.

"What's strange?" Cooper looked in the direction of the customer. "Something with the lady?"

"No. I can't sense anything from her. Can't tell what her emotions are. I've been keeping my wall relaxed so I can sense problems, but strong enough so I don't get bombarded with everyone's thoughts. When I noticed she was blank, I dropped the walls completely. Still nothing."

Something was definitely off. Not with the lady, but with me. As far back as I could remember, thoughts or feelings automatically came through. It got stronger when I grew up. Enter my psychic wall. It had been up for the past seven or eight years. Every morning after grounding, up it went.

When Drew came over before my birthday to help me re-learn everything, the first time I let the wall down, it overwhelmed me. Now, it was under control, more or less. I should have gotten some sort of vibe from the lady. Everyone in my family had it, but it was strongest with me. Part of being special.

Cooper tapped my shoulder. "You in there? You kinda zoned out."

"Thinking."

"Why don't you step outside and see if you can read anyone going by? There should be people wandering around. Walk up to the coffee shop. There's always people at Cardinal. While you're there…"

"Not so subtle hint for coffee? Maybe the fresh air will clear my mind."

The coffee shop was around the corner and the owners and staff knew me. Went in all the time before moving to the city, and had resumed the habit after Granny died. When I opened the door, I expected to be inundated with the thoughts and feelings of everyone. Like with the lady in the bookstore, nada. I got a regular coffee for me and a mocha latte for Cooper, and a couple of black bean brownies.

Walking back, I felt alone. Abandoned. *Is this what regular people feel? How do they stand it? Did the demon somehow diminish my powers so I can't stop him from getting the book and crystal? Why can't I remember the encounter better?*

SIXTEEN

I knocked on the front door with my foot, trying to get Cooper's attention. Two hot coffees and a bag of goodies made it difficult to turn the doorknob. He rang up the lady's purchase, and she held the door for me.

"Thanks. Enjoy your book." I smiled as I slipped past her.

The customer mumbled something I couldn't make out.

Cooper came over, took his coffee and the bag. "Whatcha buy?"

"Brownies." Didn't tell him they were the gluten-free ones. He'd never be able to tell the diff.

"So?"

"So, what?" I knew what he was asking, but I wasn't going to let on.

"Could you pick up on anyone?"

I sipped my coffee and took a bite out of a brownie. "Mmm. So good. Oh, the people? Nothing." My gut told me it was a big deal, but I didn't want to worry Cooper.

"Nothing? What does that mean? Side effects from being asleep for a few days?"

"Maybe." *No clue.* "I'll call Drew. Her shop should be closed by now. Then I'll call Sorcha and see if the demonologist has gotten back to her and let Auntie know." The shop phone rang. "You may as well answer that. I'll be fine."

I took my coffee and brownie into the back. When Drew answered her phone, I heard a lot of background noise.

"Hey, Marcy. On my way to Mum's. What's up?"

"Not sure. Have you spoken to Priscilla today?"

"No. Why? Have you found something?"

"Not exactly. Remember last week when I was out for a few days?"

"Do I remember? How could I ever forget? You scared us. You're okay now, though. Right?"

"Yes, and no. It kinda happened again. I think it affected me this time. I can't sense anyone. No thoughts. No emotions. I've completely lowered my wall, but nothing's coming through."

Muffed voices came through Drew's phone.

"Drew? What's happening?"

"I stopped walking, causing someone to bump into me. Almost at Mum's. This conversation requires my full attention. I'll video call you as soon as I get there."

I set up my computer on the large table and waited for the call. Ten minutes later, Drew and Susan appeared on my screen. I was kinda glad Auntie P. wasn't there, too.

"What's this Drew is telling me about losing your psychic ability?"

"Something happened when I was unconscious again." I braced myself, waiting for Susan's response. Guess Drew was too chicken to tell her that part.

Susan stared at the computer. Her mouth opened and closed a couple of times, trying to figure out what to say.

"I've already beaten myself up about this. Surprised Auntie didn't tell you. I spoke to her this morning. I went back to the woods, not thinking about consequences. Again. I wanted to see Nenka and make sure her family was all right, and we both went home. I wanted to grab a few things. Almost made it, too. The effects lessened after being away from the house for an extended time, so I thought I could slip in, grab what I needed, and exit before anything happened. With the extra crystals and the prayer to Soteria, I figured that would be enough for the short time inside. Who knew it would be that powerful?" I filled them in on the details of what I saw, at least what little I could recall.

"Mum told us you were unconscious, but you couldn't remember much. You have no idea who this entity is? It's not Montgomery again, is it?"

"No. I don't believe it is." *Do I tell her what I really saw? Was it his true identity or a mask to deceive me?. No, not yet. I need to be certain first.* "He hasn't given me any hint as to his identity. All he's said so far is that he wants his stuff back. Stuff being the ruby and dark spell book. The grimoire is still with Sorcha. At least I have all of Granny's journals, and we've found a tiny clue. As a child, Granny overheard a conversation about the coven members passing something along.

It could be the ring. There are still more books to read through, so maybe she says exactly what it looks like in one of them."

Susan shook her head. "After everything you went through this summer, you still take risks. Marcy, you have to promise to talk your ideas out. Get input from the family. Stop forging ahead on your own. I'll talk to my mother and see what's she's doing. I know there are more descendants from the old coven she's trying to track down. We'll be in touch. And stay away from the house."

We said our goodbyes and ended the call. Nothing she said was wrong. As usual, I was stupid. Thoughtless. Irresponsible. Not only had I put myself in danger, but Nenka became involved. Fortunately, she wasn't affected anywhere near as bad as me.

Next, I called Sorcha. She came over right away.

✷✷✷

"Tell me exactly what you're feeling." Sorcha dropped her bag on the floor and draped her coat over the back of a chair.

"That's just it. I'm not feeling anything. It's so weird."

"What about spell work? Have you tried that?"

"No. Haven't had any need to. Why? Do you think that might be affected too?"

"Who knows? Do something simple."

I chuckled. "Simple is about all I *can* do. I'll try lighting a candle." Several sat on the table, remnants of the séance days ago. Sorcha moved one closer. I concentrated. Nothing happened. I tried again and again. Zippo.

Next, we tried tarot cards. I'd become quite good at interpreting them. Card after card, and I couldn't read them. It felt like someone had wiped my mind clean.

Sorcha clasped both my hands in hers. "Your aura has changed. It's similar to mundanes. Do you think this entity did something to you?"

I shrugged. "Didn't think so. He seems to want his stuff returned. Can't see how he'd benefit from stripping my magick." I thought for a moment. "Could it be the crystal ruby egg? When Uncle used it, he pointed it at me. It made me weaker. Have you heard back from the demon guy?"

"Yes. I was about to call you when you called me. I included my phone number when I emailed him. I just got off the phone with him when you rang. He's available tomorrow, and he wants to see the crystal first hand."

"Whoa. It's so not safe to go into that house. I think the only people who can handle it would be mundanes. I have a friend I can trust, but I don't want to get her involved, just in case."

"Talk to the demonologist here, at the store. See what he has to say. Then we'll figure out a plan. Is tomorrow afternoon good?"

"Sure. The sooner the better. What about the spell book? Does he know about that?"

"No. That's purely magick. The fewer people who know about it, the better."

After she left, I puttered around the store, helping Cooper. A few customers noticed the symbols placed around the interior. The witches knew what they were, and expressed some concern, but the non-witches thought they were simply decorations.

Cooper found more wood and honed his skills while I made more jewellery. It was actually fun. Took my mind off what had been happening, and I got to spend down-time with Cooper, like two normal people. *Normal. Would I ever be normal?* Before my trip to the house, I'd done an internet search and found a boatload of stones online and placed a large order. They'd arrived, so I made bracelets, pendants, and a few things to hang from windows. Some hung in the back room. Several were going to be placed around my house whenever I moved back in.

The next day, Sorcha arrived at 1:30. We set up candles and incense. They shouldn't be necessary as we were only going to talk, but it made for a pleasant atmosphere. We debated whether or not to include Helena and agreed it unwise, at least until we had properly cleansed the spell book. Another thing Auntie P. was looking into. The demonologist arrived at two sharp. Cooper showed him to the back.

The introductions were short. We all wanted to get straight to the matter at hand.

"Mr. Sugden, thank you for coming. We hope you'll be able to tell us if the crystal has actually been possessed. The effects from it have been terrible, mostly on me, but it's also impacting others. I can't even enter my house without feeling it." I opened the gallery on my phone to show him pictures I'd taken over a month ago. "This is the item."

He scrolled through the pictures, nodding. "While it's common for items to be possessed by a spirt or demon, it's unusual for a stone or crystal. It can happen, though. Tell me, what are some of the effects?"

"Well, mainly nausea, dizziness, and headaches." Telling a stranger about it was odd, but I had no choice. "The brunt of it falls on me, but anyone with power can experience it. It's gotten so bad that spending even five minutes in the house is dangerous for me." I hesitated. "Um, it's also knocked me unconscious a couple of times.

"I see. Like I told your friend, I'll need to see it in person to make a determination. Only then can I recommend something. I can offer some protection to you all before we go. Are you willing?"

I looked at Sorcha. "We don't have a choice, do we?"

She shook her head. "Seems it's the only way."

"I'll have to bring Cooper." *Do I need to call Priscilla first? Yes.* "I also need to call my aunt."

Cooper took care of his customer, then closed the bookstore while I called Auntie P.

"The demonologist is here and wants to go to the house. He needs to see the crystal before he can say if it's demonic." I didn't need special power to tell she wasn't happy.

"I don't like the idea, but I suppose it can't be helped. At least this time you'll have people with you. Make sure you have as much protection as possible and get out the moment anything starts."

We all loaded our pockets with crystals. Even Cooper. Mr. Sugden brought his own protection—holy water and a blessed silver cross. Cooper gathered up some of the wood he'd burned symbols into, and I collected the crystal window hangers I'd made. We piled into Sugden's car and thirty minutes later we idled at the foot of the driveway.

Sugden turned. "How is everyone feeling?"

We all gave the thumbs up.

He continued up the driveway, stopping by the front door. "There is a demonic presence nearby. Be very careful, and speak up the moment you notice any change in yourself or one another."

I unlocked the door and entered. Once we were all in, Cooper hung one of the symbols on the nail in the front door, normally used to hang a wreath.

I pointed to the living room. "The crystal is in that room."

Once I crossed the threshold, the pounding of a headache hit hard. "I have a slight headache. It's not bad." *Liar!*

Sugden walked around the room. When he approached the display case, he stopped. "It's here. I need to hold it."

I kept the case locked, and the key was on my key chain. "I'll get it." I unlocked the case, reached in, and picked up the crystal egg, intending to hand it to him. Didn't quite work out that way.

I screamed, dropping the egg on the carpet. My hand blistered. I turned and ran outside. Cooper came after me.

"What happened?" He put his arm around my shoulders.

"Thought I was going to throw up."

"Why did you scream and drop it? You could have handed it off."

I showed him my hand. My palm was red, covered in puss-filled blisters. The pain was intense. I had burn ointment in the kitchen, but didn't know if it was powerful enough for this type of burn. I described the bottle and location to Cooper and asked him to fetch it. When he returned, I was sitting on the step.

"We need to get you home. Now!"

I winced as he spread the ointment.

"You're not going to believe this." Cooper's voice distracted me from some of the pain. "Sugden took the crystal and sprinkled the holy water over it. It actually sizzled, and I swear I heard it scream."

The front door opened and Sorcha came out. "He's going to take it and bury it somewhere for now."

"No! He can't take it away. Find a place here to bury it."

"But—"

"It has to stay here. I don't know why, but it can't leave the property."

"Okay. We'll find a place. He's got a container in the trunk." Sorcha dangled the keys. "He asked me to fetch it."

Sorcha came back to the porch and showed me the container. Wood of some sort, covered in symbols, with a lock and hinges that appeared to be silver.

Twenty minutes later, they both came out.

"Open it." I wanted to verify the ruby had been placed inside personally, and make sure it wasn't a trick. I didn't know Sugden. For all I knew, he'd bury an empty box and take the crystal home.

He lifted the lid. The crystal egg sat nestled on a black velvet cushion. I nodded, and he locked the box.

Together, we all walked to the east boundary. Cooper had detoured to the shed for a shovel. He caught up and dug a hole four feet deep. Sugden placed the box in the hole, the silver cross resting on the top. Sorcha spoke a prayer or chant in Gaelic, then Cooper filled the hole in.

My stomach settled down almost immediately. Unfortunately, the burns on my hand remained. "I think it might be safe for me to return home." I held up my right hand as Cooper started to protest. "But not for a few days. I rather like being waited on. Besides, I can't drive with a wounded wing. We can come out on the weekend and see how we both feel. Maybe Nenka can come, too."

"Don't rush it. Even if your house and property are safer, as you said, you can't drive." Cooper put his arm around my shoulders while we walked back to the car. "We'll see how you feel Saturday, then discuss it." He turned to Sorcha. "We'll all discuss it."

Sugden joined the conversation. "I wish you'd have let me take it, as I can contain it much better."

I shook my head. "No. It must stay here. That's one thing I'm positive about. Are you certain it was a demon's inside?"

"Yes, but I believe I successfully removed it. Never encountered one trapped inside a crystal before. It needs to remain underground for at least a week to ensure all the evil intent is gone. The earth will absorb the remnants of evil and cleanse it. You should be able to infuse it with…" He waved his hands, searching for the correct word. "Goodness?"

"I know what you mean. Promise I'll leave it where it is until we need it. I'm a little tired. Would you mind if we go back to the bookstore now? If you give me your email, I'll transfer your fee."

"No fee. I do this type of thing as it's a necessity. It takes a lot to get the church to agree to exorcisms, and most people need immediate help. I do not ask payment."

He drove us home, dropping us at the front door. Sorcha came in to stay for dinner. Delivery, again. I was going to miss all the attention once I returned home.

"Coop, is there any of that ointment left you've been putting on my neck? Maybe it will help my hand. The stuff from the house is just for basic burns. This looks pretty bad. Almost hospital worthy."

While he was upstairs getting gauze and the gel, I asked Sorcha about Helena. "Do you think we should bring her in now? She's probably going to be pissed we didn't invite her to come with us."

"I've had a few discussions with her about her past with the dark arts. She understands how tricky it would be if she gets too involved. I believe it's safe now. Based on her reaction when we found the book, I think she might be a good barometer to tell us if something has come back."

"I'll text her and see if she's available to come over for dinner. Cooper ordered enough Chinese for a small party."

While I texted Helena, Cooper returned with the gel and gauze. Her reply came as Cooper fastened off the gauze. I glanced at my phone. "One more for dinner. You may have less leftovers than expected.

Forty-five minutes later, Helena arrived, followed by the delivery person. She seemed to be in a peculiar funk, and her eyes were dark and sunken. She no longer wore the evil eye ring I'd given her. After burying the crystal egg, my sense of intuition partially returned. I was no where close to full strength, but I could tell she struggled with something. Sorcha touched my arm, then nodded towards Helena. She could tell we had a problem.

Now I had to figure out how to broach the subject. "Helena? Is something wrong? You look a little…out of sorts today."

"When you texted, I was trying to find a way to tell you and Sorcha." Helena bit her bottom lip, thinking. "Last night, I dug out some of my old books. You know, from before."

"Yes, you mentioned you were going to see if you could find anything useful in them. Did you find something that might help cleanse my uncle's dark spell book? Sorcha and my aunt have also been looking."

"No. I, um, think I messed up. Being exposed to the book seems to have awakened my past."

Holy Heliodore! "My aunt said you needed to be extra careful as you've only turned your back on dark magick recently. You're vulnerable. Maybe one of us should read through the books, if you don't mind lending them." I pointed to her hand. "Why did you remove the evil eye ring?"

"Couldn't help it. It was as though an outside force had control of me."

Schist, schist and triple schist. We had enough to deal with without having to bring Helena back to the light side of magick. Good vs evil. Who'd of thought I ever had to deal with that?

"There's something else." Helena picked up the large shoulder bag she brought and reached inside.

Cooper swore. Sorcha and I stared.

"When? How?" I was too shocked to form a full sentence. Helena had the ruby crystal egg.

SEVENTEEN

"I don't even remember getting it. Where did it come from?" Helena looked confused. She held the egg away from her body, looking from Sorcha to me. "Please believe me. I have no idea how this happened."

My head ached. *Residual evil still attached to the egg?* I took a few steps away. "Whatever that evil force you felt is, it must have guided you to my house once the demonologist began to deal with the evil spirit attached to the crystal. It's the only way you could have retrieved it so soon."

Sorcha took the crystal and stuffed it inside her bag. "We have to do this all over again, before it's too late."

Helena cried. "I'm sorry. I don't know what I've done, but I'm sorry."

"That egg is the source of most of my trouble." Ignoring the now fading pain behind my eyes, I put an arm around Helena's shoulder. "Not your fault." *Entirely.* "Have you had any dreams of being in a dark room with someone speaking to you?"

She nodded.

"Whatever has been communicating with me must have latched on to you. I've not been able to figure out who he is. So far, he hasn't identified himself. You need to put a dream catcher over your bed. One created by a Native American, not mass produced. Smudge the bejeezus out of your place, circle your bed with salt, maybe brimstone, and keep a couple of crystals under your pillow. Clear quartz and any black crystal. They don't need to be large."

I turned to Cooper. "Do you have any more wood? She'll need some symbols to help protect her."

He shook his head. "I can make more."

"Helena, have you ever considered getting another tattoo? One to combat evil instead of enhancing it?" Sorcha rolled up her sleeve, revealing several. "Permanent protection."

"I've thought about it, but I'm still having the bad ones removed. I'm already covered in the wrong type of symbols."

"You should start with the Helm of Awe." Sorcha lifted her thick, wavy red hair, revealing the snowflake-like mark on the back of her neck. "Vikings used to paint it on their forehead before battle. How about a small turtle or a dragonfly? I know someone who can do them. One of the first witches I met when I moved here. Perfectly safe. She can work around the bad ones. Maybe even help with the removals. Does the person who's been removing the tatts know spellcraft? The intention has to be removed along with the ink. I can call her now, if you're certain you want to do this. No time like the present, especially if you're being coerced without your knowledge." She turned to me. "Marcy?"

"You know, that's not a bad idea. I wouldn't mind a little dragonfly on my shoulder. Don't suppose she makes house calls?"

Helena sighed. "I forgot about the intention. I simply wanted them removed."

Cooper leaned against the wall, arms crossed, frown firmly planted on his beautiful face. He didn't look like a happy camper. "Marcy, you might want to give it some thought before you do something that can't be easily erased."

"The way things have been going with me, I could use all the help I can get. Besides, several of the witches Auntie P. introduced me to had them. Promise not to get anything large and gaudy."

Sorcha smiled. "With protection symbols, size doesn't matter. It's the intent that counts. Like a few other things I could mention." She winked at me.

"I'm doing it. Can you call her? If Helena agrees, we can have a little tattoo party here tonight." I looked at Helena for confirmation. Her eyes were glazed over. "Helena?"

Sorcha was closer and reached out, shaking Helena slightly. "Helena? What's happening?"

Helena blinked a few times. "What? Where?" She looked around. "The bookstore? Something tried to contact me."

"The protection around the store must be blocking it." Helena grabbed her phone and sent a text. "We need to get the tattooing done immediately. Cooper, would you consider one tiny tattoo? In case of the unexpected."

He shrugged.

I was puzzled. "When he contacted me, he wanted the book and crystal returned. Why was Helena allowed to bring the ruby here?"

"Probably to mess with you. Despite the exorcism, the egg would still possess energy. That's why it's been buried. The earth can absorb and destroy the bad energy. Since she's here, she's safe, and the ruby is also being blocked." Sorcha's phone dinged. "Text from my friend. She can come in an hour, if you're all agreeable."

I didn't hesitate. "Yes. Definitely. Helena?"

"Yes, I'll get one."

"Good." Sorcha began pulling items from her bag. "Like a boy scout, I'm always prepared. Since the tattoos will have to have intention in them, we'll need to prepare the same way we would for any spell or ceremony. Candles, incense, and as many crystals as possible. I wish we had some holy water to sprinkle on the crystal. It's impossible to say how much protection was lost when Helena dug it up."

I grabbed my jewellery supplies and quickly made up a necklace for Helena with evil eye beads and little silver spacers. When I finished, I fastened it around her neck. "Hey, how did you know where to find the ruby, anyway? We buried it on the far side of the property."

She shrugged. "Probably the same way I knew to go and fetch the crystal. Something had control of me, guiding me. It's a wonder I didn't get into an accident driving out."

"Whatever had control of you must have made sure you weren't harmed. Promise me you won't remove that necklace. Hopefully, once you've been inked, he won't be able to reach you. Or me."

Cooper closed the shop again, then headed out to get more wood. When he returned, the scent of cedar filled the store. Sorcha smudged the entire place, including Cooper's upstairs apartment. She had more experience than me and was better able to recite a powerful protection spell as she went. I managed to convince him to get one tiny tattoo—a turtle on his ankle to match the little one by the cash register. His would be the most painful.

Less than an hour later, Sorcha's friend sent a text informing us she was at the front door. I went with Sorcha to let her in.

"Marcy, this is Ashley. She's a wonderful artist."

I shook her hand. "Nice to meet you. We're set up in the back."

After all the introductions were done, Ashley laid out her ink and equipment on the table. She also brought along design books. "This book is for my special clients, like you. It's filled with symbols and spirit animals. I can also do special requests. Sorcha said you need protection. Do you know what you want?"

Helena spoke up first. "I'd like the snowflake thing. The something of Awe? On the back of my neck, like Sorcha."

"The Helm of Awe. Yes, I've done many of those. What colour? Black, blue? Something else?"

Helena thought for a moment. "Well, black is supposed to protect against evil. I'll go with that."

Ashley flipped through her book and took out the sheet with the design.

"Good. Marcy? What would you like?"

"A dragonfly. A beautiful, colourful, tiny dragonfly. On the back of my shoulder, here." I pointed to the spot. "Cooper's agreed to get inked, too."

Cooper sat at the drop-leaf table, working on symbols for Helena's home. He glanced up. "Small turtle on my ankle. Green."

I leaned in to Ashley and whispered. "Do him last. He doesn't know how much that location will hurt."

Ashley grinned. "Back of the neck is no picnic either. Yours will hurt the least. Start with you?"

My tatt took the longest as she had to change colours several times. At least it was small. Despite the surrounding redness, it was beautiful.

Helena fought back tears while her neck was inked. Cooper pretended it didn't hurt, but I saw him wince. His turtle design appeared similar to an Indigenous one, and he was quite happy with it.

When she was done, I paid for everyone's ink. *Wonder what Auntie P. will think of my tattoo?*

When Ashley left, Cooper heated up our now cold meal. We needed fuel.

As the evening light faded and darkness took over, my intuition gained strength. Sorcha went with Helena to place the symbols around her apartment, then joined Cooper and me at my home. We needed to re-bury the crystal, and I wouldn't be able to repeat her Gaelic chant error-free.

Driving up to the house, all of us felt normal. Whatever had inhabited the crystal was gone. Helena had left the shovel sticking in the ground, making it easy to pinpoint the location. The wooden box remained in the hole along with the cross. Sorcha took the ruby out of her bag and placed it in the box, then pulled a bottle out of her pocket.

"What's that?" I couldn't see any label.

"Holy water. I stopped at home and grabbed it. Better safe than sorry."

"Let me do it." I reached out. "Please?"

Sorcha nodded, gave me the container. I knelt in front of the hole. Shaking, I took the lid off the bottle. Tilting it, one single drop came out. I closed one eye and grimaced, waiting for the worst. The drop moved in slow motion. It hit its mark. Nothing. Relieved, I tilted the bottle again, letting a thin trickle of holy water flow over the crystal egg.

After Sorcha said the chant, I closed the lid, and placed the silver cross on top. Cooper grabbed the shovel and filled the hole back in. I found a small branch that had fallen from a tree and stuck it in the dirt, marking the location so I could find it next week. *Maybe I'll wait for two or three weeks.* By the time we got back to the bookstore, it was close to midnight. Sorcha headed home, and Cooper and I went up to his apartment to relax. The scent from the cedar smudge had almost faded.

Hungry, as usual, I took Cooper's hand and led him to the kitchen. Instead of the usual tingle, a warmth crept up my arm. Felt nice. Normal. Letting go, I grabbed a large handful of spaghetti and dropped it in a pot of boiling water. Cooper removed a container of sauce from the fridge.

"Hey, Coop. You aren't going to regret getting that tattoo, are you? I know you didn't really want one."

"No. I like the design she chose. I have a feeling I may end up with more. You, too."

"Actually, I was thinking about getting a few more, but I'm not going to cover myself in them. Remember what I told you about what Elsbeth told me when I was in Dorking? You know, about being special and restoring my family's dwindling power. Problems like this are likely to come up more and more. When I was over there, I spoke to some of my aunt's associates. Some of their tatts are called sigils. They're used in magick."

I sat at the table, and Cooper joined me after putting the sauce on to simmer.

"So how do you create a sigil? Are they like symbols?"

I shook my head. "No, not exactly. You write down your desire or wish. Has to be as specific as possible, but short is best. Cross out the vowels, then draw your own symbol using only the remaining letters. You can draw them upside down, backwards, or normal. They need to all be touching so they look like one symbol. It's something I'd like to learn. And don't worry. They don't have to be tattoos. They can be temporary. On a piece of paper that's burned or etched onto a candle."

"Make sure you learn from someone with experience. Don't want you watching a video and trying it alone. Who knows what you'll conjure up?"

"Promise."

After eating, we vegged on the sofa watching back-to-back episodes of *Ghost Hunters* on the On Demand channel. Sometime during the third episode, I nodded off. Something touching my face woke me. Cooper tucking my hair behind my ear. I blinked a few times before noticing my head rested on his shoulder.

"Welcome back to the land of the living." He smiled at me. I smiled back. "This is nice."

"Mm-hmm. Be nicer if I was actually awake." I yawned, spoiling the moment.

All the excitement of the day finally wore off. My eyes struggled to stay open. I wiggled away from Cooper and headed down to my make-shift apartment. *Should have grabbed my dream catcher while we were at the house.* I placed one of my crystals under the pillow along with a small piece of wood Cooper had engraved. Fingers crossed for pleasant dreams, I crawled into bed, careful not to turn onto my fresh tattoo.

EIGHTEEN

Several times during the night, I woke. Something or someone tried to enter my mind. The symbols and crystals did their job and blocked everything. Kinda wished he'd made it through. I needed to know who he was. It wasn't Uncle Montgomery, of that I was now certain. Wherever we'd sent him, he remained trapped. Or dead. Whatever.

The sense of intrusion lingered. It felt… familial. Another relative I knew nothing about? It was male. The only other male in the family was—*schist! Was the persona he showed me false? Schist, shist, schist.*

I practically flew out of bed. Tripping over discarded clothes, I race across the room for my phone. *Four in the morning.* Mid-morning in England. Priscilla answered on the second ring.

"Good morning, Marcy. How are you?"

"Fine. I think we have a major problem." I explained my feeling and suspicions.

She didn't speak for several minutes.

"How is that possible? He's been gone for centuries." Auntie's shock mirrored mine.

"Does anyone know where they sent him? Did we send Montgomery to the same place?" The only other male ever born in our family had been the boy-twin. They banished him a long, long time ago. The same thing we'd done with my great uncle this past summer. None of us knew if he'd been killed or sent to another realm or dimension. I hoped for the latter as I didn't want to think I'd killed someone.

Auntie P. broken my train of thought. "I'll go through the old hand-written journals the coven maintained. When we disbanded, many of the journals passed down through our family as our ancestor formed the coven. I can't imagine how she felt, disowning and banishing her own son. It had been hard enough for me when we did it to my baby brother." She smiled. "Funny how I still think of him as the baby, even though he was in his sixties when he returned."

"Do you think they would have recorded what happened to the twin? They wouldn't have intentionally killed him, would they?"

Auntie's shoulders raised in a shrug. "Back then, death was the most common form of punishment, but I'd like to believe they chose the other option. We've made a little progress with the artifact. It definitely is a vessel or poison ring, made from ninety-two and a half percent pure silver, engraved with runes and other symbols around the band. A black obsidian stone was set on the hinged lid.

"Unfortunately, no one knows where it is. The person I spoke to, Bronwyn, is the great granddaughter of one of the coven families.

She remembers the story being passed down, but without details of the ceremony. The ring was instrumental in how they dealt with the boy. In order to keep it safe, they passed it from member to member. Somewhere along the line, it got lost."

My hopes had raised, only to be popped. "So, it is possible that the ring is lying at the bottom of someone's jewellery box, or maybe taken to a pawnshop or auction house and sold?"

Auntie nodded. "It is possible. I'd like to believe no witch would ever sell a magickal item. The engravings on the band would alert any person born with powers like ours to what it was, even if they didn't know the intent."

"But if it was, say, stolen? That person wouldn't know, and could have seen it as something to exchange for money." A thought occurred to me. I gasped. "Worse, it could have been melted for the silver."

"Well, I suppose that's possible. However, witches protect their homes. It's not common for a thief to break in."

I could tell she was thinking about something. Her eyes darted back and forth, like she read off a page.

"What is it, Auntie?"

"Two possibilities. If the ring was being worn, someone could have mugged her. Or another witch could have stolen it, or…"

I didn't like where that thought was headed. "Or a demon?"

"Yes. Something like that. A practitioner of dark arts is actually what I thought."

My mind immediately went to Helena, but I dismissed that. She was only in her twenties. *How would she even know about the ring?*

"What are you thinking, dear?"

"Helena. I know you don't seem to like her."

"I don't dislike her, exactly. She seems nice, but there's something about her that doesn't feel right. Even though she said she's left the dark arts behind her, it's still within her."

Did I want to tell Auntie about the entity possessing Helena temporarily? Her gut reactions to people were generally spot on. If someone could affect her once, they could do it again.

"Something happened, didn't it, Marcy?"

"Yes. When we found the dark spell book, she knew she had to stay away from it. Unfortunately, something touched her. We dealt with the crystal egg, but Helena went out and dug it up pretty much as soon as we left. According to her, she doesn't remember doing it, and I believe her.

"When we went to the house with the demonologist, Helena wasn't with us. She didn't even know what we planned to do. Somehow, she shook off the hold and brought the egg to me at the bookstore. It's been reburied. I truly believe she wants to leave all that behind her. Oh, and we all got tattooed."

She raised an eyebrow. "Excuse me? A tattoo?"

I pulled my tee off my shoulder, turning to show her. "Yep. There's a witch here who does them. It's been infused with positive intention. Figured with all the stuff going on, I needed the extra protection. Sorcha and Helena got them, too. Even Cooper."

I turned back to the camera, surprised to see Auntie smiling. "We all have them. I was waiting to discuss it with you. When we do them, we have a little ceremony and celebration. Not necessary, just a tradition I started with Susan. They're all inconspicuous."

"No fooling. I had no idea. I noticed them on your friends, but didn't want to ask why you didn't have any."

"You've chosen a good one. We can talk about them when you come over. Maybe add one to your collection. A little celebration to relax before Drew's wedding will be something we all will need. I'm surprised Cooper got one."

"A green turtle on his ankle. It's really cute. I wanted to talk to you about sigils, but that can wait. I'm anxious to hear more about the ring. Do you know what it held?"

Auntie P. squirmed in her chair. She was normally straight forward. If she was hesitating, it had to be something awful. "It's yet to be confirmed, but the woman I spoke to believes it contained the evil spirit of the twin."

Whoa! Major news. If the old coven captured his spirit, then he wasn't dead. Did our banishing ceremony miss an important step? "We didn't contain Montgomery's spirit. Does that mean we killed him? Or is he able to come back?"

Auntie shook her head. "When Monty went, if he died, I would have felt it. I think I always knew he wasn't dead. That feeling hasn't changed. He's somewhere, but not on this plane. I don't want to speculate until I find out more. I keep the old journals hidden. There's a secret room in my house that only my daughter knows about. When I pass, she'll tell Drew." She paused to think.

"Actually," Auntie P. thought a moment before continuing. "When you come over for the wedding, I'll show both you and

Drew. Since our past seems to keep coming back repeatedly, you may need information only found there. If something should happen to both me and Susan, you and your cousin will need to empty out that room. Don't want the house being sold and everything found during a renovation."

So many secrets in my family. How much more would I have been told if I hadn't turned my back on our special talents in my teens? "You go read the journals. I'll visit Helena. Ask about her family. I have the strangest feeling it's not a coincidence I've met her. If she used to practice the dark arts, maybe her entire family did, too. Wonder why they let her leave? I hope they don't live nearby. Maybe they had a run-in with Granny or Mother in the past. Besides, I want to see how she's doing. Talk to you later."

I crawled back into bed, but couldn't fall asleep. I dressed and went back to the laptop to search the witchy web to see what else I could find out about sigils.

Two hours passed in a flash. The noise coming from upstairs told me Cooper was up. I glanced at the time. *After seven.* I plugged the laptop in, then joined Cooper for breakfast. My turn to cook. Assuming putting frozen waffles in the toaster counted as cooking.

After he opened the store, I borrowed his car, this time with permission, and went to see Helena.

When the door to her apartment opened, it was obvious she hadn't slept well. You could put a full wardrobe in the bags under her eyes.

"Helena! You look awful." I slapped my hand over my mouth. "Sorry," I mumbled.

Helena sighed. "Couldn't agree more. Had the same reaction when I looked in the mirror. I tossed and turned all night. Whatever took possession of me tried again. If not for the symbols Cooper burned for me, and the tattoo, I don't even want to think what might have happened. Whatever it is won't be giving up." She slumped onto the sofa and began to cry. "How could I ever have thought dark magick was a good thing? How can anyone?"

I sat beside her and put my arm around her shoulder. "Do you want to talk about it?"

She sniffled and nodded.

"What made you decide to go in that direction?"

"Family."

My suspicions are confirmed, but how did she get out? "What do you mean, family? Are your parents dark practitioners?"

"Yes. They don't believe it's evil. I used to think the same way. They're in corporate business and use it as a tool to get what they want. Some of my relatives are in politics. They see it as doing what needs to be done. It's not like they kill people or anything.

"Last Christmas I saw first-hand how it affects those without magick. It broke my heart to see families destroyed because someone in my family used a spell to win a contract or election." She grabbed a tissue and blew her nose. "One of my uncles is a contractor. He didn't need another job because he's quite well off, but he couldn't resist low-balling his bid to win. Unfortunately, the person he beat needed the job. As a result, that family is now homeless. Two small children put in care until he gets back on his feet. I packed up and took the next flight out."

My witchdar flicked on. "Flight? Where from?" I hadn't detected any accent.

"England. I've spent the last several months getting rid of my accent."

"I would never have guessed. Where in England?"

"Surrey."

"Oh. That's where my family is from. I wonder if anyone in your family knows mine. That would be quite a coincidence."

Helena laughed. "I doubt it. We come from a smallish town west of London. East Horsley."

I gasped. "My great aunt lives in Dorking. That's what? Ten miles?"

"Less. That is a coincidence."

I laughed, trying to hide my nervousness. Everyone says *small world*, but it really isn't. "I wonder if my aunt knows your family. What's your last name?"

"Davies. I don't recall my family ever associating with any of what Mamma refers to as the goodie-two shoes witches."

Couldn't help but smile at that description. It kinda fit. "It's quite possible the goodie-two shoes are aware of the witches that practice the dark arts. They wouldn't associate with them, though. The opposite."

Helena yawned.

"Why don't you go back to bed? I only dropped in to see how you were doing. I'll ask Cooper to do more symbols. Why don't you smudge or something? And make certain to surround yourself with crystals."

We hugged and said goodbye. If something wasn't done soon, Helena might get dragged back into the dark. My mind reeled at the discovery of her being from the area my family was from. I drove as fast as I dared back to the bookstore, my burned hand extra sore from gripping the steering wheel so tight.

NINETEEN

Cooper was with a customer when I returned, so I went up to his apartment and grabbed the herbal gel and gauze, then went back down to wait until he was available. Both my neck and hand needed to be re-dressed.

He put up the *back in 5 minutes* sign. I told him what I'd found out while he unwrapped the old gauze and put on the new. He seemed as shocked as me.

After being freshly mummified, I video-called Auntie again. I didn't recognize the room she was in when she answered. *Must be the secret room.*

"Marcy. Twice in one day. Have you discovered something?"

"Do you know a family nearby called Davies? Up in East Horsley?"

She narrowed her eyes. "I'm familiar with them. Why?"

"That's Helena's family."

Auntie P. swore. No matter what, she'd always refrained from using profanity. At least when I was around.

"I know, Auntie. Helena filled me in. When she saw firsthand the results of her family's practices, she hopped a plane. Are they that bad?"

"Originally, no. The last couple of generations, yes. Helena's ancestors were part of our old coven. One of the reasons they disbanded was because several members left to go to the darkness."

"You don't think… could one of them…?" I couldn't ask the question.

"No. Well… It is possible. I found a reference to the passing of the ring. I'll have to figure out exactly when the Davies family turned. They would have had possession of the ring at some point. Hopefully, it was well before they separated from us."

"What would happen if they had it?" I wasn't certain I wanted to hear the answer.

"Anything could have happened, none of it good. Now, I need to tell you what I found out about the ring and how it worked in the banishing ceremony. Somehow, they separated the evil and contained it in the vessel ring. Since he had been corrupted once, they wanted to ensure it wouldn't happen again, so they banished the physical body. So far, I've only found one reference that mentions his name. They called him Lorcan. The origin was Gaelic, meaning fierce. Supposed to refer to being a brave warrior. Unfortunately, he seemed to pledge himself to the darkness. Apparently, he was in his late twenties at the time and had already been through the initiation on his twenty-first birthday."

"What would happen if someone opened the ring? Would his life force disappear? Or go into someone?"

Auntie shrugged. "Not sure. It's not something I've dealt with. It's very old magick. The ring would have had a sealing spell attached to it to prevent it from being opened by the wrong person. If the Davies have it, I can definitely imagine what nastiness they'd do with it."

"But if they didn't know what it contained, they may have sold it."

"If the Davies were in possession of the ring when the coven disbanded, they'd know what the ring was. It's possible they released him when the spell weakened enough, then sold it. Lorcan may somehow have sensed Montgomery's dark side and sought him out. It's also possible they didn't even realize what they'd done. The symbols or runes would have indicated a witch owned it, but not know it contained anything, especially a spirit. With the annual ritual not being done for who knows how long, they managed to pry it open, hoping to find something of value. Since it's made of almost pure silver, I doubt it would have gone to a pawnshop. More likely to have been an auction house. I'll asked around, now that I have a name."

"With any luck, one of the books you have stashed away will contain a list of people who received the ring."

Priscilla laughed. "They passed the ring every year at Litha. The list would be extremely long."

"So, maybe it's a separate book? That is possible, isn't it?"

"Yes. A long shot, but entirely possible. I'll make a few phone calls, then continue reading. Susan's coming over later to help. We'll keep you posted."

After ending the call, I joined Cooper in the store. I sat in one of the easy chairs set out for the customers to browse through the books in comfort. Instead of a book, my attention focused on Cooper.

"Why are you looking at me like that?" He leaned on the counter, smiling.

"So, mister helper, can you help locate a book? We've possibly found another way to track the ring, as Auntie P. found further intel."

"Sometimes an item too close to the person's heart makes it difficult for them to locate. That messes with their mojo. The person wants it so bad, the spell doesn't work right, and you desperately want it."

"OK, I'll give you that, but desperate might be a stretch. I have a special request. Unfortunately, I don't know if the book even exists. How would that work? Or would it?"

Cooper scrunched his face, considering the possibility. "I'd have to check with my dad or even Gramps. We'd need to know as much as possible about what the book may contain and where it may be. After closing, I'll give him a call. What are you looking for?"

"A list or ledger. It would have only one entry per year, for umpteen years. Decades. Actually, probably centuries. I can find out when it would have started, if it even exists. I need to find out when something happened. Like the thing we did with my uncle."

He came out from behind the counter and sat in the chair near me. I scooted my chair towards Coop. Close enough to be cozy, but not so close he distracted me. He smiled and winked. My insides turned to mush.

"Now I'm intrigued. May I ask what this possible list is?"

I explained about the vessel ring and the information Auntie P. found.

Cooper nodded. "Are you going to tell Helena what you found out about her family's connection to yours?"

"Maybe. But not until it's all over. I think I should tell Sorcha, though. Oh, can you do more of those symbols for Helena? Something is still trying to get through to her. I think she needs one at every window. Maybe another for the front door. She's hung one on the outside of the door, but maybe another for the inside? I think at least four more. All the symbols on each board?"

"Sure. I bought lots of wood. Did some research of my own to see what trees are best used in magick? Got some Ash, Cedar, Elder, and Elm. The website was for wands, but I figure it would work for burning symbols into it. Cedar and Ash are probably the best. I rather enjoy woodburning. It's relaxing. Requires concentration, so it takes my mind off everything."

"I feel the same about the jewellery. I can understand why Drew enjoys it so much. Maybe when I get better at it, I can include small charms to go with the potions."

After speaking with Cooper, I had a long conversation with Sorcha about Helena. It became crucial she be kept away from most of what we were doing. She was still too open to the darkness. We agreed to wait at least two weeks before it would be safe to dig up the crystal egg, like the demonologist said, but the house was safe enough for Nenka and her family to return. I borrowed Cooper's car and drove out to the wooded area to find her.

"Hi, Nenka. You'll be happy to hear the house is now safe. Your family can return whenever you wish. I'll be staying at the bookstore for a little while yet, but I'll try to pop in occasionally to see how things are. Cooper wants to make sure my gashes and burns are healed before he lets me out of his sight."

Nenka still looked a little leery. The normal twinkle in her eye had been missing ever since the gnomes vacated my house. Even the promise that they could go home didn't help.

"Are you certain we can return?" She began her usual habit of wringing her hands. If she began to crumple her apron, then I'd know she was extra worried. So far, so good.

"Why don't you start with tending to the garden? If you feel safe, then you can decide for yourself. I'm not going to push you to return. I've had someone come out to fix the problem with the crystal egg. It's buried on the east side of the property and it's marked with a small branch. It's well away from the garden, so you don't need to worry about it." I refrained from telling her the someone was a demonologist. She was such a little worry wart, and just the mention of anything demon-related would send her into a tizzy. "Is there any way I can contact you without driving out? Or some way you can get in touch with me if something goes wrong?"

My little wood gnome thought for a moment. "Well, I suppose I could relay a message through the fae, but it might take a while. They don't all get along, you know."

Yes, I knew. Some were very helpful. Others wanted to play tricks. A few were down right nasty.

"We'll manage somehow until I get home. One thing I need to do is get my own car. I'll come out later with Cooper and follow him back to the bookstore. Maybe I'll see you tonight?"

She nodded. "Yes. I'll get Tinkus and we'll go over. If it feels safe, I'll tend the garden. It must be such a mess. He can go through the house. I think I'll ask my parents if Nimagg can stay a little longer." The twinkle in her eyes returned. "They do love to dote on him. Making up for the past fifty years. Now, is there anything I can get for you? Do you have enough of the ointment? Won't take but a tick to gather up more."

Trying to picture the stockpile Cooper got the last time he came out, I waved my bandaged hand. "I don't suppose it would hurt to get some more, now that I have two wounds to deal with."

I followed her through the woods while she pointed out the correct plants. I made certain to leave plenty behind for future use, suggesting I should clear a patch in the garden to add some of them so they'd be handy if ever needed. Granny had planted most, but not all, of them.

Once I had all I could carry, I walked back to the car and dumped the herbs on the passenger seat. Nenka had climbed onto the fence, sitting prime and proper. You'd think she was a queen sitting on her throne. I hugged her, then headed back to the store, taking the collection of medicinal plants up to Cooper's apartment. I washed them, then left them on a towel on the counter to dry.

As I came back down, I heard voices. *Must be a customer.* I joined them in the front of the store. When the customer saw me, she quit talking. Cooper turned and spotted me.

"Oh, don't worry about her. She's a witch, too. You probably knew her grandmother, Francine."

She looked familiar.

The lady stared at me, then nodded. "Yes. I remember you from the funeral. We never got the chance to talk."

That info surprised me. "I thought only Granny's customers had attended. Her and Mother never associated with the witches in the area. At least I don't remember meeting any. But I've been in the city for the past several years, with only short visits. I'm Marcy. You must be here to have Cooper make a special purchase. I won't get in your way. Nice to meet you…"

"Alice. Nice to meet you, too."

I headed to my home away from home in the back and continued surfing the witchy web. A few more customers came in before Cooper closed for the day and joined me, carrying two cups of fresh tea.

"So, what have you been up to? Did you see Nenka?"

"Yes. I told her she could go back to the house. I want to head back tonight, too. Instead of always borrowing yours, I'd like to get my car. Besides, it'll give us the chance to find out if the house is safe. Nenka and Tinkus will be able to sense if anything is still off. I'll also show her where the crystal is buried. It's not close to her garden, so I doubt she'll go near it, and I've told her I marked it."

After a minute or two of silence, Cooper agreed. "Provided we don't stay too long. I've been making more items to hang around for protection. Should be enough to put one at every window and door, as well as several for Helena's place." Cooper smiled. "I even made a couple of tiny ones for the fae doors."

I leaned back in the chair. "Well, aren't you the considerate one? Those gnomes do grow on you, don't they? Oh, I also brought back more of the plants for the ointment. I thought we were running low. Never hurts to have extra. Once everything settles down, I'd like to dig out a new patch in the garden and transplant a few from the woods.

"I guess Granny didn't see the need for the uncommon ones as they weren't that far away, but in an emergency, it would be nice to have them handy. Besides, Nenka's knees aren't getting any better. The shorter the distance she has to go, the better."

Cooper set his cup on the table and got all serious. "Have you figured out what you're going to do about Helena? It's going to be difficult to cut her out of everything."

"I know. She genuinely wants to help. I need to talk to my family. It should be a mutual decision whether or not to tell her that her ancestors were part of my ancestors' coven. I don't even know if there were bad feelings when the Davies left. I mean, obviously their decision to turn to the dark side of things wouldn't have gone over well, but they might have remained friends, sort of, wouldn't they?"

Cooper chuckled. "Probably not. If you had a friend who turned nasty, would you still be friends with them?"

"No, I guess not. I'll text Auntie P. and ask her to set up a time agreeable for everyone to video chat. Maybe we could include Sorcha, too. Guess I'd better tell her the latest on Helena. Even if she doesn't get a vote, we should hear anything she has to say. She's involved just as deeply as the rest of us."

"You do that, then join me upstairs to make supper. I've hardly eaten anything today. I'm starving."

After sending my text and getting an immediate thumbs up reply, there was nothing left to do but wait until they came up with a time.

Cooper was standing at the fridge, door open, trying to decide what he needed. He turned his head when I entered. "Feel like an omelet? Or maybe a western?"

"Haven't had a western sandwich for ages. Wouldn't mind that." I peered over his shoulder. "Did you shop? I don't remember having that much food."

"Grocery stores deliver, so I stocked up. Would have closed the store and popped out, but someone had my car." He gave me a lopsided grin. "Maybe it's not such a bad thing we get your car as long as you're here."

While Cooper took care of the westerns, I rummaged through the fridge and cupboard and whipped up some carrot muffins for dessert. After washing and putting away the dishes, he showed me the tiny pieces of woodwork he'd made for the fae doors.

"These are adorable. The lines are so fine. Maybe you can start selling these in the bookstore, full size. Non-witches also like putting up symbols for luck."

Cooper shrugged. "Maybe."

My phone dinged. A text came in from Auntie P. with a time tomorrow, and a yes to Sorcha attending. I acknowledged, then texted Sorcha. I'd have to fill her in before the call.

"Come on, Coop. Let's go get my car. I have to call Sorcha later to tell her what the call's about tomorrow, and that might take more than a minute."

✳ ✳ ✳

When we arrived at my house, nothing seemed amiss. We walked around back to the garden to see if Nenka was there. The rustling of plants gave us our answer.

"Nenka? Is that you?" It could have been a squirrel, but I didn't think so.

"Over here."

We followed the path around and almost tripped over an enormous pile of weeds and dead-headed blooms. "My, you've been busy."

Nenka's crisp, white apron was filthy. The little garden gloves she wore were no better, and she had a few streaks of dirt on her face. Cooper laughed, but one quick jab in the ribs from me shut him up.

"I'll get something to clean this up." He hurried to the shed, his shoulders still quivering. I looked away so I didn't start, too.

I knelt on the path near Nenka. "Since you're still here, I guess you feel safe?"

"Oh, yes. It feels like it used to. Tinkus has gone through every room and didn't feel or see anything out of place. We've moved back in, but Nimagg is still with his grandparents. He's enjoying playing with the family cat. Even wants me to ask you if you'll get one."

"I'll think about it. I want to show you where we buried the crystal."

"No need to bother. We found it and will stay away from it. The ground around it feels… off. Not bad, merely different."

"It'll take at least a week or more before it's safe to uncover it. Then the ground will probably need to heal. Once I purify it in the moonlight, I'll have to keep it in a special container, just in case. Don't know for how long. Have you thought about a suitable location for the wild plants? I can mark off and dig out an area, then in the spring, we can transplant a few of each variety."

"Someplace shady. No hurry. I've picked a few things that are almost over ripe. Would you mind taking them into the house and bringing back the empty basket?"

"Sure." I followed her through the garden to her gathering basket. "My gosh. How were you going to get that inside if I hadn't come?" The basket was overflowing with herbs and vegetables. There was no way she'd ever be able to lift it.

I bent down to pick it up and grunted. "It's heavier than I thought. I doubt even with Tinkus helping you'd have been able to drag it in. Be right back."

I walked past Cooper, who was filling the wheelbarrow with the pile of dead plant matter, and showed him the basket. "Fresh veggies and herbs. We should take the veggies back with us so they don't rot. I'll leave them in the kitchen."

"Nice. Where does all this stuff go?"

"Compost to the south of the garden. It's the only fertilizer for the veggies."

When I went into the kitchen, scuffling resonated inside the walls. *Tinkus.* I didn't often see Nenka's husband. He liked to keep to himself and mostly roamed the house at night. At least I spotted him more often than their son.

Speaking louder than normal, I called out to him. "Glad you're back, Tinkus. I'll be home in a week or so."

Two knocks sounded. I assumed he heard and acknowledged.

The herbs and half-spent blooms went into the workroom to dry. I tied them into little bundles and hung them on the line strung across the space. When I turned to leave, the scent of rosewater drifted by.

"Granny? Is Mother with you?"

A warm breeze kissed my cheek.

"I need your help again. We're trying to locate a family heirloom. A poison or vessel ring. Um… do spirits talk to one another? Do you have any way to find out where it might be?"

Two words whispered in my ear. "We'll try."

The breeze kissed my cheek again, then the rosewater vanished.

"Thank you."

As I exited through the front door, I spotted Cooper walking to the car, arms full of the veggies I'd left on the kitchen table. I went to say goodbye to Nenka.

She was in the same area as before, so I left the basket on the path near her.

She smiled when she spotted me. "Come home when you're ready. You need Cooper to tend to your wounds. Tinkus and I will be fine. Won't be any different from when Francine was off travelling and collecting more antiques and books."

"With the help of the ointment, I'll heal extra quick." I waved goodbye, then joined Cooper.

"Hey, whatcha do with our harvest?" He stood beside the car, but he no longer had our bounty.

"In the trunk. Did you remember to grab your car keys?"

I pulled them out of my pocket, jangling them in front of him. "Race ya back."

TWENTY

I got into town first, but since Cooper only had one designated parking spot behind the store, he beat me inside. I took the harvest from Cooper up to his apartment while he took care of a few emails. Some of the regular *special* customers needed him to order in items. It amazed me how many witches didn't enjoy flying and visiting other countries.

My phone beeped, indicating a video request. *Mr. Barker!* I accepted the call and plopped onto the sofa.

"Marcy, dear. How are you?" He looked so much better now that he'd retired.

"Not bad, considering. You look well. Cooper's taking care of a few special requests, but shouldn't be long. He's settled in here nicely."

"Good. I have news of the item you're looking for."

"The ring?" I sat up straight, my heart racing. "You found it?"

"Not exactly. Someone sold it at an auction house back in the twenties. Nineteen twenties, that is. Unfortunately, a fire destroyed the records so we don't know who bought it."

I slumped. "So, it's been out of the coven family for about a hundred years? Schist."

Mr. Barker chuckled. "I love how you swear with crystals and minerals. Anyway, I've started going through newspapers from the time to see if it was written about. It's unique enough it might have warranted a story. Not all the local papers are online, though. You may need to enlist your family to search over there."

The apartment door opened, then closed. I turned the phone towards Cooper. "It's your gramps."

Cooper stood behind the sofa, leaning over my shoulder. "Hi Gramps. Where's Mom and Dad?"

"Newspaper duty. Marcy will fill you in. You take care of her or I'll disown you. Guess I should get back and help. We'll talk later."

I ended the call, set my phone on the table, then filled Cooper in on the latest about Helena.

Before we did anything else, Coop insisted he change my bandage. Any more serious injuries and I'd be able to audition for *Return of the Mummy, Part IV*, or would that be *Part V*?

"Oh!"

Cooper stopped unwrapping. "What? Did I hurt you?"

"No. I was thinking of mummies, which reminded me I haven't spoken to Missy lately."

He raised an eyebrow and resumed his doctoring.

"Mummies…Egypt…Missy."

"Bit of a stretch, but I get it. Call her when I finish. Does she know about your wounds?"

"No. Not sure how to explain it. She's well aware of some of my abilities and bits and pieces of the thing with Uncle Montgomery. I trust her, but what if whatever this new entity is latches on to her? These things like harming friends and family until they get what they want. That's why Helena can't be heavily involved. The dark magick is already affecting her."

I sucked in air when Cooper put the ointment on my wounds. "You been keeping that in the freezer? Next time, let it sit out a bit, will ya?"

He chuckled. "Nenka said to keep it cool. There. All done. I need to mix up more. Why don't you go down to your little nook and call Missy and Sorcha?"

Cooper had become quite adept at mixing up the ointment, so I left him to it. Once in my room, I dug out a scarf to hide the wrapped gashes on my neck before making the call. Missy preferred video chats, and I still hadn't decided whether or not to fill her in on all my wounds. I retrieved my phone and started a chat.

"Hi Marcy. Was planning to call you." Missy leaned closer to the screen. "What's with the scarf?"

What would I tell her? My hesitation lasted too long.

"Something happened. Tell me. I may not have your abilities, but I know when something's wrong."

"Just trying to protect you, Missy. There are things you may not be prepared for."

"I'm a big girl. And I've seen some unexplainable things. Egyptian curses and all that. Spill."

For the next ten minutes, Missy stared wide-eyed at the screen while I spilled.

"I wanted to tell you, but didn't think it fair to draw you into all this." I took a deep breath and unwrapped Cooper's handiwork.

"Wow! Are those stitches?"

I nodded

"If I was still in Cairo, I'd think Apophis was behind it. He had an army of demons at his disposal. They buried the dead with spells to protect them from him. You probably don't have an Egyptian demon harassing you, but if you'd like, I can see if I can dig up a spell."

"Any little bit of help would be great." *And would make her feel involved.*

"Thing is, they were written for the specific person. If I can find a translation, it can act as a guide to create a spell for you. I'll send out some emails to friends in Cairo."

We spent the next half hour chatting about totally useless stuff. It was a good distraction. Finally, we said goodbye.

Next, I called Sorcha to tell her about the video call with my family to see if she could join. She had remarkably little to say about Helena's family being former members of my family's coven.

Sorcha remained expressionless while I spoke. "I'll have to let that sink in. Not sure if it would have any baring on anything. Best you have a private conversation with your family about how to deal with Helena. But thank you for the invitation."

Could she somehow have sensed a connection?

After ending the call, I joined Cooper in his apartment for an evening of movies. When he spotted the bandages hanging loose, he shook his head and re-wrapped me without saying anything. At least my burned hand was almost back to normal. The tingling sensation when he touched or hugged me no longer jarred. It was now comforting and natural. Nice. More than nice. Much more.

When I returned to my room later that evening, the scent of rosewater filled the air.

"Granny? We need to figure out a way to communicate. A word here and there won't cut it any more."

I lit a candle and set it on the big table. "Can you make the flame flicker or change colour?"

The flame increased to a height of two inches, did a little dance, then turned pink.

"Cool. That's good for yes/no. Can you manipulate stuff? I remember reading a cozy where the dead aunt could write in a book left out in one of the rooms. Can you do anything like that? Green flame yes, red for no."

The flame turned bright red.

"No need to yell. Hmm. What about the laptop or cell phone? They run on electricity. Can you manipulate power?"

I watched the candle, waiting for a response. It flickered, but didn't change size or colour. Was Granny thinking? Finally, the flame began changing. Instead of green or red, it stayed the same basic flame colour, only brighter.

"Does that mean you don't know?"

Green.

Fist pump. "Yes! Try sending me a text."

My phone dinged. A text from unknown.

Hi

The scent of rosewater faded.

"Did that sap your energy?"

Light green flame.

"Rats. Maybe we can find a way to boost you. We'll stick to yes/no for now. Have you located the ring?"

Red

"I found out something from Mr. Barker. It was sold at an auction about a hundred years ago, but a fire destroyed the records. He's going through old newspapers online to see if he can find a story. We still don't know if it's going to help us, but it would be nice to get it back."

Granny's perfume became barely noticeable.

"You recharge." I yawned. "I need to recharge, too."

The flame shot up, then went out, leaving a tendril of green smoke.

I changed into my PJs, then crawled into bed.

TWENTY-ONE

Someone called my name, but I couldn't see anyone. I recognized the voice, though.

"Why don't you show yourself, coward? What do you want?"

"My name is Lorcan. You know what I want." The voice surrounded me.

"Is that name supposed to mean something to me?" *Should I let him know I know who he is?* Looking around gave me no indication whether or not I was still in the back room of the store. "I don't have the book, and the ruby is gone." A half truth.

A high-pitched scream almost pierced my eardrums, followed by a swoosh. My stomach burned. Another swoosh. Something lit my back on fire.

I curled into a ball. Instinct told me to try to protect my stomach, my organs. A hot wind whipped around me. The burning on my back increased. I tucked my chin as close to my body as possible to protect my already damaged throat. My body felt like a million bees stung at once. I screamed.

"Marcy! Marcy! Wake up."

I tried to sit up. Screaming in pain, I fell back. When my back hit the bed, I screamed again.

"Don't move." Cooper grabbed my phone and made a call. "Doc. Something has attacked her again."

I watched through half-open eyes as he explained, listened, nodded, then ended the call.

"He's on his way. There's so much blood."

Cooper gently lifted the sheet off me, blanching at what he saw. I gritted my teeth and propped myself on my elbows to look.

My PJ top and the single white cotton top sheet were both shredded. My arms were covered in scratches where I'd attempted to protect my stomach. I could only imagine what the sheets under me looked like. The blood had already begun caking on my skin, making it impossible to see the extent of my injury.

"My back," I croaked, half rolling over so Cooper could check.

He gasped. "The same. Can you sit up?"

"Maybe."

With his help and a little time, I sat on the edge of the bed, head spinning. Cooper raced upstairs to get a clean cloth and a bowl of warm water to clear away the blood before the doctor arrived.

"How am I not still bleeding?" I winced when he dabbed the slashes.

Twenty minutes later, Doctor Barnstable arrived. Not many interns got the sort of extra practice he was getting.

"You should be in a hospital."

"No. No hospital."

"I know. They'll call the police. I understand, but you need more care than I can give you here."

"Do your best."

He pulled a syringe from his bag, along with a tiny vial.

"Whoa. What's that?" I wasn't a fan of needles.

"You need a lot of stitches and it will hurt. A lot. This will knock you out for about an hour. You'll be sore when you wake, so I'll leave something for the pain."

✸✸✸

When I woke, the young intern was gone. He wasn't kidding about being sore. The scratches on my arms had been cleaned, but didn't require stitches. Still hurt, though. The sun shone through the window, almost blinding me. *An hour my eye.* Someone had put clean sheets on the bed, and a fresh pair of PJs on me. How embarrassing. *Please let it have been the doc and not Cooper.*

My phone sat on a small end table at the head of the bed. Wincing, I stretched for it, knocking over a little silver hand bell. *Coop's going to regret leaving that.*

Before I could pick it up, Cooper appeared at the door. "You rang?"

"Not exactly. But while you're here, can you help me up?"

He scooped up the bell and put it back on the table. "Barnstable doesn't want you moving any more than necessary. Whatever you need, I'll take care of it."

"Oh, really? What I need right now is the bathroom."

His mouth opened and closed a couple of times. I could tell he was trying to think of a snappy reply.

"Will you help me up?" Fortunately, the bookstore had a two-piece bathroom on the main floor, saving me from the stairs.

By the time I got to my feet, about an hour passed. Or maybe five minutes. Felt like an hour. "What time is it?"

"Around ten thirty."

Store's open. "Any customers?"

"No. You're in the clear. No one will see you."

When I came out, Sorcha had taken Cooper's place outside the door.

"Cooper told me something psychically attacked you again, but didn't give any details. What happened?"

I filled her in between winces. Once Sorcha noticed the tiny steps I took, she started to put her arm around me.

"Whoa. Take my arm. Remember what my throat looked like?"

She nodded.

"Back and stomach the same. Worse, actually. Under my jammies, I look like a mummy. I spoke to Missy last night, and she mentioned a demon called Apophis and the Egyptian spell books for the dead. That was before this attack, though. I believe this is personal, same as the last time, but it's not my great uncle." *Should I tell her?*

Sorcha led me back to my bed, but I tugged her to the large table. "If I lay down, I'll never get back up."

Cooper came in, carrying a tray containing a mug of soup, ointment, and a fresh roll of bandages. Sorcha took it and shooed him out.

"You take care of the store and I'll play nurse. I've nothing on all day." She turned to me. "If you don't mind me staying."

"If you're certain it's not an inconvenience." Cooper looked from her to me.

"Go." I waved him away. "You look after your customers. We can brainstorm."

When he left, Sorcha shut the door tight. "Keep out the noise." She rooted through the oversized bag she always carried and pulled out a bundle of sage and a lighter, then walked around, smudging the room.

"Think that'll help?"

She shrugged. "Can't hurt, and it smells nice. Now, off with your top so I can re-wrap you."

I turned sideways in the chair so my back was accessible. One by one, I undid the buttons of my pajama top. She gasped at the sight. I'd been wrapped from armpits to waist to ensure all wounds were covered.

"You weren't kidding about the mummy look."

First, she removed the gauze from around my neck. "That's healing nicely. Looks like the stitches have begun dissolving."

Next, Sorcha unwrapped my torso. As the gauze unwound downward, I placed one arm across my bare chest.

"These look deeper than the ones on your neck and throat. I'm surprised the doctor didn't call an ambulance and have you admitted. He used staples instead of stitches."

Wasn't expecting that. "Staples? No wonder he gave me a knock-out shot. Will they hurt to remove?"

"Probably. Don't think you'll be worrying about that for a while."

"As long as they're out before my cousin's wedding in December."

"Should be."

Neither of us spoke while she worked. This time the ointment wasn't ice cold. Cooper must have taken it from the fridge when he got up. It took over a half hour before I was ready for my sarcophagus.

"Thank you. Guess I should call my family and let them know."

"Do you want me to step out while you chat?"

I shook my head. "No. You're part of this, too. You're also moral support."

"Did you find out anything new when he invaded you?"

"Only his name, Lorcan, but Auntie already found it."

"Lorcan? I've not heard it before. Sounds like a Celtic name, probably not a demon."

"He's a long-ago banished relative, but based on the one glimpse I got of him, he's turning into something else. Can a person be turned into a demon, or do they have to be born that way?"

She shrugged in reply.

I pulled the laptop closer, opened Skype, then sent Auntie a text to see if she was free. A moment later, a call notification appeared. Taking as deep a breath as I dared, I answered.

"Marcy, dear. How are you? And Sorcha. Nice to see you again."

"Been better, Auntie. Tell you about that later. It is Lorcan who's attacking me."

Her eyes went wide. "Lorcan? You're certain? That's the name of the banished twin."

"Had another visitation while I slept last night. He said his name is Lorcan, and I don't recall another with that name."

"No. I know of no other. Interesting. So, I guess that means wherever he went, it wasn't to his death. That makes sense now."

"What does?"

"One of my friends has an old book from the days of our coven. It's sort of a diary or journal. Belonged to her great grandmother. It mentions the banishment. Apparently, Lorcan had a dark grimoire that vanished shortly after the ritual. I don't mean literally. Someone stole it. That must be the book Sorcha is keeping for you."

I turned to Sorcha. "Have you noticed anything in it indicating whose book it is?"

"No. The first few of pages are stuck together, magickally. Haven't been able to reverse the spell yet. Must be concealing ownership."

This was beginning to get interesting. How would Montgomery get his hands on the old book? Did it get shipped to Canada? When? Why? By whom?

"Auntie, is it possible that someone deliberately sent it to Montgomery? You said some of the coven turned to dark magick. Is it possible Monty found them after he grew up and formed some sort of allegiance? If Lorcan came back, could your brother, too?"

Aunt Priscilla sighed. "Much as I'd like my baby brother back, I know he's grown worse. I now understand his actions at such a young age are why my parents sent him away. Since he tracked you down, it's not out of the question he also found the old coven families and formed a pact. Lorcan might be the cause of our dwindling powers. It's also possible he was intentionally released by someone who knows about the old coven. You know it started well before I was born. The journal my friend has mentioned Lorcan reciting a curse before he vanished, but it doesn't specify what he said."

Sorcha leaned closer to the laptop. "If your powers are dwindling, and have been for a while, it's probably a good guess it was the curse."

I turned to her. "Sorry we hadn't told you about that. It's not something any of us speak of. I'll fill you in on the family history." I looked back at the screen. "If Auntie P. agrees, that is."

Auntie smiled weakly. "It is rather embarrassing, but it's not exactly a secret. Tell Sorcha whatever you're comfortable with."

"To heck with comfort. If she's going to help us, she needs to know everything. Warts and all." I raised an eyebrow. "Assuming I know everything."

Priscilla smiled. "I believe you do. Now, is there something *you're* not telling me?" Her eyes twinkled, a sure sign she knew I held back. That twinkled would disappear as soon as I filled her in.

"Yeah." I took a deep breath, reached up, and gently unbuttoned my top.

Auntie's jaw dropped. "Marcy…"

"Yes, it was Lorcan."

I pushed my chair away from the table and finished unbuttoning. "Lorcan is much more impatient than Uncle Monty. He lashed out when I said the ruby egg was gone."

"Gone? What have you done with it?"

"Not gone, gone. I've re-buried it. We should be able to retrieve it in a week or so."

"The answer must be in that book." Priscilla hesitated, thinking. "If only I could feel it. Better yet, if we knew someone who was at the original banishing."

I knew where this was going. "Fiona."

My great aunt nodded.

"I don't want to involve the Grey Haired Grannies in the séance this time. I know Missy would love to participate. Sorcha?"

"Of course. But not Helena."

"Definitely not. She may still have an attachment or some other influence from Lorcan. Maybe Cooper? She needs our energy to materialize properly." *Wonder why her spirit isn't in the Dorking cave with the others? Are the others trapped, or can they all travel at will?*

"You make the arrangements and let me know what happens. Meanwhile, I thought of something we can try at this end. I'll get the ladies together and go to the caves. Maybe one of the ancestor spirits has information that will help. Skype can wait."

I ended the call and filled Sorcha in on my family history. At least everything I knew. Even told her about Elsbeth, the palm reader, and her revelation it would be me who restored the power to my line.

TWENTY-TWO

Mid-morning the next day, I'd spoke to Auntie, asking if they'd restarted the old coven yet, and if I could join long distance. These past few months made me realize the importance of close friends and connections.

"We're talking about it, dear. We've agreed it's in our best interests to form the coven again. Still working out the details." Auntie sounded a little evasive, but I let it go. She had a lot on her mind.

I headed to the coffee shop for a large coffee and Morning Glory muffin. On my way back, I thought about the upcoming séance. It needed to be arranged soon. I wasn't certain Fiona would appear, but she was our only hope. Sorcha's calendar was wide open, so I texted Missy and arranged the séance for the next evening. I'd tell Cooper later. He wouldn't be overly thrilled, but he'd oblige—as long as I didn't try something dangerous.

Needing to speak with Sorcha, I approached Cooper about going to her place. He didn't want me leaving the store.

"I'm a grown woman. You can't keep me locked up." I crossed my arms and glared at him. "We aren't going to do anything. Promise. Just have a look at the contents of the grimoire. No spell casting, only reading."

After almost a half hour of going back and forth, he relented. "I'm terrified something will happen and I won't be there to help. You mean so much to me."

Knowing he was concerned about my wounds, and not being possessive, helped ease my temper. I could sit at her place just as easily as in the back room, and he knew it. We had to see what else was in that spell book. I promised again that we'd do nothing dangerous. I flipped the store sign to *open* when I headed out.

Ten minutes later, I sat at Sorcha's kitchen table, the dark grimoire in front of us. When I first entered her home, the atmosphere was light, welcoming. She lead me to the kitchen and the feeling changed. Despite the bright yellow walls, the room seemed dark. I turned and looked at the book sitting on the table. It radiated bad vibes, even though she'd done her best to cleanse it. *She did say a complete cleanse wouldn't be possible.*

She opened the cover and showed me the stuck pages. "Hold your hand over them. The magick is strong."

I did as instructed. Wasn't expecting the force that emanated from it. My hand tingled about four inches from the book. It pushed back, not allowing me to get closer.

"Wow!" I pressed down, but my hand didn't move. "Good luck breaking this spell without knowing what it is." I closed the book to examine the cover, in case it held a clue. The light hit it in a way that revealed a faint outline. "Hey, it looks like a handprint."

Sorcha picked up the book and moved it around, looking for the shadows. "Oh, I see it. I wonder …"

"What? Don't keep it to yourself."

"Sorry. Sometimes, instead of a spell, family members can seal things in a way that only they can release. Occasionally, a drop of blood. Since this is a handprint, it may be a sort of DNA thing allowing any family member to access it. Try it."

She put the book down and slid it in front of me.

"Could it really be that easy?" I was skeptical, but it was worth a shot.

The outline was a left print, so I held my left hand over the cover. Instead of being pushed away, the book seemed to draw it down. I didn't fight. The impression was too large, but the magick pulled the heel of my hand into place. My fingers splayed to snuggle into the correct position, and the print shrunk to hug me.

My wounds immediately ached, but my hand stopped tingling. Instinctively, I touched the book with the evil eye ring on my other hand. The aching subsided, but didn't completely go away.

A couple of seconds later, the sensation stopped. I lifted my hand and opened the book. The front pages were no longer stuck together. Sorcha gripped my arm, gasping in surprise.

The first page resembled the illuminated pages I'd seen in very old books. The first letter was inside a thickly outlined box, the rest of the writing in fancy old English scroll, the words in a language I didn't know. The page was covered in brilliantly coloured pictures, scrolls, and symbols. At the bottom were two words: Lorcan Adamah.

We both sat staring at the page. I couldn't read the text, but Sorcha could.

"It's Gaelic. Looks like it's some sort of affirmation."

"So, nothing to say why the first several pages were sealed?"

Sorcha shook her head. "Nothing to indicate any secrets."

I reached for the next page. "Should I?"

She nodded.

Mindful of the old paper, I took the corner of the page and turned it.

More Gaelic. I made another mental note to learn it, as it seemed to pop up regularly. This probably wouldn't be the last time I needed it.

Sorcha mumbled as she read. When she stopped, she turned to face me. "This sounds like a curse, but it's a riddle of sorts. Clues as to how to reverse it. It may be the cause of your family's power drainage, but I can't be certain. It seems to be written in an older version of Gaelic, which makes it difficult to read. Partly old Irish, which has been out of use since the tenth century. I can make out enough to understand it. Let me write it out."

Sorcha retrieved a notepad and wrote out what she could. "I believe it says the curse will remain as long as the person making it exists, either on this plane or the other."

My heart raced. *Could this be the solution to everything?* I let that sink in, realizing what the last line indicated. "Are there more planes than here and the afterlife? Doesn't that make the curse kinda permanent?"

"Well… maybe not? I think *the other* actually refers to the underworld. Some people believe there are multiple planes. Multiple universes where we all have a different life."

"And how are we supposed to find an entrance to one of these planes? Assuming they really exist."

Sorcha shrugged. "I don't believe it's possible to create a curse that can't be reversed eventually. They may have a seemingly impossible solution, but there will be one."

"Great. Let's hope you're right. How about we shelf this for now and see what's on the other pages that were sealed? Fingers crossed it's not all old Irish." *And fingers crossed we don't get sucked into an alternate reality.*

My thoughts went to Drew's upcoming wedding, then to my possible future with Cooper. *If we get this wrong… My heart raced again. This time, not from excitement. I tried not to think about that.*

Only two more pages had been sealed to non-family, all in the extinct Gaelic, and Sorcha said they looked to be spells for taking control of people.

That got my attention.

"Could that be what happened to Helena? Does it list any way to stop or block it?"

She read it again. "No, but since we have the spell, between Priscilla and myself, we should be able to figure out how to reverse it. Might take a while."

I rubbed my temples. Another headache, this time a regular one. *I think.* "OK. I'm feeling a little tired, so I'm heading back to Cooper's. Make sure you copy down everything you need off those pages. The book will likely seal them once you close it. I'll line up a call with my family to brainstorm a solution to the curse."

My walk back was slower than expected. Partly because my gashes ached as soon as I touched the book, which I didn't mention to Sorcha. *Why didn't I tell her? Because she'd tell Auntie, and I didn't want that.* The farther from Sorcha's I got, the better I felt, but only slightly. They ached regardless. Maybe once I got inside with all the wood-burned symbols Cooper hung around the shop, more of the aching would go away. *Maybe another tattoo or two?*

I found the bookstore void of customers when I arrived. Cooper sat in one of the comfy chairs set out for customers to look through books before purchasing. He looked up from his phone when the over-the-door bell dinged.

"Back so—" He dropped his phone when he turned towards me. "What the hell?"

"What?" He looked like he saw a ghost.

"Have you been attacked again?" Cooper rushed over. He extended his arms to hug me, but stopped mid-way. "Where does it hurt?"

"What are you talking about? I'm fine." *Liar.* As I suspected, the moment I stepped through the door, most of the aching stopped. My stomach felt warm, though. *Did I start bleeding again?*

I looked down. "Schist!" The front of my blouse was crimson instead of cornflower blue. *When did that start?*

Cooper flipped the lock and ushered me into the back. Without bothering to ask, he unbuttoned me. I didn't stop him this time. The one good shirt I'd brought from the house lay bloody and crumpled at my feet. My wrappings were deep red and dripping from over-saturation.

Once the shock wore off, he half-smiled, raised an eyebrow and told me to unwrap.

"Nice try." I grabbed the roll of gauze off the table, then headed up to the bathroom in Cooper's apartment.

I removed all the wrapping around my torso, wincing as they partially struck to my skin. I dropped them into the garbage. Turning to try to see my back in the mirror, the staples appeared to still be in place, so I took a quick, warm shower. The water stung when it hit the wounds, but I sucked it up. Took longer than normal to dry off, trying to avoid catching the towel in the staples. Even though my neck hadn't bled, the gauze got waterlogged, so it joined the rest in the garbage.

I pulled on my pants and covered my chest as best I could, then called down to Cooper to finish the job.

From the sound of the heavy thuds, he ran up from the store.

I smiled and called out. "Door's unlocked. Come on in."

He opened the door so fast it bounced when it hit the wall. His grin disappeared when he looked at me. "Oh, you're half dressed. You take all the fun out of everything. Hang on while I grab the ointment. It's going to be cold."

I sucked air every time he dabbed it on, but it made the healing speed up, so I refrained from complaining. Mostly. He'd brought up another top for me. A thought crossed my mind as I slipped the tee over my head.

"Will these leave scars?"

"They're pretty deep, so I'm guessing yes. Wear them proud. You've been through a battle and survived."

"Battle ain't over yet. Why don't you go and re-open? I want to lie down, then arrange another video chat with the family."

About two hours later, I woke fully refreshed and re-charged. I grabbed my phone and sent a group text to Auntie P., Susan, and Drew. It was early evening in Dorking, so they were all home and available immediately. I gave them ten minutes to gather at Priscilla's, then opened the chat.

Auntie P. answered right away. "Hello, dear. Susan and Drew should be here any minute. How are you feeling?"

"Oh, you know. Not a hundred percent, but I'm doing fine. You look tired, though."

A door slammed at her home, then my cousins appeared on the screen. We spent a couple of minutes talking about Drew's wedding before getting down to business.

"As I said in my text, we need to brainstorm. We found the curse. At least we think it is. Sorcha thinks it's old Irish Gaelic, but at least she was able to translate most of it."

Auntie's and Susan's eyes widened, smiles grew on everyone's face. Drew fist-pumped the air. Then they spoke over each other.

"It'll be over before my wedding!"

"I'm so relieved."

"It won't be easy to break." Leave it to Auntie to be a downer. The smile had left her face as quickly as it appeared.

I filled them in on the little gleaned from the translation. "Any suggestions? Is there a third plane? Or forth, or fifth?"

They looked at each other, shrugging and shaking their heads.

My great aunt finally spoke. "Anything is possible. You should know that by now. Sorcha is certain it said not this plane or the other? Other was singular?"

"Yes, but I'll double check. Why? Is that important?"

"If it's singular, we can send him to anywhere except the underworld, once we figure out how." Susan looked to her mother for confirmation.

Auntie agreed. "The other generally means the underworld. If the curse said *not here or the other*, all we need to do is find a third plane."

Drew leaned forward. "Otherwise, we'll have to kill him outright and that would put a damper on my wedding."

I grinned. "Yeah. Not really wanting to do that. Is Lorcan actually dead, a demon, or simply back from another realm? And is it possible he's being turned into a demon of sorts? Don't suppose any of you have any clue where the door to somewhere else is?"

(add discussion about Lorcan being turned demon)

"Hey. I had a thought. What about the caves?" Drew looked at her gran. "Maybe the ancestors there can help."

When exploring the caves months ago, I awakened our ancestors when I touched the walls. They weren't flesh and blood and hadn't revealed themselves physically. *Could they be on another plane?*

"Auntie, what do you think? Where do their spirits exist?"

"I'm sure I don't know. It's too late to go tonight as the sun will be setting soon. I'll go tomorrow." She turned to her daughter. "Are you available tomorrow?"

Susan nodded. "I'll make time. You're not going in there alone."

Since I stumbled across the cave entrance last summer, literally, the local witches started using them again. They'd even confirmed one of the tunnels led west towards Stonehenge, like we'd guessed. Three of them had rented little scooters and rode the eighty-odd miles through the tunnels. The exit was in a small wooded area at Vespasian's Camp, about four miles from the Henge.

"Can't wait to hear what you find out. And I'd love to re-visit the caves. Maybe we can squeeze in time after the wedding?"

That prompted further discussion on the plans for the wedding that lasted over an hour. Cooper came in to see if I was ready for supper. It took another twenty minutes to end the call.

TWENTY-THREE

The next day I took it easy. The most I did was prepare for the séance. Arrangements had been made for Missy to spend the night at Sorcha's rather than driving back to Peterborough in the dark. She wasn't working the next day, so we all planned to hang out together. I'd already warned Sorcha to expect a barrage of questions from Missy.

At 10:00 p.m., the four of us sat at the large table. Cooper and Missy were both curious, as they'd never been to a séance. Missy was super excited, practically bouncing in her chair.

"Do we hold hands now?" Missy reached for Cooper.

"We don't need to do that. If Fiona appears, she'll draw energy from us so she can materialize. We'll have to join hands if you want to hear her, though. So far, only I've been able to hear her after she manifests. My family had to link before they heard her speak. No guarantee it'll work for non-family, but we can try."

We grounded, and I closed the circle.

"Fiona? Are you here?"

The candle flickered.

Missy's eyes went wide. "Behind you."

I felt her presence before Missy spoke.

"Take all the energy you need."

I stood and turned to face her, watching as she slowly took form.

"If you guys want to listen, stand with me and join hands. Hopefully, it works for you like it did for my family."

Cooper stood to my left, Sorcha and Missy to my right. No one spoke.

As Fiona drew our energy and materialized, the white glow she gave off brightened.

"Fiona, these are my friends. Can you allow them to hear you? We need your help. Lorcan has managed to come back, and he's dangerous. Moreso than Montgomery. Do you know how to break his curse and send him elsewhere?"

As before, no features were discernible, but she had the definite shape of a fully grown woman. The white glow changed to blue briefly at the mention of her wayward son.

A wave of sadness radiated from her. "Lorcan? How can that be?"

The gasps let me know they heard Fiona's voice.

Sorcha addressed my ancestor. "In order to break the curse he put on your descendants, he needs to go to some other plane, we think." She recited the curse, speaking in the old Irish dialect.

I turned and looked at her, surprised. She'd said earlier that she didn't understand most of it.

Sorcha grinned. "I can pronounce it in Gaelic, but can't translate all of it.'

"Whatever. Fiona, do you understand it? Particularly the part about this plane or the other?"

"Yes. As long as his spirit is in your world or the underworld, the curse remains. If he should cease to exist, either in the flesh or spirit, the curse will end."

"That's what great aunt Priscilla thought. I'm not prepared to make him not exist in flesh, as you say. Is there some other plane or realm we can send him to? Auntie P. and cousin Susan have gone to the caves to speak with the ancestors."

"Yes, I know. You are on the correct path. Many things are awaking, now that you've discovered the old caves. Good things. They can guide you."

Her glow weakened. "You must go to the caves. Only then can you continue your mission. Be alert and be careful."

She faded away.

"That was beautiful." Missy continued to stare at the now empty space where Fiona had appeared. She reached out, latching onto Sorcha. "Whoa. Little dizzy."

"Guess she drew a little more energy than expected. We should stay seated for a few minutes. Missy, rest your head on the table. Could you all hear her clearly?"

Cooper and Sorcha nodded. Missy, her head on the table, gave a thumbs up.

Sorcha removed one of her quartz bracelets and slipped it on Missy's wrist. "She affected you more than the rest of us. I'll fix up something for you when we get back to my flat."

Cooper had been quiet the entire time. I tapped his hand.

"You okay?"

"Mmm. That was… amazing."

I gave him a gentle rap on the arm. "Stick with me, kid. You'll be amazed more than you can imagine."

Cooper cocked an eyebrow, grinned, and opened his mouth to make what I knew would be an inappropriate remark.

"Don't even go there, buster."

He feigned a hurt puppy-dog look. "I only wanted to ask about the caves."

"Sure you did."

Sorcha sat listening to our cajoling, but the mention of the caves got her attention.

"What are the caves she mentioned? Are they near here?"

I shook my head. "Nope. England. There's a cave system in Dorking. That's where my great aunt and her family live. The local museum has tours of sections of it. Apparently, the system is much larger than the locals know about. It used to be used by the witches. When I visited a few months ago, I stumbled across a hidden entrance. Auntie P. and her witchy friends have been exploring it ever since."

I hesitated, deciding if I should mention the rest. As Granny occasionally said, in for a penny, in for a pound.

"Um. The caves aren't exactly empty. The spirits of the local witches' ancestors are there." I described how I awakened them by touching the walls.

Her eyes widened when I got to that last bit. "So, you have to travel overseas to get ride of this Lorcan *duine olc*?"

Duine olc? Doesn't sound pleasant. Not bothering to ask for a translation, I quickly reviewed what Fiona said. "Sounds like we need the caves to break the curse. Maybe I can trap him here somehow. I don't want to make two trips over so close to one another, but I don't want to wait until December to trap him, either."

"Sounds like we need another brainstorming session." Cooper pushed his chair away from the table. "I'll start the coffee."

"Remember that containment spell we saw in the hidden pages of the grimoire? I'll pop home and fetch it." Sorcha grabbed her jacket and headed out.

Missy's eyes practically popped from her eye sockets. "Um, I don't want to be a Negative Nelly, but isn't that book evil? You haven't told me much about it, so I could be wrong. If it is evil, should you even consider using it?"

"You're correct. It is evil. Sorcha can't even completely cleanse it. Unfortunately, that one spell may be our only chance. I'll text my family. They'll be up in a few hours." She was halfway down the hall, so I didn't know if she heard me.

By the time Sorcha returned, the coffee was ready. She placed the book on the table.

That done, I put my hand on the cover to release the first few pages, then she opened it at a page flagged with an envelope. "This must be what he used to imprison the demon in the ruby. It also has a release spell. If the demonologist wasn't completely successful in ridding the ruby of it, this may come in handy. May also need it if he latches on to Helena again."

While Sorcha flipped the few pages and read parts of the spell, Missy half-raised a hand to inject a comment, but waited for my new Scottish friend to finish. "How? The cover… did I see a handprint?"

"Yes." I couldn't help but grin. Missy wasn't afraid, simply awestruck. She'd mentioned seeing things in Cairo, but never said anything specific. I'd have to get some stories from her later. "We think there's a sort of DNA lock on the book, so only family can open it."

Cooper missed the magick trick with the book and simply raised an eyebrow at our conversation as he passed around the coffee mugs. "What will you use to contain him? It will have to be something you can easily get through customs."

"We'll figure that out later." I blew on my coffee before taking a sip. "Let's go over the spell and see what we need."

"Short list…" Sorcha read it out. "Sea salt, spring water, dried roses, and thirteen rose thorns. And something to trap him in. The spell is for containing a demon, but it should work. Just change the chant, replacing the name of the demon with Lorcan."

"Sounds easy enough." I read over the instructions. "Then we'll bury the item with him in it until the trip over for the wedding. I have a feeling sending him to another dimension will be a lot trickier."

When I woke the next morning, I'd received a couple of replies to the group text I'd sent last night. Auntie suggested a video chat at two, their time, nine in the morning here. It was already eight-thirty. I dressed and gobbled down some cold cereal.

As usual, Auntie started the call on the dot. Looked like she was at Susan's this time. Because it was a workday, Drew called in from her store.

"How are you doing, cuz?" Drew made jewellery while chatting.

"Little sore, but getting better. So, what do you guys think of our plan?"

"Concerned." Auntie was always concerned. "I don't like the idea of you using a spell from a dark spell book."

Susan agreed. "It's a dangerous book, Marcy. I do wish you'd put it somewhere safe."

Drew glanced up at the screen long enough to nod, but didn't say anything.

"Normally, I'd agree with you. The book is extremely dangerous, but I honestly believe it's the only option. Once we've contained Lorcan, Sorcha can put a permanent lock spell on it, and I'll bring it with me when I come over."

"Not the wedding gift I was hoping for." Drew put down the pendant and joined the discussion. "Seriously, though. Why bring it here?"

Susan and Priscilla had backed away from the laptop, heads together discussing something.

"I thought we could contain it in the cave. Fiona said I needed to go there. That little alcove with the altar, possibly? Maybe one of you can ask the ancestor spirits?"

My great aunt and her daughter finished their discussion. Auntie took the lead.

"Neither of us can come up with another solution. It will be necessary to contain Lorcan and bring him over. Extra strong protection will be required. We may have to request help from one of the gods or goddesses. Since we don't use those types of spells, you have no other option but to use the grimoire. Promise Sorcha will be with you when you perform the ritual. I'll call her and discuss it with her. Protection will be of utmost importance."

"For sure. I'll throw the book at it, no pun intended."

Drew smiled. Priscilla and Susan did not.

"I promise I'm taking this seriously. If I ever forget, my mummy wraps are a great reminder. Auntie, you have your chat with Sorcha. We need to get rid of Lorcan immediately, if not sooner."

Auntie P. had said she'd make calls, but didn't mention any names other than Sorcha.

Knowing Sorcha would call or text after chatting with Priscilla, Drew helped me at the bookstore. A few special orders had been delivered, so I contact the witches who'd made the requests. Some of the titles sounded interesting, so I skimmed the contacts, ensuring not to leave signs they'd been read.

Sorcha finally called over an hour later. We discussed what object we could use to contain Lorcan in case we weren't able to find the original ring. She also had suggestions for the ritual.

"We need to wait until the moon is waning." Sorcha opened her calendar app. "That's the time for spells to banish evil influences, neutralize enemies, and remove harm."

"Well, that all fits. When is the next waning?" I remember that a waning moon's light decreased, so with the fading light, the evil dies. Fingers crossed, it was soon. The last thing I wanted was another nighttime attack and more gashes.

"The next full moon is October 9, so we can perform the spell up to three days after that."

"That's not too far away. Fingers crossed Lorcan doesn't attack again. Don't think my body can take much more blood loss."

Sorcha placed her hand over mine. "It will give us some much-needed time to prepare and allow you to heal more. We can also try to find a way to prevent further intrusions."

"Another tattoo?" I kinda liked the idea I could have protection on me all the time. Jewellery could easily be lost. Skin art wouldn't fall off or get stolen. "Since he's been attacking me in my dreams, how about a dream catcher?"

"I'll set up an appointment. Maybe get you a witches ball, too. An actual ball, not a tattoo."

That sounded familiar. I searched my brain. They were intended to ward off evil spirits, witches, and evil spells. I grinned.

Sorcha cocked an eyebrow. "What's so amusing?"

"Witches balls are meant to ward off witches. Does that mean neither of us would be able to set foot in the bookstore?"

She laughed. The sound was light and musical. It made me happy, almost enchanted. When she saw the dreamy look on my face, she stopped.

"Sorry. I should have told you. I have an ancestor who was a siren. Sometimes my laugh affects people, similar to how a siren song enchanted sailors."

I sat back in the chair, gobsmacked, as Auntie would say. Sorcha waited while I processed the info.

"So, you're telling me one of your male ancestors married, what? A mermaid?"

"Basically. We're all excellent swimmers, but few of us have the song. It gets weaker with each generation. The gene surfaces periodically. One of my cousins has the actual song and it's still pretty strong. With me, it's my laugh. Not easy to control. Anyway, we're getting off track."

"Right. I'd love to hear more later, if you don't mind talking about it."

"Certainly. Now, the witches ball. Despite the name, it has no effect on flesh and blood witches. The name is actually a corruption of watch ball. The strands inside the ball are said to trap the evil, not the body. And they're quite pretty. Available in many colours."

"Can we use it to trap Lorcan?"

Sorcha shook her head. "No. It's too easy to break glass. It has to be something we can seal, and won't break."

"Right. And something customs won't question. The original ring would be perfect, but it's unlikely we'll be able to find it in time, if ever."

A call notification rang on the laptop, interrupting our conversation.

"It's Priscilla. She must have news."

Sorcha moved across the room in case the call was personal. I told her it wasn't necessary, but she insisted. I accepted the call. Auntie was in a room I didn't recognize. With her were the twins. Couldn't recall their names and still couldn't tell them apart.

"Sorry. Don't know which of you is which." Easiest way to get their names without embarrassment.

Auntie waved a hand, dismissing my comment. "Doesn't matter. They have their great grandmother's journal and found something."

"Wait a minute. Are they descendants of the old coven, too?"

"Yes. Everyone you met when you were here is. Now listen. The ring did hold Lorcan's spirit originally. When he poofed, as you put it, the evil portion of his spirit trapped into the ring."

I started to say something, but she gave me the same look Granny used to shut me up and kept on talking.

"The ring was passed from family to family annually. The coven gathered and re-spelled it with a sealing spell to keep him inside. After the coven disbanded, the ceremony gradually died off, with the members performing it only occasionally, until eventually, they completely forgot about it.

One of the twins spoke. "Great Grandmother wrote about the ceremony they performed when they passed the ring to the next family. Unfortunately, the last family mentioned has died out. We don't know who had the ring last as it was her final entry before passing."

I began to get the picture. "So, the spell wore off, someone opened the ring, and out he popped."

The other twin spoke. "Most likely. If we can find the ring, we can put him back."

"My boyfriend's grandfather is trying to track it. It was sold at an auction about a century ago, but a fire destroyed the records."

The twins looked shocked and spoke at the same time.

"An outsider knows?"

Auntie P. explained about his family being helpers. They nodded their approval.

"We can help."

"You know, that might not be a bad idea. Cooper's grandfather is going through online newspapers, looking for a write-up, but not all papers are digitized. Can I give him your number?"

Auntie smiled, her eyes twinkling. "Be careful ladies. He's quite the charmer, and a widower."

The ladies giggled, then gave me their number and email. They were still giggling when we signed off.

"If they can find the ring in the next week, like I said earlier, it would be the perfect thing to trap him in." Sorcha joined me and tapped her fingers on the table. "There may still be residual spell in it."

"I'll video call Mr. Barker. Chances are, he's on the laptop, going through online papers."

He answered right away. Even though they only met briefly before his heart attack, he remembered Sorcha. I explained the reason for my call.

"A contact in England would be most helpful. Two is even better. Twins, you say? Interesting. Afraid I've run out of leads, so this is most serendipitous."

I gave him their contact info and let him get on with the research.

Sorcha tapped my shoulder. "Your aunt forgot to tell the twins how handsome Cooper's grandfather is. It's easy to see looks run in the family. You said Cooper's father as well?"

"Yep. You should see the three of them standing side-by-side. Mind-boggling. Can't help but wonder if they're somehow related to Johnny Depp. The resemblance is uncanny."

"A project for after we resolve this. Do you want me to arrange an appointment for your tattoo? Then we can get some witches balls."

While Sorcha did that, I thought about Uncle Montgomery. We hadn't contained him inside anything. *Did we actually kill him?* Somehow, I'd have to figure that out, no matter how long it took. My musing was interrupted when she touched my hand.

"She can fit you in this afternoon. You okay?"

"Yes, just thinking about something. Let's get some of the balls you mentioned. Oh, we also need to go to my place and let Nenka know I won't be back as soon as expected. We can start drying some rose flowers and collect the thorns while we're there."

We headed out and bought a four-inch green witches ball for the back room at the bookstore in my temporary residence, and a six inch blue one for the store window. Then we moved on to my inking appointment. I chose a smallish dream-catcher, full of colour.

The perfect size for my left arm. The tips of the feathers would peek out from my t-shirt sleeve.

Ashley was reluctant when she saw all my wrappings. I assured her I was fine, drinking plenty of fluids, and taking the prescribed pills. Because the tatt had more colours than my dragonfly, even though relatively small, it would take several visits and a few hours per visit. Once Ashley finished with me this visit, I decided to get Cooper to drive me out after he closed shop. It was too late for Sorcha to go with me to see Nenka.

TWENTY-FOUR

The bookstore was empty of customers when I returned, so I filled Cooper in on the video call with Auntie P., then showed him the start of my new tattoo.

"Are you positive there won't be any ill effects from the tattoo? You've got more than enough punctures already." The look of concern on his face was both heart-breaking and sweet.

"I've been taking the pills the doc prescribed. The trany-something."

"Tranexamic acid. That was only to stop the bleeding. Didn't he say he'd prescribe something to help regenerate the red blood cells once the bleeding was under control?"

I nodded. It was nice having someone looking out for me. Even though initially it kinda annoyed me, it always seemed to have been spot on. Might look less like a mummy if I'd paid attention to his concerns. "Thanks for being a worry-wart." I shoulder bumped him. "Bleeding's almost stopped. The bandages are mostly white when changed. I'll text him."

Cooper waited while I sent my message, one eyebrow raised as my message was long.

"Told him about the amount of bleeding, then the tattoos. Also asked about iron pills. And we need to go to my place after you close up. For the spell, we need to collect rose thorns, pick some rose blooms, and start them drying. Hope there's enough time for that. Nenka can help pick them. We can't try to contain Lorcan until early October. That gives us a week and a half to dry the roses. Cutting it close, but should be doable. Might need to get an electric dehydrator." With nothing to do but wait, I grabbed one of the books retrieved from the workroom last week and snuggled in one of the cozy chairs in the store.

The doc finally replied, scolding me for getting tattoos so soon, but he sent a prescription to the drugstore and suggested I start taking iron until fully healed.

The pharmacy was only a block up Main Street, so after getting my pills, I stopped at Cardinal and bought a couple of coffees and two slices of coffee cake to take back to the store.

Our snack was interrupted only once when someone came in for one of the special orders. It gave me the opportunity to meet another local witch.

"Oh, yes. I knew of your grandmother. Never met her, though. I understand she mostly kept to herself."

"Yeah. Don't know why. My family in England is the exact opposite. I'm trying to make friends, now that I've moved into Granny's house. Both wiccan and… non." I resisted the urge to call them muggles, but no other word came to mind.

"I'm certain we'll run into one another again. I'd love to chat, but I have other stops to make. Nice to meet you, Marcy."

"Nice to meet you too, Carol."

Cooper finished making notes in the order book used for helper business then put it back in the drawer under the counter. "That's four new friends you've made in just a few weeks. It's not so hard, is it?"

"Two friends and two acquaintances. What about you? How many friends have you made? Oh, that's right. Zero."

Cooper grinned. "Well, if you'd stop getting into trouble, we could go out and meet people."

"Low blow, Coop. Tell you what. Once everything settles down, you can hire part-time help, like your gramps did. Then, we can take weekly breaks together. The coffee shop has game nights. There must be tons of other things we can do around town. I bet one of the seniors would love to work a few hours here."

He came out from behind the counter and gently hugged me, sending tingles through my body. "How about we get you healed first?"

"It'll be our New Year's resolution. If everything goes as planned, it *will* be over after Drew's wedding. Can I at least ask the ladies if anyone at the senior's place would be suitable and interested? Must be at least one resident able to handle cash who has an interest in books."

"Sure, but can you hold off for a month or so?"

After supper, we drove to my place to chat with the gnomes.

"Good evening, dear. Are you moving back now?" Nenka sat primly in her little mini-chair in the dining room, hands folded on her lap. Cooper and I occupied two dining chairs.

"No, afraid not. It's going to be a little longer than planned." I didn't tell her about my most recent injury.

"Oh, dear. The house feels quite empty without you."

"I wanted to let you know about the delay, and also to ask if you could collect some roses. Only need the flowers, no stems. We need to have them dried to get rid of the person, spirit, whatever, that's been attacking me."

"Roses? Most of them have finished blooming." Nenka slid off her chair. "Let's go check. I'm certain there were some still in flower when I dead-headed a few days ago."

We followed her out. As she said, most had finished for the season. Fortunately, there were a lot of rose bushes and we got a half dozen suitable blooms, some already drying up. Nenka directed, I snipped, and Cooper collected the thirteen thorns. I snickered every time he swore. A little hydrogen peroxide would take care of his minor injuries.

We stayed and visited for about an hour. Tinkus and Nimagg even came out for a few minutes. When I mentioned Nimagg coming home, Nenka said they decided it would be safer if he stayed with her parents. Looking around, I realized there wasn't any place for my gnome family to hang out, except the lone padded little chair in the dining room. *I need to fix that.*

After Nenka went back to doing whatever she did in the evenings, I went to my room to gather up more clothes. Cooper stood in front of the display case where the ruby had been kept, and was still there when I returned.

"What are you going to do with the evil egg when it's dug up?"

Hadn't thought that far ahead. "Well, if it's no longer possessed, it can go back there." I pointed to the ring of crushed brimstone still sitting on the shelf. "Guess I should clean that up… eventually."

"Don't be too hasty, in case there's still a problem." He pointed at the small travel bag over my shoulder. "That all you're getting?"

"It's enough. Not like I'm moving in with you."

"You could." He waggled his eyebrows.

The thought of staying with Cooper wasn't exactly repulsive. The tunnel vision I first got when I looked into his silver eyes had stopped now that we were sort of a couple, but those eyes still fascinated me.

"You could move into *my* house after we're married." *Did I say that… out loud?*

If it wasn't attached, his jaw would've hit the floor. "Is that… did you just… what? When did we become engaged?"

"Um, well, my family believes… and yours agreed. We get along." I leaned against the door frame. "Oh, schist. Did I totally screw everything up?"

The shock wore off and the corner of Cooper's mouth twitched. He pulled me away from the door frame and hugged me. Tight.

"Ow. Ow. Ow. Wounded, remember?" A warmth seeped into my body, the same way it did a few weeks earlier when the ruby egg made me woozy. I relaxed and let it flow through me, practically melting into his body.

"Sorry. Got so excited I forgot about your gashes." He eased up, but didn't let go.

"Wish you'd done that sooner. Remember when your dormant healing ability kicked in before?"

He nodded.

"Happened again, just now. You need to learn how to control it. Talk to your folks and see if they can help. Maybe Drew, too."

With nothing left to do at the house, we headed back to town. Cooper called his dad, and I decided to do a little online shopping, since it was way too late to call England.

Most of the doll furniture was for the twelve-inch dolls. Too small for the six inch gnomes. The larger stuff was too expensive. A few ads popped up for doggie furniture. *Why not? Looks perfect.* A little pricy, but not too bad. Granny left me well off, so why not spread the joy? I ordered a sofa designed for a large breed, displayed with a lounging Great Dane, big enough for all three gnomes to sit comfortably on. The top of the seat cushion was about a foot from the grounds, and the legs were only a couple of inches high. Also got a few matching padded chairs. Once winter kicked in, they'd be perfect around the fireplace in the living room. Even found what looked like a chaise lounge for the sunporch. My tiny family should have no trouble getting on and off the furniture.

Cooper came down shortly after I finished, carrying two mugs of hot chocolate and some fresh gauze.

"Dad doesn't know much about my ability, but Gramps remembered a little. He's not certain, but he thinks it's either for calming or healing. Seems I got the healing one. Unfortunately, he has no idea how to control it."

I took one of the mugs, smiling at the mini-marshmallows floating on top. "You remembered. Why don't we call Drew before you open up tomorrow? I doubt she could control her calming initially, either."

"Sure." He glanced at my laptop and saw the pictures of dog furniture. "Not even going to ask. Now, drink up, then we'll get your wrappings changed. Need to buy more gauze tomorrow."

"I can do that. Did your gramps mention if he'd contacted the twins?"

"Yes. They're taking a train up to Oxford tomorrow to see if they can find anything at the Oxfordshire History Centre." He glanced at his phone to check the time. "I guess it's already tomorrow over there. Apparently, it's closed Monday and Friday. The ring is old, so it may have warranted a mention somewhere They think it's from the 17th or 18th century."

"Fingers crossed. If they can find out where the ring is, maybe the owner will sell it and we can re-trap Lorcan in it."

"If they can't locate it in time, use something else. You can't afford to sustain any more injuries. Now, drink up, so we can play 'wrap the mummy'. All talk of Lorcan is banned for the rest of the evening."

For once, I had an eventless night. Cooper was moving around upstairs, so I knew he'd be calling me for breakfast soon. I sent Drew a quick text to ask if she could spare fifteen minutes for a quick chat in about a half hour, then headed up to devour whatever Cooper was making. Drew replied with a thumbs up icon.

Cooper and I had settled into a morning routine. He made breakfast and I did the dishes and cleaned up. Less than thirty minutes later, I called Drew for a video chat, quickly explaining the reason.

Drew listened, nodding while Cooper talked. "It's only happened twice. It really surprised me. Is there a way to control it?"

"Don't see why not. I remember when it first manifested in me. After talking to Mum, we realized it happened when my emotions were heightened. Afraid or concerned."

Cooper thought about the two times. "First time, I was both concerned and afraid for Marcy. Yesterday I was… happy? No. Excited." He turned and winked at me.

Drew looked from Cooper to me. "What am I missing?"

"Nothing. So, what does Coop have to do to control it?" My face grew warm. Drew must have noticed the change in colour.

"I know you're lying, but I'll let it go. For now." She shrugged and turned to Coop. "In order to control it, concentrate on what you want to do. If you're trying to heal someone, envision the wound healing and fading. I draw the anxiety into myself. Not exactly sure how that works for healing. Maybe the wound temporarily appears on you and is absorbed. Has that happened?

"No, not that I've noticed."

"After, you'll have to ground and let whatever you took from Marcy flow into the earth. Marcy can help with that. Picture the wound sinking into the earth. You'll need to recharge and rest afterwards. Healing uses much more energy than you'd expect."

Cooper touched my arm. "Got the perfect guinea pig to practice that."

A little bell tinkled in the background. Drew glanced away. "Customer."

"We won't keep you. I'll let you know how it goes. Thanks, Cuz."

I closed the laptop and turned to Cooper. "Guinea pig, eh? More guinea than pig, I hope."

He waggled his hand. "More or less. Why didn't you tell Drew you proposed to me?"

"What? I didn't, did I?" I thought about what I'd said at the house. "Guess I sorta did. You never actually agreed."

"Wanted to give you a chance to change your mind. As you've pointed out more than once, we only met a few months ago."

"True. We don't need to rush into anything." I shrugged. "Get to know each other better first. It's our decision. No one else's."

Cooper had been joking about us getting together pretty much since we first met three months ago. Both our families had made more than one comment that we belonged together, and they were very serious. He nodded. "I can wait as long as necessary."

Part of me was glad he didn't take me up on it. A larger part was crushed. When I looked at him, I got the impression he was keeping something from me. His silver eyes looked different. *Was he hiding something from me?*

Normally, when he got mischievous, they twinkled. Now? More like a bright sparkle. *Did that go with his awakened skill, or something else?*

Cooper snapped his fingers in front of my face.

"What? Sorry. Did you say something?"

"Yes. I asked if you want to try it now that Drew's told me how. See if I can finish healing your neck."

"Sure." I started to remove the fresh gauze. "Easier to see the before and after."

Cooper reached over and finished taking off my wrappings. "Stand up. I want to take a picture."

I did as instructed, turning so he could get shots from all angles. He put the phone down, then enveloped me in a bear hug.

"Drew usually touches a hand or arm, not that I'm complaining."

"This is better." His breath tickled my ear. "Now hush and let me visualize the wounds closing."

Wrapping my arms around him, I melted into him, soaking up the warmth. The usual Cooper-tingle spread through me, but no new sensations. Standing like this wasn't a problem, healing power or not. The minutes ticked by.

"Don't think it's… wait." My throat felt hot. I tried to pull away.

"Stand still."

"I can't. It feels like a million fire ants are crawling on my neck."

Cooper released me, took a step back, then lifted my chin with his hand. "You've got to see this." He picked up his phone and took another picture, then reached for my hand, practically dragging me to the bathroom.

"Look."

"Holy Heliodore!" The skin on my throat moved, knitting the remainder of the wound together. "Why don't I feel it on my torso?" The last bits of dissolving stitches were absorbed into my skin.

"Only concentrated on the first wound. It's half-way healed, so I thought it might be easier." Cooper leaned against the wall, eyes half closed. "If a small heal takes this much out of me, I can't imagine what a large one would do."

"You look wiped. Don't forget to ground. To release it from your body. Drew said she needs to recharge after healing. I think you're gonna need a lot more time than she requires. I can give you some crystals to help, but it won't be enough. Do you have any of those sports drinks?"

He shook his head no.

I quickly showed him how to ground. "Take a few slow, deep breaths. Visualize roots extending from your feet, digging into the ground. Imagine a white light around you. Probably should have done this first to gain energy. Too late. Now picture my wound being pulled down out of you. We can refine the technique as we go."

He followed my instructions, but neither of us knew if it would work.

"No." Cooper slowly slid down the wall.

"Whoa! Hold on. We need to get you to a chair."

Once I had him wrangled onto the sofa, I gave him a chalcedony, quartz, and amethyst, then headed to the store.

Not being familiar with what sports drinks actually did, I got one of every colour.

Cooper chuckled when I sat the rainbow of bevvy's on the table.

"What? Won't these work? I figured one of the colours would be appropriate."

"They all do the same thing. Just different flavours and colours to make them more appealing." He took the one closest and guzzled it.

TWENTY-FIVE

The next day, my neck had completely healed, and Cooper was back to his normal energetic self. I had a short chat with Drew to show her my fully restored neck. Not even a scar. My torso wouldn't be so easy.

Late afternoon, Mr. Barker video-called. I went into the store so Cooper could listen.

"I've got some good news. The twins struck gold at the historical centre. You were correct. Because the ring is unusual, there was a lot of interest in it. They found a write-up in the archives. Unfortunately, the descendants of the purchaser have since sold it."

My heart hit my feet. "So it's still lost?"

Mr. Barker shook his head. "Not exactly. The ring stayed in that family for quite some time. They only sold it twelve years ago. Sheila has asked them to contact the new owner to see if he's interested in selling it." He cleared his throat and looked like a little boy caught doing something naughty. "I know I should have asked you first, but I told her the cost wasn't much of an issue."

Granny had left me plenty of cash, but I wasn't exactly a billionaire. "That's okay. I probably would have said the same. Getting the ring back isn't a deal stopper as we can use any object, but there's likely residual magick still in it, and it would work better than a regular item. Let's hope the owner isn't greedy."

Cooper put his arm around my shoulders. "Good work, Gramps. Thank Sheila and Stella for us."

Mr. Barker cocked his head. "You look different, Marcy. Can't put my finger on it."

"It's the healing power." Cooper lifted my chin. "Look."

"Well, I'll be. It's been so many generations since it's manifested in our family, I've lost count. Well done."

"Got help from Drew." I gave Cooper a little jab in the ribs. "Now he needs to fix the rest."

"Don't rush it." Mr. Barker seemed concerned. "Let me do a little research into our family and helper community. There must be another around with that gene." The worry lines smoothed out, and he grinned. "You're going to have special children."

Cooper and I exchanged a quick glance before responding. "Why is everyone so insistent we're going to marry?" *Not that it would be a bad thing.*

We chatted a little longer. Cooper's parents came to the laptop, so I let him visit, and I took care of the customer that came in.

The next two days were uneventful. Sorcha and Helena came with me to drive up and surprise Missy. I felt bad not including Missy and Helena on the latest goings on.

"I'm looking forward to seeing the displays and the drive is lovely, but next time we take my SUV." Helena sat squished in the back of my Smart Car.

I hadn't told Missy or Helena about my latest attack, and made certain none of the wrappings were visible.

When we arrived at the museum, Missy gave us the grand tour, proudly showing off the new display on crystals and fae. Afterward, we sat outside with coffee. The fall weather was settling in, but today the sun shone.

"I have a surprise." I unwound the silk scarf to reveal my scarless neck. "All better."

After explaining about Cooper, Sorcha suggested he get another tattoo, spelled to help with his energy levels.

"Don't know if he'll go for that. He was reluctant to get the small turtle in the first place."

"It doesn't have to be big, just spelled properly. How's your new one healing?"

I removed my sweater and rolled up my shirt sleeve to show them.

"That's beautiful. Wish I was brave enough to get one." Missy wrinkled her nose. "Not a fan of needles."

"If you do, make certain it's something you can live with." Helena rolled up her sleeve, revealing several tattoos in various stages of removal. "It's a long and painful process. I got these and many more when practicing the dark arts. In my case, they need to be un-spelled as they're being removed."

"If I did, I think it would be a tiny ankh. It represents eternal life." Missy laughed. "Growing up in Cairo, I have a deep love of all things Egyptian."

We spent a half hour more with Missy before she resumed her duties. Instead of heading straight back to town, I led Sorcha and Helena through the woods. The trail ended at a stream and lookout area with a bench. The stream babbled louder than the last time I visited. The recent autumn rain raised the water level at least two inches, making the flowing water more talkative. We all inhaled the fresh, earthy scent.

"This truly is a beautiful place." Helena seemed more relaxed than before. Hopefully, getting her tatts removed properly, and a new positive one inked, helped. Lorcan didn't seem to be affecting her any longer, but we would continue to keep her out of our plans for now, as a precaution.

We sat in silence, absorbing energy from nature. A Great Blue Heron landed on the water, fishing for a snack.

"That's a good omen." Sorcha nodded. "They represent inner strength, luck, and determination."

"That's appropriate." I stood. "We'd better head back so we don't get caught in rush hour traffic."

Cooper called as we made our way back to the car.

"Hey, Coop. What's up?"

"Gramps called with more news. When will you be home?"

"About an hour. Good news or bad?" I crossed my fingers.

"He didn't say. See you soon."

I shoved my phone in my pocket. "Hmm. If he wouldn't say, does that mean bad news that he needs to tell me directly?"

"Ever the optimist." Sorcha opened the passenger door. "The sooner you get back, the sooner you'll find out."

By the time I dropped off the girls, rush hour in town was in full force. I found a spot by the community centre, way in the far corner, and walked around to the back door.

Cooper spotted me, put up the *closed for an hour sign,* and locked the front door. "Let's take the call in the back. Don't want someone spotting us through the window and knocking." He dimmed the interior store lights and joined me at the large table in my temp abode, then opened the video chat. His gramps answered right away and got straight to the matter at hand.

"I have good news. The owner is willing to sell the ring." He told me the price.

"Wow! That's a lot more than I thought."

"Is he willing to negotiate, Gramps?" Cooper was more shocked than me at the cost.

"Yes. I've done some research and those types of rings can command a good price, but not what he's asking. No special provenance with yours. He wants to negotiate directly with you, Marcy."

"Um, I've never done that before. Can you join the call? You have all the research." *My stomach knotted at the thought of haggling with the owner.*

"Certainly. How about I set up a call for tomorrow?"

"Sure. Fill me in on what you found, so I don't sound like a dunce."

Cooper went back to the shop, and I stayed on the call with Mr. Barker. Apparently, poison rings range from under a hundred all the way up to several thousand dollars. More if it belonged to someone famous.

We arranged the call for ten the next morning, my time. Since I'd only packed one dressy top and it was covered in blood, I put on my best tee. At least the tee was clean and didn't have a stupid saying on the front.

Mr. Barker called me first, then added the owner to the call. "Mr. Smith, this is my friend, Marcy Adhamh. The ring used to be in her family."

Smith's eyes lit up. "Ah, a family heirloom. You must be anxious for its return."

I could practically see the dollar signs in his eyes. My gut told me this Smith character was a real wheeler and dealer, and undoubtedly crooked.

Stay cool. "It would be nice to get it back, but it's been out of the family for so long, it really holds no sentimental value." I shrugged, hoping to appear indifferent.

Smith slumped, more than a little disappointed. At least one dollar sign left his eyes. He held up the ring. "It's quite lovely, as you can see. Well worth ten thousand pounds."

I did a quick calculation. Over sixteen thousand Canadian. *Nope.*

"Yes, it is lovely, but way over priced. A poison or vessel ring owned by Julius Cesar sold recently for less than seven thousand

Canadian. This ring has no history even remotely close to that. A Victorian emerald and diamond vessel sold for a little over eight. I'm sure you've noticed this ring isn't gold and has a solitary onyx stone. Not terribly valuable. Comparable rings run between one to three hundred. I'm willing to offer five hundred British pounds. More that you spent to purchase it."

Mr. Barker smiled and sent me a text.

Well done, Marcy.

Smith said nothing.

"Why don't you think it over? If you agree to the price, contact Mr. Barker and I'll arrange payment. Have a nice day."

"Wait. Five hundred pounds? Cash?"

"If that's how you want to be paid, yes. I have family over there. They can complete the transaction on my behalf."

I already knew he only paid two-fifty for it. The ring was unique, but not expensive. He had no clue about the symbols etched into it or what its true purpose was. I waited while he thought it over. If he did any research, he knew the true value was probably less than one hundred. He'd overpaid and now had a chance to make it up, plus some.

"Yes, five hundred British pounds in cash."

"Agreed. I'll contact my aunt and make the arrangements."

He left the call, but Mr. Barker stayed. "You did very well, Marcy. Sounded very professional. I'll give you his contact info so you can pass it along."

"I don't mind telling you I was scared to death. Mr. Smith is a very greedy man. Thank you for your help. I'd better contact Auntie P. Talk to you later."

My great aunt answered right away. I filled her in and asked if one of them could make the exchange.

"Of course, dear. I'm curious to see what the ring looks and feels like. Hopefully, it still holds power. I'll see if Susan will come with me."

She suggested a public, but quiet, place. I relayed the info to Smith, and he agreed. I forwarded a picture of my family, mentioning Priscilla would possibly bring her daughter.

After confirming with Auntie that Smith agreed, I e-transferred enough money to cover the current exchange rate. She said she'd courier the ring after examining it.

I called Sorcha to tell her we'd have the vessel ring soon, and didn't need to find anything else with which to capture Lorcan.

"That's great news. You can wear it and customs won't give it a second thought." She paused. "Maybe you shouldn't wear it. Let me mull that over."

"We'll have it in plenty of time for the spell. The exchange is tomorrow. They'll probably examine it for a day or two, then pop it in a courier bag."

With nothing left to do but wait, I drove home to see if the roses had dried. They were half dead when plucked, so fingers crossed, they were ready. As soon as the ring arrived, we were going to do the spell.

While checking the blooms in the workroom, Nenka popped in. Satisfied the roses would be ready, we went into the living room to chat. Much as I enjoyed living in close quarters with Cooper, I missed this old house.

Holding my head high, I asked Nenka if she noticed anything different.

"Oh! Your wounds have healed. That is wonderful."

"Only my neck. The rest of me still hurts like the dickens." I didn't tell her that I'd almost bled out after touching the spell book, or the extent of my new gashes.

"I'll need more ointment soon. May as well collect more ingredients while I'm here. Are they still growing?"

The diminutive gnome nodded. "Yes, but their season is almost done. I hope there's enough to heal you."

"When it's done, it's done. At least it'll have helped immensely." I snapped my fingers. "Don't know why Granny never did it."

Nenka cocked her head. "Did what?"

"Put up a greenhouse. The common herbs for cooking are grown inside in window pots, but not everything would take to planters or being indoors. This property is huge. More than enough room. A project for next spring. I'd like to do it now, but there's too much going on."

"She did mention it a time or two, but never got around to it. She thought somewhere near the sunporch."

I nodded. "Far enough away to get full sun, but close enough not to freeze your buns collecting specimens."

Nenka giggled.

"Maybe a nice stone path leading to it? I'll have all winter to research." The mantle clock chimed four.

"Is it that late? I'd better get the plants and head back. Cooper doesn't like me being away too long. He thinks something might happen to me."

Nenka smiled. "Doesn't it usually?"

"Touché."

We gathered up the last of the plants for my ointment, making certain we left the roots intact, then I headed back to Antique Books.

TWENTY-SIX

Cooper turned the lock and flipped the closed sign over. "Delivery came for you. It's in the back. Please tell me you're not planning on getting a dog. At least not one large enough to fill that furniture."

"Oh, good. We'll have to go out to the house again. The furniture is for Nenka and her family. They have total run of the house, but nowhere to sit and enjoy it. There's that lovely fireplace in the living room I'm sure they'd enjoy. Once you show me how to light it without filling the place with smoke, it'll be quite cozy."

Cooper shook his head. "You're something else. How do you know they want to sit around the house?"

"If you lived inside walls, wouldn't you want open space occasionally?"

"Suppose. Did you want to go tonight?"

I mulled that over a moment. "No. Tomorrow. Kinda tired. After supper tomorrow, we can drive out. I'll distract Nenka and you can sneak the furniture in and set it up in the living room."

Cooper bowed, making a grand gesture. "I am but your humble servant."

"And don't you forget it."

I grabbed one of his utility knives and went to slice into my purchases. There was little to assemble. Just taking them out of the boxes, screwing in legs, and dropping on the cushions. Easy, peasy.

Cooper's mention of a dog got me thinking. I'd never had a pet. Did I want the responsibility? How would it affect my gnomes? Nenka said Nimagg enjoyed his grandmother's kitty. I'd sit in the sunporch with Nenka tomorrow to discuss it. The perfect distraction.

I spent the evening researching greenhouses with Cooper. We decided on a large one, but Cooper declined my suggestion of him putting it up.

"I'm busy with the store seven days a week. Besides, I know nothing about them. Your granny left you enough to hire the right people to install it and lay a stone path. Tomorrow, make a few calls and get some estimates. That'll give you at least six months to get over the shock of the cost."

✳ ✳ ✳

Late afternoon the next day, Auntie video called. "I have the ring." She held it up proudly so I could see. First time I'd seen her smile so much. "I've called the descendants of the old coven, and we'll be meeting in an hour to examine it. Also, we'll continue discussing re-establishing the coven. Tomorrow, the ring will be on its way to you."

Auntie's smile faded, and she got a funny, unfamiliar look on her face. "Are you hiding something?"

"Whatever gave you that idea?"

I tried to read her, but she blocked me. "You're up to something, but I won't push it. It's obviously a surprise."

"If you say so, dear."

Humph. "Okay, so, can you feel any power in the ring?"

"Only a little. There's an essence that I believe lingers from Lorcan. The spell that sealed the ring is gone. Someone must have finally managed to open it, releasing him. Impossible to say how long ago."

"That's what I figured. We'll have to do a better job this time. When do you think the courier will arrive?"

"Sending it special delivery today, so it should arrive mid-afternoon tomorrow."

"Don't forget to give them Cooper's address."

"Not senile, dear. I know where you are."

"Sorry. A little anxious. Let me know what your friends say."

I went back to my list of greenhouse designs and prices, then started looking for someone to install the stone path. Flagstone seemed to be best, and would look lovely with the old house.

After supper, we loaded Cooper's car with the dog-gnome furniture and headed to my place. Like she normally did, Nenka appeared out of nowhere. Her husband and son were typically absent. *Is Nimagg back at his grandparents?*

"Come, sit with me in the sunporch. I want to talk to you about something." I led the way, grinning.

The white wicker chairs were too high for her, but the matching foot stool made the perfect step. The sun sat low enough for the trees to block the sun, and the solar lights engaged one after another.

"I love this view. Won't be the same nice once winter settles in, though."

"And will get rather chilly. What did you want to discuss? Nothing bad, I hope?" Nenka's brow furrowed.

I settled back in the chair. "No, nothing bad. I wonder… how would it affect your family if I got a pet? Would you be safe?"

Nenka leaned forward. "What type of pet? Witches do frequently have familiars, and we get along fine with most of the wildlife. Except the coyotes."

I shrugged. "Not sure. You mentioned Nimagg enjoyed the cat at your parents', but a dog might be good protection."

"A vicious dog? Oh, my. I don't know."

"No, nothing like that. Something that *looks* mean. Or maybe the stereotypical witchy pet cat, but not black."

The conversation ended when Cooper joined us. He nodded at me.

I rose. "Nenka, we have a surprise for you and your family. This chat was to keep you busy while Cooper set it up. Get your family and join us in the living room."

Five minutes later, Nenka and her husband showed up. I looked around for their son.

"Nimagg is still visiting my parents, but I found Tinkus."

Cooper and I stood in front of the fireplace, hiding the doggy chairs and sofa. We'd moved the recliner across the room out of sight. We stepped aside.

"Oh, little-people-sized furniture." Nenka stared, head cocked.

I couldn't tell if she was happy or not. Tinkus' expression rarely changed, so I couldn't read him either. Except when their son went missing in the summer, he always appeared stoic.

"Since you're part of the family, you deserve a place to sit. I can't imagine living inside a wall. I can move the furniture anywhere you like." I pointed across the room. "There's a chaise lounge, too. I thought maybe that could go in the sunporch in the spring and summer so you can enjoy the flowers."

"Oh, my." Nenka's eyes watered, and she dabbed them with her apron.

Tinkus put his arm around his wife. "Very nice. Thank you."

"Full disclosure. It's actually dog furniture, but it's quite nice. Sturdy, too. And I promise, it comes without a dog." *Maybe next year.*

My gnomes approached the little sofa and pressed down on the cushions. Satisfied they were soft enough, they climbed up. Since the doggy sofa cushion sat about three inches from the ground, my tiny gnomes had no problem getting on, even if awkward. *Note to self, little step stool.*

"Very comfortable. With winter approaching, the fire will be perfect." Nenka slid off and tried one of the chairs. "Very nice indeed."

Tinkus stretched out on the sofa, head against the arm. "Could get used to this." He actually smiled.

Cooper moved the chaise to the sunporch. Fortunately, the wall facing the garden was almost completely glass, so Nenka would be able to see the spring and summer blooms. We left the gnomes to relax in their new space outside the walls.

Back at my temp home, Cooper practiced controlling his healing on me. Since this required hugging, I didn't mind being his guinea pig.

Priscilla had emailed while we were out, updating me on the meeting with her friends. Nothing new on the ring, but several women were open to re-establishing the coven. Apparently, more meetings were required to discuss details. We watched a movie, then called it a night.

I spent the next day pacing around, waiting for my package to arrive. Auntie hadn't sent a tracking link, so I couldn't tell where it was. A few minutes past four-thirty, someone rang the buzzer on the back door. *The courier should have come to the store.* When Cooper came out from behind the counter, I waved him off.

"I'll get it. Maybe Priscilla gave instructions to come to the back."

When I opened the door, Drew stood in front of me. "What? Why?" Too surprised to form a sentence, I grabbed her arm and pulled her inside.

"Gran, Mum, and I talked it over and decided the spell would work better with another family member. Gran still has issues flying, and I wanted, no, *needed,* a break from everything. Mum is watching the store for me. I thought I'd stay at your house."

I led her into the back room. "My thought exactly." I waved my arm around the room. "There's only the small bed here, and Cooper's apartment only has the one bedroom. Maybe he'll agree to me going home since I won't be alone."

Drew set her luggage by the back room door and looked around. "Quite different from the last time I saw it. Less hospital-like." She turned to me. "And since when do you ask permission to do anything?"

I shrugged. "Maybe I'm finally growing up. Anyway, when Cooper said he was returning from Nova Scotia, Missy helped me put everything back the way it was before his gramps' heart attack. Fortunately, we hadn't gotten around to doing anything about the bed. We'd shoved it against the wall to get it out of the way."

"And the reason I'm here." Drew reached into her shoulder bag and pulled out the ring.

"Oh, let's show Cooper. Wait. Did he know you were coming?"

"Not as far as I know."

"He's been hiding something from me. I thought maybe he was in on it."

"Nope."

We joined Cooper in the shop while I tried to figure out what he was up to. He looked more shocked than me.

"Well, this is a surprise. A pleasant one. How long are you staying?" He gave Drew a quick hug.

"Only a week. We should be able to capture Lorcan by then."

"She's going to stay at the house. I thought I'd move back."

Cooper's smiled faded. "So soon?"

"Had to happen eventually. I'm half-way healed, and once we contain Lorcan, there will be no danger." *I hope.*

"Right." He looked so sad.

"We'll spend time here, and you'll still have to give me my daily healing hug."

"How's that coming along?" Drew turned to Cooper. "I'd like to see how the wounds are healing. I can assist you with that. Provide an energy boost, even though I don't heal physical wounds."

"It takes quite a bit out of me, and the repair is small, but at least I can get it to surface on command." Cooper put his arm around my shoulders. "Being tired is worth it."

"Good. I can try to help you with that while I'm here. Eventually, you'll feel less exhausted, but that feeling will never completely disappear.

"I'm due for another dose of Cooper-hugs tonight. Let's get you settled at the house. My wonderful healer can bring over takeout when he closes." I reached up and took his hand from my shoulder, twisting out of his half-embrace. When I looked at Drew, she stared, one eyebrow cocked, a questioning look on her face. I still held Cooper's hand and quickly released it. "Deal?"

"Like I have a choice. Let me lock up and I'll take Drew's bag to your car."

Drew and I linked arms while we walked to the parking lot, Cooper trailing behind. The single, large suitcase filled the tiny trunk of my lava orange Smart Car. Cooper waved us off and headed back to re-open the store.

Traffic was light, so the drive didn't take long. The thought of moving back home lifted my spirits more than I imagined. For the first time in ages, I had a place that truly felt like home.

"You and Cooper have become quite cozy. Will your arrangement become permanent?"

I glanced at Drew. "What do you mean?"

"Living over the brush."

"First, we are not living together. Second, why is it called that? And third, who still says that?"

"Picky, picky. You're living in the same place. If I recall, it's called that because when a couple couldn't have a church marriage, they simply held hands and jumped over a broom or straw brush. We Brits love our sayings."

I made the final turn onto my drive. "As Dorothy said, *there's no place like home*. Nenka will be happy to see you."

With the ruby crystal egg safely buried at the edge of the property, my nerves remained calmer when I passed the doorway to the living room. Still had a touch of pterodactyls, but only baby ones. Nothing bad had happened when Cooper and I were in there with the gnomes, either.

"Want the same room you had last time?"

"Suits me fine." Drew paused at the living room door. "Is that dog furniture? Are you getting a puppy?"

"No. Not exactly. Come on." I tugged her sleeve to get her moving. "Yes, it is doggy furniture, but I got it for Nenka and her family." As we ascended the stairs, I filled her in.

"Gran would have a fit if one of us got little furniture and invited any sort of fae to live with us. She was rather smitten with Nenka, though."

Most of the remainder of the afternoon, we chatted about her wedding. Well, Drew chatted, I listened and nodded. She showed me a picture of her in the gown. The one her mother wore. I'd seen pics of it, but this was the first time with Drew wearing it.

A vision of me wearing it flashed through my mind. *No. Not my style.* I shook the image away, refusing to consider it… yet.

"One of Mum's friends is altering it. Still needs tucks here and there." Drew pointed out something I hadn't seen before. "Little change every time I go in. Mum insisted she take a picture every time I try it on. Can you come over a week early? She's going to make your maid of honour gown. The friend, not Mum. No bridesmaids, only you. Look."

She swiped through her photos. "I hope you have no strong objections to it."

"Holy heliodor." The dress she chose had a deep-green halter top with a flowing skirt in variegated shades of green. "It's beautiful, but won't I freeze in a halter in December?"

Drew laughed. "It'll have sleeves and a full top, but I couldn't find a better picture. The green will fade from dark at the top to light at the hem. The dress will be full length like in the picture, with the sleeve cuff having a large, pointed opening."

She obviously didn't like the face I made.

"Oh, I'm not describing it properly." Drew scrunched her face, trying to remember the name of the sleeve. "Angel? Or butterfly?"

A quick search on my phone solved the mystery. "Angel sleeves. Very wizardly looking. I love it."

Once that was done and Drew emailed my measurements to the dressmaker, it was about time for Cooper to close up. He texted asking about the food. We settled on good old burgers and fries.

While waiting for dinner, I phoned Sorcha and put her on the speaker. "Hi, Sorcha. Got Drew here with me. Can we arrange a time for you to come to the house tomorrow to talk details? She brought the ring with her. I'd like to trap Lorcan right away."

Drew leaned over my shoulder. "Hi, Sorcha. Can't wait to meet you in person."

"Drew. *Braw*! Can't wait to meet you in person, too."

I looked at Drew. "*Braw*?"

Sorcha laughed. "It means wonderful, fantastic, brilliant. Keep forgetting you're not well versed in the necessary languages. You should really start learning Gaelic."

"It's on my to-do list. Latin, too."

We set a time for the ritual, and Sorcha told us what we needed to do to prepare. Luckily, I had everything required.

As we ended the call, Nenka came in. "Drew! How lovely to see you. Are you staying long?"

"It's nice to see you, too. I'll be here about a week."

"Congratulation on your upcoming wedding. I look forward to seeing pictures. Wiccan and Pagan weddings are something I've never seen before. Even though I have a lot to do, I wanted to say hello."

She scampered off seconds before Cooper texted.

Out front. Need Help.

I opened the door. Cooper stood on the porch, arms full of take-out bags and a bakery box.

"How did you manage to text? Use your feet?"

"Texted from the car. I may have over-ordered."

Drew took the bakery box and lifted the lid. "Black forest cake. This won't last long. I'll have to jog miles tomorrow. Maybe even the next day."

"And you'll be doing that on your own." I took one of the bags from Cooper and headed to the kitchen.

While we devoured the burgers, I told Coop we'd arranged to do the ritual in a few days.

"Full moon is Sunday, so we'll do it the next evening. That way, if it doesn't work, we'll have a few more shots at it while the moon is waning and Drew is still here."

Around 8:00 p.m. Drew began yawning. "Sorry. It's well after midnight at home. By the time I adjust, I'll be on a plane back. Would you mind if I cleansed the house before my eyes snap shut?"

Both of Cooper's eyebrows shot up. "Do you think there's still some evil lingering?" He touched my arm. "Maybe you should come back to the shop."

"The house feels like it used to." I turned to Drew. "Are you sensing something?"

"No. Simply a precaution, and it smells nice."

Couldn't argue with that. The scent of cedar or sage burning smelled heavenly. Most incense smelled heavenly.

"Let's do it. After you visit the sandman, Cooper can re-wrap me." I smacked my forehead. "Schist! I forgot to grab the ointment and stuff."

Cooper stood. "I noticed. You get your witchy stuff and I'll go to the car and grab the make-shift first aid kit I created. Should be enough to last the week."

Five minutes later, the three of us walked single file through the house. Drew led the way, fanning the smoke. We circled the living room twice since that's where the ruby crystal sat for the past few months with its resident minor demon. Neither of us felt any lingering effects, but an extra pass wouldn't hurt.

Next, across to the dining room. When we started down the hall to the kitchen, Drew paused, reaching to find the button to open the hidden doorway.

I reached up and tapped her shoulder, whispering. "No, he's not family."

Drew nodded, let the sage linger a moment, then continued. First floor done, we ascended to the bedrooms. Halfway up, Drew stumbled.

"Let me finish before you break your neck." I took the bundle from her. "We'll do your room first. Then you crawl into bed. Me 'n Coop can finish up."

She didn't argue.

When we reached the top, I froze, causing a three-person pile-up.

"What the—" A dark cloud settled around me. Not an actual cloud, more like a heavy feeling. A bad, heavy feeling.

Cooper waited patiently for one of us to let him in on what happened. He cleared his throat.

"Sorry. Bit of bad mojo up here. I can't be certain, but I think it's residual."

Drew agreed. "Yes. There doesn't seem to be any physical attachment to it. Once the house is done, leave the rest in a bowl near the top of the stairs. Let it burn out overnight. Wide awake now. Let's continue."

Only the area at the top of the second story staircase felt off. When the second and third floors were done, Cooper fetched a large glass mixing bowl from the kitchen for the sage to safety burn itself out.

"Bit of overkill, don't ya think? A plate would've sufficed."

Cooper shrugged. "Didn't want to risk burning ash getting onto the hardwood floor. Where'd Drew go?"

"Bed. I think I'm about ready to call it a night, too. But first, time to play Wrap the Mummy, after I shower.

Once dried, I joined Cooper in the kitchen. I'd put on PJ bottoms and my housecoat. I'd taken a large piece of gauze with me and wrapped my chest. Coop could do the rest. When I removed my housecoat, Cooper shook his head at my partial wrap and laughed.

"What? We're not married. Not even engaged, since you didn't say yes when I asked."

Cooper smiled. "Didn't say no either."

Once fresh ointment and gauze were applied, time for my favourite part; the healing hug.

"Mmm. You're getting good at this." I snuggled closer, enjoying the warmth.

"Marcy, when this is all over, we should get married."

I let go and took a step back. "Married?"

"We both know it's going to happen. And you did propose. Why put it off? Next spring? Beltane or Litha?"

"Seriously?" The pterodactyls returned. Why was I surprised and nervous about this? It was me who proposed originally.

The huge soppy grin on this face told me he was serious. I half shrugged.

The pterodactyls left. "What the heck. Why not?"

"Not exactly the reaction I'd hoped for, but I'll take it." He reached into his jeans pocket and pulled out a ring box.

"I've been carrying this around for a few days." He opened the lid, revealing a white gold ring, with a two-carat round emerald mounted in the centre. Simple. Elegant. Beautiful.

That's what he's been hiding. I held out my left hand so he could slip the ring on my finger. He dropped to one knee and placed the ring.

"It's perfect."

Cooper pulled out a second box and opened it. "Wedding bands."

Matching white gold bands with tiny trees of life raised around the band. Mine had a two-millimetre-round emerald between each tree.

"These had to be custom made. How did you get them so fast?"

"Had them made in Nova Scotia. I knew this was happening, even if you didn't." Cooper bopped me on the nose.

He put the wedding bands back in his pocket. "So, it's official?"

"Definitely." I threw my arms around him. "We're engaged."

His lips found mine. Every inch of my body tingled.

When we finally separated, I could barely breathe. We agreed to keep it secret until after we captured Lorcan.

TWENTY-SEVEN

Letting Drew sleep in the next morning, I sat in the sunporch with my coffee, and stared at my engagement ring. When my cousin entered the kitchen, I quickly removed it and slipped it into my pocket before she joined me. "Morning sleepy head. Did you notice? The heavy feeling is gone."

"Coffee first. Talk second." Drew popped a pod in the machine, set a mug under the spout, pushed the button, and leaned on the counter until it finished. "Ah, liquid magick!" She wrapped both hands around the mug and inhaled.

I nodded, totally agreeing. "Something we have in common. Sit. We need to prepare for Monday. How do we call Lorcan so we can imprison him?"

Drew blew on the coffee as she walked through to the sunporch, then took a sip before sitting. "Mmm. Better. Well, he wants the grimoire and ruby. It's not safe to dig up the crystal yet, so maybe we can use the book as bait. Sorcha will be bringing it, anyway." She looked around, noticing I didn't have food in front of me. Rare sight. "Whatcha got for breakfast?"

"French toast?"

"Sure."

I got up to start breakfast. One of the few things I could make from scratch "I think we have all the ingredients in the workroom. We'll have to triple up on protection.

Drew followed me into the kitchen, then gasped, stopping abruptly and slopping her coffee. "I just remembered the workroom! We didn't smudge it last night."

"I did after Cooper went home. Left some of the cedar burning down there, just like at the top of the stairs. Circled the dish with the spell ingredients to ensure they were contamination-free."

Drew sat back, examining my face. "You're unusually happy this morning. I can sense there's something you're not telling me, and I don't need to be a witch to get that."

"Happy to see my cousin. And what I'm not telling you is what your wedding gift is." Not that I actually had any clue what to get her and Randy.

"Why don't I believe you?"

"Because you're a highly suspicious person?"

"Fine. Keep your secrets. I'll find out soon enough."

"Not until your wedding day." I glanced at my empty finger. *Or later this week.*

After breakfast, we video-called Sorcha to iron out the last of the details.

"Have you decided on a location for the ritual? Should be somewhere neutral, if at all possible." Being relatively new to the area, Sorcha still didn't know where most things were.

"Guess it should also be somewhere secluded. Would the woods around my place be considered neutral?"

"Technically, yes. But it would be better to put a bit more distance between Lorcan, your home, and the ruby."

I wracked my brain. There were plenty of woods and trails around, but they had no gates or locks, so anyone could go in and interrupt at any time. There wouldn't be a high probability someone would wander around in the dark, but why take a chance?

"How are you at tricking surveillance cameras?" I looked from Drew to Sorcha.

Drew shook her head. "Not part of my skill set. Sorcha?"

"I believe I can manage it. After making your uncle's hide-out appear normal, a camera would be a piece of cake. What are you thinking?"

"There's an abandoned house on Davis, not far from here. Fenced in and boarded up. If we can get in and out undetected…"

"No, that won't work. I believe I know the place you mean. It's too close to the main road. Too exposed. Since we're going to use the grimoire for bait, why not do the ritual at the house where we found it? It's not neutral, but it should be easier to get him someplace familiar to him."

I shuddered. "Do you remember how that place felt? It practically reeks of evil. Remember the effect it had on Helena? There must be a better place. You said neutral was best, so why suggest it? He likely trained Uncle Monty there. His imprint is all over that place. Wouldn't that make it worse, familiar or not?"

"I agree with Marcy." Drew leaned closer to the laptop. "She told me what happened. I realize Helena was more susceptible with her background, but he could still get hold of any one of us."

"Well, I have an idea to negate all that, but it will take a day or two to arrange. If what I'm thinking falls through, we'll go try the abandoned house on Davis. *Mo ghealladh sòlaimte.* My solemn promise. I need to speak with someone first."

Even though I'd only known Sorcha a few weeks, I trusted her. Partly a gut instinct, partly because Auntie P. trusted her. But how could she make Monty's house safe in such a short time?

I thought about the extra protection we needed. *Should I get another spelled tattoo?* "I wish my dreamcatcher tatt was complete. I've only had one appointment so far. Maybe one of the other ones would have been a better choice before starting the dreamcatcher. Maybe a small Helme of Awe? Too late now. How about you, cuz? Ready for some more skin art? And before you return home, I want a look at whatever tatts you have hidden on your body."

"Well, Mercury is the god of commerce, among other things. That would be good for my store, but I wouldn't want anything too large."

"How about just his winged feet?" Sorcha made fluttering motions with her hands. "The intention is as equally important as the design, more actually. But you know that."

"On my ankle. Perfect. Too bad there isn't time to arrange the type of ceremony we do at home. We can do one when you come over, for all the new tatts."

We chatted with Sorcha a few more minutes, then signed off after getting the tattoo artist, Ashley's, contact details. She had the entire afternoon available, so I made arrangements for Drew and a series of appointments for me to finish the dreamcatcher.

We puttered around the house, then went into town to bother Cooper until our appointments.

Ashley worked out of her home. One of the rooms on the main floor had been renovated and resembled any tatt store I'd seen on TV, except smaller.

Drew did hers first, since it was a much simpler design. She jumped when the first needle prick touched her skin.

I snickered. "Oh, did I forget to mention the ankle is one of the most sensitive parts of the body? Suck it up, Sunshine. Concentrate on the intention. That'll take your mind off it. At least yours is a one-shot. I have to come back three more times to finish mine."

Once Ashley finished Drew and did the second round on me, Drew wanted to visit the Garden Witch. She'd packed only a few gemstones and wanted more, especially since it seemed a possibility we'd be going into Monty's old hideout. *Please let her plan fall through and we use the house on Davis Drive.*

We both purchased a large, clear quartz, and a wire pendant cage so we could wear them around our necks. A rack of gemstone bracelets, like the black tourmaline bracelet I'd gotten for both of us in the summer, caught my eye. With several to pick from, we grabbed the last of the black obsidian and black jade. The obsidian to attract positive energy, and the jade to avoid negative people. The last wouldn't work for the ritual because we had to deal with a mega negative entity, but it would be good to have.

As we paid, I thought I saw Sorcha in the back. *She shops here, too. Maybe she's chatting or putting in a special order. Not my business.* Transaction complete, we headed back to Antique Books.

When we approached the abandoned house Monty used, I pointed it out.

Drew shivered. "That place is chalk-full of bad intentions. It hit me before you showed me. I hope whatever Sorcha has in mind works. It will have to be strong protection to overpower it."

"I kinda hope she fails and we use my suggestion."

Drew mumbled an agreement as we hurried past the house.

Since we skipped lunch, I texted Cooper to see if he wanted food. He figured he'd forgotten to eat again. I picked up Greek along the way. Coop was finishing up with a customer, so we headed to the back to wait.

When he joined us, we filled him in on Monday's plan. He was not pleased. Major understatement.

Cooper shook his head so much I thought it might fall off. "No way. You're not going back into that house."

"Not your call. We have a back-up location, but it's not an ideal spot. Too exposed. That abandoned house on Davis. It's a busy road, and it might have security. Hiding our activity will take a lot of energy. Energy we need to fight Lorcan. Even though I hate to admit it, Monty's hideout is the logical place. Lorcan knows it and will come easily. Monty probably had called him there more than once.

He wants the book, and it's the perfect place to lure him. If whatever Sorcha has planned won't work, we'll call it off for another day."

"I have an open plane ticket, and I'll stay until we finish this. Marcy needs my help." Drew pushed her food away. "You know I won't let anything happen to her."

Cooper glared at both of us.

Let him be mad. Wasn't going to change my mind. Fingers crossed, Drew would survive to get married in a few months.

As he'd chosen not to speak to us, we left right after eating, leaving the mess for Coop to clean up.

TWENTY-EIGHT

*B*efore we called it a night, we needed to prepare the vessel ring to ensnare Lorcan. Fingers and toes crossed the spell modification worked.

I removed a glass bowl from the kitchen cupboard and took it down to the workroom. So far, I think I'd managed to hide my fear from Drew and Coop. Fear. That didn't even begin to describe it. Were we seriously planning on defeating such an ancient and evil being? Lorcan already injured me beyond belief, and he wasn't flesh and blood… yet. Family fighting family. An awful thing. But if we didn't try, the consequences would be dire. I took a deep breath and joined Drew at the worktable.

She poured the sea salt into the bottle of spring water. I dropped the rose thorns into the bowl, one at a time, reciting the modified spell. *With this thorn, I bid farewell. Lorcan Adhamh, inside this ring you will forever dwell.*

After the thirteenth thorn landed in the bowl, I ground them, probably with much more force than necessary. Next, I added the dried rose petals, crushing each one in my hand before dropping them in. Drew tilted the bottle and carefully poured the salt water in.

Lastly, I took the ring from my pocket and plunked it into the mixture to absorb the intention overnight. Even though it wasn't required, I sat it on the sill of a window on the top floor where it could soak up the moonlight.

"Granny, Mother, are you here? We need your help. If this doesn't work, friends will be injured, or worse. Our family will all end up dead if we fail."

No scent of Granny's rosewater perfume. No gentle touch on my cheek from Mother. *Were we on our own this time?*

When I came back down, Drew sat in the living room chatting with my gnomes, still minus their son. Since inheriting the house, I think I'd seen Nimagg, or parts of him, only two, maybe three times. The first sighting of his foot inside the fae entrance in Granny's room still haunted me. Nenka and Tinkus sat side-by-side on the doggy couch, holding hands.

"Glad to see you're enjoying the new furniture." I plopped beside Drew on the grown-up couch. "If there's anything in particular you'd like, let me know. I know I promised to add more lights and mini-furniture around the door in the willow a few months ago, but I was a little busy not dying. Next spring should be good, knock on wood." I rapped my head.

It was nice to have a family to enjoy. Not wanting to intrude too long on my gnomes leisure time, I excused myself and headed upstairs.

Drew followed close behind. "Do they know about Monday?"

"No. I don't want them to worry, especially Nenka. She gets upset easily. Wonder what would've happened to them if Granny had no one to leave the house to?"

"They're resourceful. Besides, regular people can't see them. No reason they couldn't stay put, provided the house didn't get torn down or renovated. You said she has family close by. They could've also gone there temporarily. What made you think about that?" Drew touched my arm. "Is there something you're not telling me?"

I dropped onto the stair, hugging the closest baluster. The flood gates opened, releasing all the tension and fear. I blurted it all out. "What if something goes wrong? Even though we've never mentioned it, the ritual could go bottoms up. Lorcan will stop at nothing to get his two items back. And he's more powerful than anything either of us has ever had to deal with. Next time he attacks, I may bleed out, permanently."

"Banish the thought! Nothing is going to happen." Drew sat beside me and hugged me. "We dealt with Montgomery and we can deal with Lorcan." She pulled out some of my despair, without overloading herself, then loosened her grip.

I relaxed a little. "But Granny and Mother appeared and helped us with Uncle. Lorcan is stronger. It took an entire coven to banish him last time. This time there's only three of us, and I'm the weak link." I sniffled and ran my arm under my nose.

The look in Drew's eyes told me she agreed, but wouldn't admit it. It strengthened my resolve. "All negative thoughts have to be buried by Monday. Even though I'm still a newbie, I do know that much. If Lorcan senses any weakness, he'll use it. Don't worry,

Drew. I'll concentrate on the task at hand. There won't be any time for doubt."

"Good." Drew hugged me tighter, drawing more of my negativity out.

"Too bad you can't also heal like Cooper. I really could use the extra dose."

❋❋❋

By Monday morning, Cooper still hadn't responded to my texts. I figured he was still royally pissed. What a way to start our engagement. I need his support more than ever. Since the ritual wouldn't begin until six-thirty, Drew and I stayed at home.

All day I stomped around the house. Actually broke a plate while washing up after breakfast. Every time Drew tried to relax me, I waved her off. Meditation didn't help, since I couldn't concentrate. How could Coop ghost me at such a critical time? By mid-afternoon, I'd settled enough to hang out with Drew.

I showed her my plans for the greenhouse and almost let news of my engagement slip. The fewer distractions before tonight, the better.

All day I kept checking my phone. Still no word. At five-thirty, I tried one last time.

Could use a healing boost. ❤

Stop in on your way.

I turned my phone so Drew could see. "Got a reply, but no response to the little heart emoji. He's still mad."

"At least he replied. May as well head over now. Anything from Sorcha?"

"Yeah. A short text to say everything was set and to meet her at Monty's old haunt at six. Guess her plan didn't fall through. She better know what she's doing." *Why couldn't she have failed?*

Because I was still learning all the best times and moon phases for spells, Sorcha had explained that clock hands facing down would be the best time for banishing. The farthest the hands could point down was six-thirty. That's when the ritual would begin.

While Drew gathered up all the necessary crystals and talismans to help protect us from negative energies, I headed to the third floor for the ring, careful not to spill the water on the way to the kitchen. I left the full bowl sitting by the sink and dried off the ring before wrapping it in one of Granny's hankies, sprayed with rosewater. They were one of the few items I'd kept when clearing out her non-witchy things. "Please help, Granny." I kissed the hanky and put it in my jeans pocket.

We both went to the workroom to ground ourselves while standing on the earthen floor. Too cold to do that outside. Barefoot was best, even though not necessary, and doing that at Monty's house wouldn't work. Too much negative energy.

Grounding helped stabilize our energy and draw up energy from the earth. We'd have to do it again after the ritual, assuming we survived. Once complete, we put our shoes on and piled into my little Smart Car.

When we arrived at Antique Books, Cooper stood at the counter typing on his laptop. He looked up when the over-the-door bell tinkled. He gave me a short nod.

"Look, Coop. If you have a better idea, now's a good time to tell us. I know it's not ideal, but there isn't enough time to find a private location. It's not neutral, but it's familiar to Lorcan."

He closed the lid and came around the counter. "I've been a jackass. You have no other option. I get that. Don't have to like it, though. I could have handled it better. You guys are doing something dangerous and I'm worried for your safety. Angry that there's nothing I can do to help."

He wrapped his arms around me. Immediately, his healing seeped into my body. Mixed in with the healing weaving around my gashes was a softer warmth. The familiar tingle I got any time he touched me.

"Stop that. I can't afford any distractions."

He whispered in my ear. "Make me." His breath ramped up the tingle and sent a shot of electricity through me.

I absorbed some of his energy, both healing and non. Love was powerful, and we needed so much more power. Reluctantly, I finally pushed him away. "Later."

Drew stood, arms crossed over her chest. "Well, that was embarrassing to watch. It's almost time. Let's go."

The walk to the abandoned house Montgomery used didn't take long. We could both feel the familiar glamour Sorcha placed around it to mask our activities the closer we got.

"She must be here already." Drew stood at the entrance to the walkway. "Where to? Backyard?"

"Yep. The door is boarded up, but Monty re-attached the boards so it still looks inaccessible. It swings open like a door. Sorcha spelled it to lock so no one can sneak in."

When we entered the backyard, I stopped short. Drew collided with me.

"Who are all these people?" I spotted Sorcha and walked over.

She waved her arms towards the crowd. "This is what I had hoped to arrange. I know I should have asked you, but I figured it's better to ask forgiveness than permission. Since we don't have a coven, I've recruited help via the ladies at the Garden Witch."

Just like the Grinch, my heart grew. All these strangers coming to help me and my family. I smiled and nodded, trying not to cry. A quick head count told me she'd found a baker's dozen of extra witches. "I thought I saw you in the back of the store yesterday. Guess this is the reason. Wish I'd thought of it myself. Thank you all so much for helping. Lorcan is powerful, and we need all the assistance and power we can get." I took a deep breath. *This may actually work.* I squeezed Sorcha's hand. "Thank you."

Everyone introduced themselves before we filed inside. I recognized Carole and Alice. Since we didn't have Helena and her illumination skill, we brought flashlights. The glamour outside would prevent anyone from seeing the beams. The sixteen of us barely fit in the altar room where we'd found the grimoire. Everyone stayed away from the pentagram on the floor. I estimated the room to be about twelve by twelve feet square, with a six-foot pentagram painted in the centre. With some furniture and an altar that looked like it'd been taken from a church, the room barely had room for people.

With the help of my family overseas, we'd been able to cobble enough bits and pieces together from the entries in the old journals written by past coven members to come up with something. Together with the ritual used to banish Monty, we had a plan of attack. Sort of.

"Um, Sorcha? When we went over how to do this, it involved only the three of us."

"That's why I asked you to come at six. I knew only a few were positive yeses. Since I didn't know if enough would make it, I kept *sàmhach*, quiet. Didn't want to get your hopes for help raised. Our plans won't alter much. Think of them like car jumper cables. They'll boost the energy level. Strength in numbers."

I pointed at myself. "This wreck of a car needs all the boosting possible. So, how do you think this will work?"

Drew chimed in. "How about if the ladies form a circle around us without stepping inside the pentagram? There's been too much dark magick used to make it safe. If we were outside, maybe your mom and Granny would show up again."

"Why don't you call them to join us?" Alice waggled her phone.

"They're both deceased. Not sure how much Sorcha told you, but we've done a banishment before. Mother and Granny showed up as… what? Spirits? Angels? Something. We basically had two sets of Maiden, Mother, and Crone, as Drew's mother and gran were with us."

"Oh! One set of the trinity is powerful. A double set would more than double the power."

What was her name? Patsy? Penny? My brain was too distracted to remember names, never mind putting them to the correct face. We were still going to use the chant that banished Monty, with a slight tweak. We needed to specify Lorcan in order for him to return to the ring.

The ladies formed a circle around the room, leaving a gap by the door for Lorcan

"How do we know he'll appear in human form?" Drew had a valid question. "He's been gone for such a long time, and we don't know when he escaped from the ring."

"Well, Mother's been gone eight years, and Monty said he was responsible for her death. He needed to be powerful enough to mask himself from her or she would have protected herself. Lorcan must have been released long enough ago to locate and train Uncle. We also don't know how long Monty studied the dark arts before Lorcan found him. Might not have needed a lot of extra training. Conservatively, at least fifteen years, I'm thinking. Unless he started learning the dark arts young. Lorcan should be able to materialize if he expects to actually take the book." I turned to Sorcha. "Doesn't he? Could he be able to poof the book away?"

Sorcha smiled. "In a book or movie, yes. But in the real world? No. Either he must take the book or ..."

Never good when someone suddenly stopped in the middle of a sentence and got that *Oh, schist* look. "Or?"

Another of the witches finished the sentence. "He could send someone. How long since you banished your uncle?"

"July. Only a few months ago."

"Then whoever this entity is that trained him likely hasn't found a replacement. Even if he has, he needs time to train them properly, to a point where they're trustworthy and controllable. That takes more than a few months."

Sorcha agreed. "Lorcan wants control of the coven, even though it's disbanded. He'll go after their descendants and try to take control that way. He'd do best with a family member, but there aren't any who've gone to the dark side." She looked at me for confirmation. "Just you and Drew's family remain?"

Drew nodded her confirmation. "No family members have turned, except Lorcan and Monty."

"He may have gone after another of the old coven members who left to practice the dark magick, but fortunately all of those descendants had the good sense to turn their back on that." *Except Helena's family.*

"Are you positive, Drew?" Sorcha looked skeptical.

"Yes. Well, no. But they're in England. Hang on."

Drew pulled out her phone and sent a text. "Asking Mum if any of the old coven members have left the country recently. It's a pretty tight network, and word would have gotten out quicker than social media. Every one of our trips was common knowledge before we had our bags packed."

Her phone dinged.

"Everyone's where they should be. Only us two in Canada."

Three, actually, if we counted Helena. No need to tell them. She's doing everything possible to stay on the light side of witchcraft.

Sorcha checked the time. "Five more minutes. Sprinkle the brimstone."

Just like at the Big O, I laid one ring of brimstone around the outside of the circle of witches, and a second overtop the ring of the pentacle, leaving a gap for Lorcan. I left a small pile of the mineral at the open end, so the witch closest could close it up after he passed through.

"What's stopping him from entering before we're ready?" I glanced at Sorcha, who hadn't produced the book yet. The ring still sat snuggled in my pocket.

"I've placed a spell at the front door that only allows us through. He'll be able to break it, but it'll delay him briefly. I've added a hum to the spell, so we'll have enough of a warning. There's also a spell on this door, minus the hum."

She reached into her bag and took out the grimoire, placing it on the altar. I couldn't help but chuckle when a snippet of the movie *Mary Poppins* ran through my brain. Her satchel seemed to be bottomless, just like Sorcha's. What couldn't she fit inside?

The baker's dozen of witches began mumbling. They probably felt the power from the book like I could. The barely visible hand print on the cover glowed.

I placed the ring beside it.

A steady hum hit our ears. We all turned. It didn't last long. All eyes watched the door as heavy footfalls sounded on the stairs.

TWENTY-NINE

A figure appeared at the door, much younger and more handsome than I expected. His blackish-green skin had turned almost white. *Could time in this realm be turning him human again?*

"You must be Lorcan. Your resemblance to your mother is astonishing."

Even though Fiona wasn't able to maintain form long, I'd never forget her. Outstandingly beautiful. Bright green eyes, porcelain skin, and long, almost white hair. Lorcan had the same appearance, minus the long hair. *This must be what he looked like before being banished.*

He took a step and stopped, reaching out with one hand. He felt the second barrier and smirked. "You think this will stop me? There isn't strong enough magick anywhere to keep me from this room." Lorcan stared at me. "We are related. And there's another."

Drew put her arm around my shoulder. "Yes, there's two of your relatives here, and we *will* defeat you with the help of our friends."

His laughter shook the room. Literally. The floor rumbled beneath my feet. Lorcan placed both palms on the invisible shield and pushed. The room filled with the odour of burning… magick? Rotting flesh? I swallowed a bit of bile that tried to escape.

The spell at the door sizzled, then released with an audible pop. He stepped into the room and approached the circle.

"Ladies." He smiled, making him even more handsome, then took the hand of the witch beside the gap in the brimstone, Alice, and kissed it. She pulled away, shaking her hand. Her burned flesh permeated the air. Even from across the room, I could see blisters forming and her skin reddening.

Lorcan glanced down. "Brimstone. How quaint."

As he walked closer, the now-marked witch bent to fill the gap, taking a bit of brimstone and rubbing it over the fresh wound. *That has to hurt.* I could almost feel her pain. The sensation was strong enough to make me look at my own hand.

He kicked aside the brimstone covering the outer circle of the pentagram and walked towards the altar. His smug look disappeared. His eyes narrowed. He approached the altar, frowning. "You've done something to my book."

Sorcha stepped away from the altar. "Yes. I modified one of your own spells. Only I can open it now."

He reached for it, but whatever she'd done to it appeared to be much more powerful than the door block. A force around the book repelled his hand.

She stepped forward and moved the book slightly. "Guess it likes me now."

The handprint glowed brighter, turning a sickly puke-green.

Before I even saw him move, he grabbed my arm and pulled me to the altar. Lorcan tried to place my hand in the print, but it wouldn't allow my touch either. Only Sorcha's.

He finally noticed the vessel ring sitting nearby.

He released his grip on me. "Ah. Home sweet home. I will not go back there. Release my book. Now!" The force of his voice vibrated throughout the room. The floor shook beneath my feet. I grabbed the altar for support.

"Sorry, dude. Ain't happening." I began reciting the modified chant we'd used for Uncle Monty. Drew joined me, then Sorcha and the makeshift coven. It seemed to have only the tiniest effect on him.

"Stop! I command you." The shaking of the floor grew worse, making it difficult to stand in place.

Raising one hand to my nose, I gave him the bird, continuing with the chant.

"We now push away all spirts, evil, and astral nasties.

With the strong influence of Saturn, this will never occur.

By the element of fire, we banish you."

Lorcan raised a hand, pointing at me. Pain ripped through my sides and stomach. It's a good thing I'd put on a black tee since my wounds reopened. I felt it cover my chest as the blood trickled out. I dropped to my knees.

"Marcy!" Drew tried to help me up.

"Don't stop. I'm fine." Through gritted teeth, I resumed chanting.

Drew screamed. Three long, deep gouges sank into both her arms. Blood dripped to the floor. One by one, each witch cried out, maimed, but they persevered.

The floorboards absorbed our seeping blood. Lorcan stood in a grounding position. *What is he doing?* Slowly, he raised his arms.

We all gasped.

A red glow appeared around his feet. He raised his arms higher, and the glow crept up his legs. Lorcan took a deep breath and continued. The glow climbed. His body grew taller, more muscular. When his palms touched over his head, he quickly swept them down again, forming a red halo around his entire body.

"What in holy heliodor is happening?"

"He's taking energy from all the blood." Sorcha's brow furrowed. "He's much stronger than I imagined. He must have found where his physical body was sent and is trying to reunite with it. Could there be eternal life in other realms? We need to finish this before he completes the joining."

I looked around the room. Every witch had been injured. "How are we going to manage? He's sapped most of the energy from everyone but us three. I don't think good always wins over evil."

"You can't give up." Drew placed a bloody arm around my shoulders. "Our family and new friends are in danger. Stay positive."

"I'll try."

Lorcan lashed out. Items flew around the room. A small statue hit someone, knocking her out. A pen impaled Carol's hand, but she never stopped for a moment. Not everyone ducked in time, but no still-conscience witch gave up. With a community this strong, I wondered once again why Mother and Granny kept to themselves all those years. *We are so much stronger together.*

Over the crashing and smashing, thunder roared above. I glanced at Drew. "Did you hear that?"

She nodded. "You think they're helping again?"

I called out, hopeful. "Mother? Granny? Are you here?" Rain smacked against the window, washing away all prospects of celestial help. "Just a storm. Schist."

Lorcan shoved the altar, sending the book and ring flying.

"The ring! Where'd it land?" I crawled in the direction it flew, wincing from my now-open wounds. The mineral particles ground into my gouges as I crept over the brimstone, causing them to burn. Sucking in air, I continued.

The ring vibrated, directing me. A bolt of lightning flashed at the window. Light glinted off something. *The old desk.* Reaching under it, my fingers probed, finally brushing the ring. I scooped it up, using the desk to help me stand.

I gasped at the trail of blood I'd left behind. Now that I had the ring, a little of the anxiety left, clarifying my situation. So much blood loss. My head spun. The ring vibrated faster, heat intensifying so much I almost dropped it.

A multitude of moans caught my attention. I surveyed the room again. Some of the witches lay crumpled on the hard wooden floor, motionless. *Are they all still alive?* Others heaved on all fours, expelling a thick, dark vomit. The rest persevered. The remaining six stood, hands joined with Drew and Sorcha, circling Lorcan. They recited the chant, louder and louder.

I made it halfway to the overturned altar before excruciating pain circled my throat. I fell to the floor. A wave of penetrating heat rolled over my body. Each breath became more difficult. My head spun. The voices of the make-shift coven faded. My vision blurred. Right before I lost consciousness, something shadowy whizzed past me. I dropped the ring and everything went black.

Distant voices weaved through my brain. My head throbbed. *Focus, ignore the pain.* The voices got louder, clearer. One eye opened, then the other. *In my bed at the bookstore.* Cooper sat on the edge of the bed. I moved my arm, reaching for him.

"Hey, she's awake."

I tried to sit up, but failed. My head spun, my stomach roiled. I flopped back down. "What… happened?" The pain in my throat was unimaginable.

Drew and Sorcha came over. Even from my prone position, injuries were noticeable. Pink-tinged gauze covered their arms. Stitches ran across their cheeks and foreheads like train-tracks. Based on what I recalled of my lacerations, the rest of their wounds were under their clothing.

Sorcha smiled. "It's over. When you passed out, we forced Lorcan back into the ring."

"Is that why it felt so hot? Was he the shadow I saw before I blacked out?" My words were little more than croaks. *What did he do to my throat this time?*

"Before the ring sucked Lorcan back in, he made one final effort to kill you." Drew looked more worried than usual. "Not only did he re-open your neck wound, he added to it. Almost severed your head right off."

I raised an eyebrow. "Severed? And you didn't bother taking me to the hospital?"

"OK. Maybe I exaggerated, but the gash is deep and goes about three-quarters of the way around. He actually nicked your carotid artery. Bled plenty, even though it was the smallest of nicks. We managed to stay the flow long enough for Cooper to begin healing. Thought you were a goner. How can you even speak? You really need to rest your voice."

"Like that's ever going to happen. You know how stubborn I get." The words coming from my mouth were little more than squeaks. "I'm going to look like a mummy at your wedding. What about you two, and the ladies? I remember seeing several on the floor in a heap."

"Everyone is fine, more or less." Sorcha had stitches on her lower arm, continuing up under her sleeve. A horrible-looking shiner circled her left eye. "We all returned here, with help from Cooper. He called both Barnstable and the wiccan physician he recommended. He knows another intern who's also a witch and the three of them took care of everyone."

"Guessing they pumped me full of drugs. I think it's wearing off. Tell the docs to send their bills for everyone to me. It's literally the least I can do. Where's the ring?"

Sorcha went to the table and picked up a jar. "In here, with some of the brimstone."

Cooper had been silent since I came to. He looked drained, barely able to open his eyes. It must have taken a lot to deal with my almost severed neck, if it really was that bad. Drew was prone to exaggeration. He radiated mixed emotions. Too many to tell how angry he was.

He nodded at the jar. "Where do you plan on keeping that thing until you go to England?"

Good question. "Maybe bury it with the crystal ruby?"

"How about I take it and the grimoire back with me? Mum or Gran will know what to do." Drew glanced at the jar. "I can put the ring in a baggie with the brimstone and ditch the baggie before boarding. I'll wear the ring. Don't want to let it out of my sight."

"Might want to have it in the baggie in your carry-on." Sorcha yawned.

"You've done so much. I can't thank you enough. Please, get some rest." She wavered and reached for the back of a chair. "Go home, Sorcha. You need to recharge.

Sorcha nodded. "Despite the wounds, it was quite the experience. I'll leave the spell on the book for now. I can remove it before Drew goes home."

Cooper walked her out so he could relock the door. He had his car keys in his hand when he returned.

"I'll drive Drew back to the house." He glared at me. "You're staying here until the doc says you can move around. For now, it's bed and bathroom only."

He was in no shape to drive and I didn't want to think about him getting in an accident. "You need to recoup, too. Do you have the strength to drive there and back? You look ready to pass out. I'm sure I can do it." *Have the drugs worn off enough for me to drive?* Breathing began to hurt. Talking was almost impossible. Driving home would cause me more pain than I wanted to think about.

Cooper waved off my concerns. "Running on adrenaline right now, and you're still doped up. I'll collapse when I get back." Cooper walked to the door, jingling the car keys.

Drew said good night, and I closed my eyes.

When I opened them, Drew was at the table across the room, chatting on my laptop. *Schist! She's talking to Auntie.* Sun shone through the window. *Morning? Afternoon?*

"Drew? I thought Cooper drove you to the house."

"He did. I took an Uber back after lunch." She picked up the computer and brought it over.

"After lunch? I only closed my eyes a minute ago."

"More like twelve hours ago." She turned the computer so I could see Priscilla and Susan. They both gasped when they saw me.

"Hi Auntie, Susan," Once again, my voice croaked. "Did Drew tell you we trapped Lorcan?" I winced when I tried to turn my head. "Feel like Frankenstein's monster."

Auntie P. was unusually quiet. Fortunately, she didn't appear angry. *Too bad I couldn't read minds. Well, maybe not. Feelings were more than enough.*

My eyelids grew heavy, droopy. "Think I'll have another nap."

"Barnstable said he'd stop in after his shift. He called in a prescription for the pain. I picked it up for you. It's on the little table." Drew walked over to it, calling over her shoulder as she headed back to the Skype call. "You need a lot of rest in order to heal."

✳ ✳ ✳

The next time I woke, someone poked and prodded me. *Better be the doc.* One eye opened, then the other. The young intern sat on the side of my bed.

"Hello, Marcy. Do you think you can sit? I need to check your neck wound and change the wrapping."

"Gonna need help."

I sucked air as Dr. Barnstable slowly helped me up. "How's it look? Do I resemble Mary Shelley's monster? Anyone got a mirror?"

"I've taken pictures for my records. Not certain you want to see them."

Recalling Drew's comment about my head practically being severed, I shuttered. *Did I want to see? Yes.* "Show me."

He took a few more pictures then opened the gallery on his cell. The first batch were totally gross. He'd snapped them before cleaning up the wound. Then I saw the ones he just took. "I was right. Frankenstein's monster. Only thing missing are the neck bolts. Hey Drew, will my dress for the wedding have a high collar?"

"She'll be able to fly by December, won't she?" Drew looked worried.

The doctor laid me back and turned to my cousin. "She'll be well on her way to recovery by then, provided she doesn't get into any more battles."

Once he'd examined all my wounds, he headed to the door.

"Hey, doc. How are the other ladies?" If they were seriously injured, I'd never forgive myself.

"You were the only one seriously injured. Everyone else's wounds are minor. Superficial in comparison. I believe most have gone to their regular physicians by now. Keep using that ointment you made up. I'll check on you in a few days."

Cooper's mood had changed somewhat. Still pissed, but his concern over-rode it. He'd returned to the back room after letting Barnstable out.

"You don't need to hang around me, Coop. You're losing business. Open up after I get one of your healing bear hugs."

"Afraid not. You've got too many stitches. Wait a few days so the ointment can begin working its magick. I hope we've got enough. The plants are pretty much done for the season. Drew brought back the stuff I took to the house, but it doesn't look like it's near enough."

"Good thing you're planning on building a greenhouse." Drew always tried to find the positive.

"So, I have to heal the old-fashioned way when the ointment is gone. No biggie." I grinned at Cooper. "At least I'll still have the hugs from my fiancé."

It took a second for that last word to register with Drew. "Hugs are always welcome from your… what did you say? Fiancé?"

Cooper nodded, that huge, soppy grin spread across his face, his anger and concern forgotten.

"When did that happen, and why am I only finding out now?" Drew stood, hands on hips, foot tapping, pretending to be miffed. She couldn't stop smiling.

"Just a couple of days ago. Didn't want to say anything until we'd ensnared Lorcan. The plan was to call your mum and Gran to tell them we'd done it, then let you all know together about the engagement. Ring's on my dresser in its box. Can you grab it and bring it tomorrow? It's gorgeous. You can peek."

Cooper dashed up to his apartment and returned with the wedding bands. "You can see these now." He opened the box and proudly handed it to Drew.

Her face lit up. "It's exquisite. Mine and Randy's are simple white-gold bands. I love the tree of life circling around."

"And the emeralds will enhance my engagement ring. Coop has wonderful taste."

"Of course he does. He picked you."

"Naturally." Cooper took the box back from Drew. "Gonna open up for a few hours." He ran upstairs to put the rings back, then clomped down and out to the store front.

I reached out to Drew. "Help me sit, then call the family. If I wait any longer, they'll have my guts for garters, as Granny would say."

"Not yet. Hand over your car keys. I'll get the ring and you can wave your hand around on the call. See how long before one of them notices."

I tossed her the keys, calling out to her as she rushed down the hall. "Remember, drive on the right. Don't want my little car turned into an accordion."

Now that Drew knew, it made my engagement official. I stared at my empty ring finger and smiled. *That gorgeous ring will be a permanent fixture soon.*

Drew returned in record time and handed me the box. "Couldn't he find a bigger stone? I'm jealous, but I still love my ring." She wiggled her fingers.

Her engagement ring had a one carat flawless rose quartz, surrounded by two-millimetre-round white quartz stones for protection. They sparkled like diamonds.

It took about two minutes to get me upright and comfortable on the edge of my bed. Drew brought over the small drop-leaf table that usually sat between the wing-back chairs and placed my laptop on it. Gently, she sat beside me and texted her mother and Gran.

Update on Marcy. Skype now?

Two thumbs up came back.

We called them both, but only Susan answered. Auntie P. was already at her daughter's house. I sat cross-legged, resting my left elbow on my knee, hand on chin, displaying the ring.

Drew's mum stopped writing in her journal. "We were discussing what to do with the grimoire and ring." Susan frowned. "I hope you feel better than you look."

I wiggled my fingers. "So-so. The doc said I'd be fine by the wedding. Might have a scar or two."

Priscilla leaned closer. "Looks like we got two weddings coming up. That's quite the rock."

"Oh, my gosh. How did I not notice that?" Susan's eyes grew wide. "It's beautiful. When did this happen?"

"Couple of days ago. Like I told Drew, didn't want everyone distracted before we dealt with Lorcan. The news kinda slipped out a little while ago, so I figured I'd better tell you now. We're thinking either Beltane or Litha. Cooper's not fussy when, he just wants it to happen, sooner rather than later."

Drew shoulder bumped me. "Since Cooper's coming to my wedding with you, we could make it a double."

"Thanks for the offer, but it's *your* day. Besides, that's too soon for me. And it's a discussion Cooper would have to be in on. Randy too. No. I'll wait until next year. Gives me time to get used to the idea."

"Well, congratulations. So, back to the business at hand." Susan nodded at her mother to take over.

"If Drew can bring both items over, we'll find a safe place to hide them until we figure out the riddle in the curse. We'll need to spell-protect them so they don't affect the plane."

"What do you mean, Auntie? How would they affect anything without being prompted?"

Auntie P. sighed. "When Drew resumes your training, maybe she should focus on handling spelled artifacts. Anything and everything is possible. Double so when dealing with what is commonly called black magick. Sorcha can help with that. Does she still have the book?"

I turned to Drew. "She kept it, didn't she?"

"Yes. When Lorcan went back into the ring, she scooped up it and the book, then stuffed them in that bag she always has. I called Cooper. The ladies that were still conscious called their spouses or whatever, then came here. That's when we put the ring in the jar."

"Why don't you call her to go over transporting the items?" Susan checked the time. "We have a meeting with Randy's parents to discuss wedding things. Can I tell them when you'll be back?"

Drew nodded. "I'll catch a flight day after tomorrow."

"Good. Send the details and I'll pick you up."

Drew ended the call and pushed the little table away from my bed.

"Down, please. Now." I winced. Every wound and stitch pulsed with pain and my throat ached.

My cuz turned me, then lowered me onto the bed. "Are you all right?"

"Not really. If that call lasted any longer, I'd have lost it. I can't even begin to describe the pain. Why don't you call Sorcha while I lay here and die?" I pointed at the prescription bottle.

"Drama Queen." Drew giggled. She handed me the bottle and a glass of water, then searched my phone for Sorcha's number. "Got it."

I downed two pills, set the bottle and glass on the floor, and was out before she finished dialing.

THIRTY

When I woke hours later, no sunlight shone through the window. "Anyone here?"

Silence.

Taking a deep breath, I bellowed as loud as I dared. "Hello!" My throat screamed at me. *Too soon to raise my voice.*

An elephant thundered down the stairs.

"Marcy. What's wrong?"

No elephant. Just Cooper. "Nothing's wrong. I wondered where everyone went."

"Drew's making dinner. You must be hungry. She's fixing a special soup for you."

"Nice." I raised my arms. "Bathroom."

With Cooper's help, I hobbled down the hall. I never knew going to the bathroom could be such an ordeal.

Coop waited in the hall, but I discovered I couldn't get up because of the pain when my muscles contracted. I hollered just loud enough to be heard through the door. "Need help. Get Drew."

I swear he laughed when he went to fetch her. A minute later, Drew knocked and came in.

"Can't get off the throne. And don't say a word."

She helped me stand, laughing the entire time, then waited in the hall with Cooper while I washed up. By the time I came out, I was laughing too.

"I'll install some assist bars tomorrow. I think some of the older customers could use them." Cooper helped me back to my temp apartment, then went with Drew to bring our meal down. She filled us in on her conversation with Sorcha while we ate.

After the dishes were cleared, Drew made me an herbal tea infused with her magick for my throat. I drank, listening while she talked. The tea tingled all the way down.

"We'll wrap the book in burlap to protect it and set it on top of a layer of crushed brimstone inside the box. We can stick to my idea of putting the ring in a baggie with more brimstone, then place it on top of the book. A simple spell will mask the actual contents. I hope you don't mind, but I'd like to scavenge the brimstone from your place. Sorcha is coming over with the book tomorrow."

"Certainly. Take whatever you need. There's plenty already crushed in the display case and more uncrushed in the workroom. I bought way more than necessary, just in case."

Cooper listened as she relayed her chat with Sorcha. "I'll be glad when those things are gone and Marcy can continue to heal." He disappeared upstairs when the conversation turned to Drew's wedding.

After one last trip down the hall, Drew used my car to go to the house, returning early the next morning. She seemed comfortable driving on the right side of the road, unlike the first time in the summer. I could still imagine her mumbling *right side* over and over.

"I come bearing food." Drew held up a bag from *Subway*. "Breakfast wraps. Hope you like them."

"Love 'em. What time is Sorcha due to arrive?"

"Eleven. I've got the brimstone and ring in my purse. She said she'll provide the box."

Sorcha arrived promptly at eleven. I'd already set up candles and incense. Drew brought a sage bundle from the house. All we needed now was coffee, and that was brewing. Drew headed upstairs to wait for the brain juice, allowing me and Sorcha to chat.

"You seem much better. It's amazing how quickly you've healed in only a few days." Sorcha smiled. "Guess a lot of that is courtesy of your *fian*."

"I'm guessing that's Gaelic for fiancé? How did you… Drew. I promise I was going to tell you, but had to tell the family first." I held my left arm towards her.

She took my hand. "Of course. Your ring is beautiful."

"Thanks. No plans yet. Have to deal with all this stuff first." I waved a hand at our stitches. "I think I hear Drew coming. Ready?"

Ready.

I lit the incense and candles while Drew brought the coffee down. No way I'd be able to navigate the stairs carrying a tray. The doc didn't want me going up and down, anyway. Sorcha circled the room, fanning the smoke from the sage. The room smelled wonderful. We were ready to begin.

After we all grounded, Sorcha removed the grimoire from the box and covered the bottom with a thin layer of crushed brimstone. She placed the book on top. It fit snuggly inside so the brimstone shouldn't move around too much. Another layer went on top, then Drew placed the baggie containing the ring into the box, leaving the lid off.

"This will be easy. I don't need any help, except from the god Lugas, sometimes called Lugh." Sorcha explained briefly. "He was king of the gods in the Celtic pantheon. In addition to being a warrior, he was also a trickster, and a trick is what we need to mask the brimstone in the box."

Brimstone is sulfur, which is prohibited on planes, but we didn't have a large amount, and it was absolutely necessary in order to transport the items. The several-hundred-year-old witch trapped inside shouldn't show up on the security machine. All the x-ray would see would be a book and ring inside a box. They might wonder why the lid was so tightly wrapped in packing tape, though.

I lit more sage, inhaling the hint of pine it released. Drew lit another candle. She'd already scratched protection and purification symbols into the wax. Sorcha began the short incantation.

"Lugas cast your trickster net wide,

we have an item we need to hide.

Please help us make this crushed brimstone

to all mortal eyes unknown.

As I will, so mote it be."

One final trip around the room with the sage for good measure, and we were done.

"I'll be so glad to get that to Gran." Drew cast a wary eye at the box. "She's had several conversations with her friends about what to do. According to Elspeth, the curse can only be broken if you solve the riddle. Entrapping him won't be enough."

"Is Elspeth a high priestess?" Sorcha was a little out of that particular loop.

"No." I sighed. "She's the palm reader in England who told me I'm responsible for breaking the curse and restoring my family's dwindling powers. Another few generations and we'll be plain old earthlings."

She smiled. "A plain old earthling? Can't have that, can we, *a sheòid?*"

"Excuse me?"

"It's an old Scottish term of endearment that translates roughly to my hero or valiant warrior. I know I'm repeating myself, but you really should learn Gaelic. Many old books were written in it. They do come in handy, but only if you can translate them."

"It's already added to my never-ending to-do list."

"Has anyone spoken to Helena recently?" Drew topped up her coffee mug. "How's she doing?"

Sorcha held her empty mug out for a refill. "I spoke to her a couple of days ago. The effects of Lorcan's spell seem to have worn off. She wishes she could help, but knows it's too dangerous for her."

"Hey, I've got an idea. Since Drew is leaving tomorrow, why don't we all go out to dinner tonight? I'm well enough to sit and move around a little now. The ointment has helped me immensely, so I'll be fine to sit in a restaurant." *Not to mention Cooper's healing hugs.* "Don't want to drive, though, so Drew, you'll have to drive my car again. Eating won't pose a danger to Helena or us. I'll call Missy and see if she can drive in. I'll even ask her to stay over at the house so she doesn't have to make the long trip back in the dark. Company for Drew. With any luck, she'll be too tired to inundate her with witch-related questions."

"Fabulous idea. I'll text Helena now." Sorcha reached for her phone and I did the same.

"Seven OK? If Missy's free, it'll take almost an hour for her to get to town." I paused before hitting send.

Drew nodded. "Perfect. I won't mind a bit of company, but Missy will have to lock up the house, because my flight is early."

I shrugged. "Not a problem."

"Yes, seven's fine." Sorcha texted Helena. Her phone dinged almost immediately. She read the text and laughed before turning it so we could see. Helena had responded with a yes, followed by seven exclamation marks.

Twenty minutes later, Missy gave me a thumbs up.

We chatted for a while, then Drew went around the corner to Malt+Chip to grab us lunch. While waiting for her return, I told Cooper about our dinner plans and invited him to join us.

"Listen to five women gabbing for hours? Pass. Did you tell Drew to bring me back some lunch, too?"

"Of course. Can't have you salivating while we eat."

When Drew returned, I gave Cooper his takeout order. Drew and I ate in the back, then went to my house with Drew to help her pack. Took forever to get up the stairs to her room, even aided by Drew. The flight out was very early, and she didn't want to waste time in the morning. All she'd have to do was throw her nightie and toothbrush in the suitcase after she dressed, then wait for the taxi.

"I'd offer to drive you, but I'm too sore to tackle that distance. I couldn't even do the short distance here."

"I don't want you getting up that early. You need all the rest you can get. A taxi will be fine."

We spent the rest of the afternoon talking about my unexpected wedding announcement, and trying to figure out when to have it. I was leaning towards spring. Since Cooper had already said he didn't care when, it would be up to me to decide.

Drew drove us back into town to wait for Missy. She'd meet us at the bookstore. Sorcha and Helena were going directly to the restaurant. Missy had only met Helena a few times, but they seemed to get on fine. I think Missy was fascinated with the dark side of magick, but I'd cautioned her not to discuss it.

We avoided talking about the recent events, focusing mostly on Drew's wedding and my engagement. Missy brought up the failed love spell she'd tried, so Sorcha offered to help her write a better one, even though she said Missy shouldn't need one to attract a mate. We were simply a bunch of ladies, not witches, out to enjoy themselves.

Sorcha told Missy she could stay overnight with her instead of going out to my house, since Drew would be up way too early for Missy. The evening sped by, and at nine, Drew announced she was calling it a night as she wanted to get as much rest as possible. She drove my car to the parking lot by the community centre so I'd have it when I was better, then called for an Uber to pick her up outside the bookstore. A taxi would arrive at four in the morning to take to her the airport. She was anxious to be rid of the items and didn't want to take one of the many flights later in the day. That way, she'd be home early enough for Auntie P. to take the package off her hands.

Feeling wiped out, I called Coop to pick me up and left about a half hour after my cousin, leaving the two witches and Egyptologist swapping tales and guzzling down cocktails. *They'll feel that in the morning.*

When I woke, there was a text from Drew letting me know she made her flight. I checked the time. She should land late in the afternoon, my time.

Around 4:30, she texted she'd landed safely and was waiting for her mother. A quick calculation told me it would be around 10:30 p.m. her time when she got home, depending on the traffic, so I wouldn't hear from her till at least tomorrow.

THIRTY-ONE

Over the next month and a half, there'd been numerous video chats, mostly with Auntie P., updating me on the formation of the old coven. She'd been to the caves with Susan and spoke with the ancestor sprits about the curse. Unfortunately, nothing could be completed until I arrived in December. Auntie stashed the ring containing Lorcan, along with the book, in a location she wouldn't disclose, confirming that he would not be able to escape.

Now that Yule was less than two weeks away, the medicinal plants needed for my healing gel had long since begun their winter sleep. Cooper and traditional medicine were my only options to finish dealing with my wounds. My neck had knitted back together now that Cooper's healing power seemed to be at full force, and miraculously had not left a scar. Everything else was about ninety per cent healed.

Once I could drive without pain, I moved back home with my gnomes. With Drew back to England, I didn't feel right staying in the house alone until much better healed. Cooper gave me a healing hug when I arrived at the bookstore every morning, and another at the end of the day. I missed being waited on and having my own personal chef, but by spring that would change. Once Drew was married and the rest of the witches finally dealt with Lorcan, my wedding plans would begin.

I held my hand up to the afternoon light shining through the display window at Antique Books, smiling. Mrs. Marcy Barker-Adhamah. Or would that be Adhamah-Barker? The thought of being married no longer scared me. No more running from things. No more throwing up my wall every morning to block out all the thoughts of people around me. At least not the full wall. Leaving it down completely still overwhelmed me.

The time to fly to England had arrived. Eight days until Yule and Drew and Randy tied the knot. Cooper and I boarded our flight to London. I told Auntie not to pick us up. They still had much more to do. Naturally, when we landed, Priscilla stood right at the exit so we wouldn't miss her.

"Auntie, I told you we'd get a cab."

"Nonsense. Most things are in place. Susan is making last-minute calls to confirm the flowers and cake will be ready. Now hurry along."

As we followed her to the car, I whispered to Cooper. "Make sure you fasten your seat belt tight."

"I heard that." She didn't even bother to turn around and glare.

"Hey, you got a new car."

Auntie P. had stopped beside a brand new SUV. No more trying to avoid that loose spring in the front passenger seat.

"I'll be expecting Drew to provide a great granddaughter soon, and will need a safe vehicle." She looked from Cooper to me. "Maybe even a great grandniece." Her eyes twinkled.

I glanced at Cooper and rolled my eyes. "Someday, Auntie. Don't rush it."

Cooper grinned, keeping any comments to himself. "Thanks for the lift, Mrs. Adhamh."

"None of the Mrs. stuff. Call me Auntie. You'll be family soon enough. Now, get in. You've got a dress fitting this afternoon, Marcy. Susan will pick you up."

Drew had kept me up to date on the progress of my dress, and even sent a picture of it on a dress dummy. It looked gorgeous. Hopefully, it didn't need much alteration. As I healed, my appetite came back. Fingers crossed, I hadn't put on too much weight.

The drive to Auntie's house on Myrtle Road was as frightening as before. Auntie P. drove like a demon, but we arrived in one piece. While Cooper and I settled into our rooms, she made several phone calls. Couldn't make out what she said, but I heard my name a few times. *She doesn't sound agitated, so I guess I shouldn't worry.* I joined her in the living room after my fitting, hoping to find out what the earlier phone calls were about.

"You're probably tired after your flight, but I've asked the ladies to come over. We need to begin planning." Auntie arranged chairs around the dining room table.

I wanted to put my feet up and do nothing, but Priscilla was right. The grimoire and the ring had to be put somewhere permanently. Then, the riddle about the curse needed deciphering.

Auntie had Lorcan safely stashed, but none of us had figured out where we needed to take him to break the curse. If not in this world or the other, what was left?

Auntie'd been to the old cave system several times with the local witches, but all they'd determined was the grimoire should be left hidden in the alcove I'd found last summer. Only Auntie's witchy friends knew about it, and no one not related to the coven descendants could enter it.

The ladies arrived shortly after Drew and Susan, some in pairs. Twenty minutes later, we were all seated at the table. Instead of hanging around, bored, Cooper decided to explore Dorking, leaving as the last witch arrived. He winked at me and closed the door.

Priscilla began with an announcement. A surprise, but something I'd hope for. "We've officially re-established the old coven." She chuckled. "No original members, obviously. We haven't chosen a high priestess yet."

Something was brewing, and it wasn't in a cauldron. Everyone, including my family, wore a suspicious-looking grin. Almost everyone. One or two of the witches didn't seem particularly thrilled about whatever wasn't being said. I'd grill Drew later.

"So, how do you choose her? The oldest? The most powerful? A combo of the two?"

Auntie shrugged. "Depends. Frequently, it's someone who's studied the craft for many years, then is initiated. In some covens, it may be familial, like the royals. Princes and princesses take the crown when the king or queen passes or steps down. Since we're starting from scratch, more or less, we haven't come to a decision. Everyone here is a descendant of the old coven, and our family descends from the last high priestess."

"OK, sounds reasonable. So, either you, Susan, or Drew could claim the title?"

Auntie nodded. "If we decide to go that way. I've already taken myself out of the equation. Don't want the sudden responsibility at my age. Everyone here is more than qualified. We agreed not to decide until we've taken care of the task at hand. Now, about that." She gestured across the table. "Viktoria, you have the floor."

Viktoria looked to be about Susan's age. Maybe late forties, early fifties, with a gorgeous mane of strawberry-blond curls resting gently on her shoulders.

"It's nice to finally meet you, Marcy. We're all so grateful you stumbled across the hidden entrance to the caves."

I grinned. "Stumbled is correct. Did they tell you I leaned on what I thought was a mound and fell through the opening?"

"No, they skipped that part. I look forward to hearing all about it. Anyway, we've all been back to the caves many times and have mapped out most of it. When Priscilla explained about the curse and the old spell book, we tried communicating with the sprits of the elders. We've had some success, but they seem to be awaiting your arrival before revealing all."

Great. "Why can't they just tell you? They're your ancestors too." I looked at the ladies sitting around the table. No one volunteered anything. Not even my family. *What am I missing?* I turned my attention back to Viktoria.

"The spirits have told us we should seal the grimoire in the alcove, but haven't given us any details." She hesitated. "We're aware of what Elspeth saw in your palm. That you will be the one to restore your family's power. How to deal with Lorcan will be revealed only once you come to the cave."

Oh joy. "Why does that not surprise me? How about I go out tomorrow with whoever wants to join me? If we can come up with a plan before Drew's wedding, we can get started after Drew and Randy leave for their honeymoon."

Drew half-pouted. "I really wish I could help, but I think I'll enjoy my time with Randy more." She waggled her eyebrows.

"We can video the ritual." One of the twins. Stella? Sheila? Still don't know how to tell them apart.

"Really, Stella. Video indeed." Priscila wasn't much into tech.

"You know, that might not be a bad idea." Auntie glared at me. "In the event he escapes again. Something could get missed when writing it down. A video would capture everything."

Priscilla huffed. "By the time he gets out, if ever, the technology will likely have changed drastically." She thought for a moment, then partially conceded. "We'll see."

Four of the ladies volunteered to go to the cave with me. The rest had to work, including Drew. With nothing more to discuss, the house emptied. Cooper didn't return until well after the witches had gone home, so we filled him in.

Susan poured him a glass of wine and he joined us in front of the fireplace. Before he had a chance to sit, she inquired about his walk. "So, what do you think of our little town?"

Cooper thought for a moment, then sat and sipped his wine. "Quaint, charming, friendly, and quiet. Gramps would love it here. Those twins that giggled when I met them, they're the ones who helped find the ring?"

"Yes. Maybe your grandfather can visit some time." Susan winked at me. "The twins would love to meet him."

"They'd like to do more than meet him."

Cooper choked on a mouthful of wine.

"Drew!" Her mother pretended to be shocked, then smiled. "You're not wrong."

I nudged Cooper. "Think he can handle them?"

"Probably give him another heart attack. He was quite taken with them, though."

We finished our wine, then I headed for bed, leaving Cooper to my relatives. No doubt he'd be grilled. With his help, my wounds had pretty much healed. The stitches and staples had long since been removed, but the gashes were deep and, even though now closed, were still a little red. The worst of the wounds left slight scars, mostly on my back, out of sight. Cooper continued with the healing hugs, not necessarily only to help my wounds.

Susan joined us for breakfast, since she would be coming to the caves with us. We sat at the table while Cooper prepared our meal. *Nice to know I'll be well fed after we marry.*

He doled out portions of eggs benedict and sat beside me. "Do you really think I'd be able to come, too? I've heard so much about this cave system, I'm anxious to see it. Or is it witches only?"

"He's a helper, Auntie. It's not like he doesn't know about us."

"I don't mind. I'll make some calls after we eat." She took a bite. "Delicious."

Cooper's cooking was so scrumptious, none of us spoke much until we'd cleaned our plates. They barely needed washing. I helped with the dishes while Auntie made her calls. From the sound of a few of the conversations, she had to do a bit of persuading, but at the mention of Cooper's helper status, they seemed to change their minds.

At 10:30 a.m. Susan, Cooper, and I piled into Priscilla's new SUV and drove to the forest, parking along the shoulder of the A25. We followed a slightly beaten path directly to the cave. It still looked like a vine-covered mound, the entrance not noticeable. We arrived a half hour before the others were due.

Cooper looked around when we stopped walking. "Nice pile of dirt. Where's the cave?"

I pointed at the eight-foot-high mound. "In there. Go ahead. Reach out and feel the side."

"Seriously?"

We all nodded.

He walked to where I pointed and reached out. He patted to the right, then the left. "This is a joke, right?"

I shook my head. "Nope. Concentrate. Reach out with your mind."

The opening wouldn't appear for him.

"Let me." I walked over and stepped through. Cooper's gasp reached me through the earthen walls. Placing one hand on the wall, I addressed the spirits. "Ancestors, it's Marcy. Will you allow my fiancé through? He's not a witch, but he *is* a helper."

My hand began to tingle. A warmth crept up my arm. I felt them probe my mind.

He is welcome.

"Thank you." I stepped halfway out and reached for Cooper. "It's okay. You can enter now."

He took my hand, but hesitated. "Are you certain I can walk through?"

"The ancestors said you're welcome. Come on."

Priscilla stepped up and gave him a shove, then she and Susan stepped in, colliding with Cooper. He'd stopped the moment he entered, standing open-mouthed, staring at the walls. "Amazing."

I shone my flashlight ahead. "Hey, I had to crawl through this section."

"We've been busy. Most of us are a little old to be crawling, so we had it excavated. The workers won't remember, the same as when Francine had her workroom built." Priscilla looked pleased with their work.

"I wasn't looking forward to crawling, anyway. You've added wall torches, too." They were wrought iron and made to match the original ones farther inside the caves. Whoever made them did a fabulous job.

Susan and Priscilla lit them and we made our way to the alcove. It looked the same as when I found it, right down to the melted wax on the altar. Someone had placed fresh candles around the room.

Susan unfurled a map, using the altar for a table. "This is what we've explored so far. We each have a copy."

"Holy heliodor. It's ginormous. And you still have more to survey?" I traced the lines with my finger. The longest line went south-west and had a tiny drawing of Stonehenge near the end, exiting at the image of a castle tower. Each line ended with a drawing or open end, except one.

"Is this one you still need to explore?" I pointed to the one that seemed to dead-end. It wasn't far from the door we'd found during the first exploration, before I went back home last summer.

"No. Unfortunately, someone already sealed it. Too much work to reopen it. According to the GPS reading we took, it would join up to the caves in town that are open to the public. We have no intention of reopening it. Viktoria spelled it so no one can access it."

We all turned when a voice echoed down the tunnel. "Hello?"

"The ladies are arriving." Priscilla went out to greet them. The twins and two others joined us in the alcove. *Must learn all their names.*

The twins were happy to see Cooper. The other two, not so much. Easy to tell which one's Auntie had to convince.

One of them nodded at Cooper, lip twisted in a sneer. "I see they allowed you entrance."

I'd have to have a chat with Auntie later. If they were part of the coven, they'd have to accept Cooper's presence. He wouldn't be a coven member, but he wouldn't be kept shut away like an embarrassment. *Did they treat Randy the same way?*

"Yes, the ancestors allowed entrance. *They* aren't prejudiced against non-witches." I glared at her. The twins snickered. I could feel Auntie's eyes boring a hole in the back of my head. Too bad. I wasn't ever going to apologize for sticking up for Cooper.

Susan broke the tension. "So, this is where the ancestors said we could hide the grimoire. We don't know where or how. None of us has been able to find a cubby hole or anything."

All will be revealed.

Cooper looked around. "Who said that?"

The witches gasped, including me. "You heard that?"

He looked puzzled. "Hard not to. It was loud enough."

"That was one of the ancestors. When I was here before, we needed to be in contact with the walls to talk to them." I looked at Auntie P.

"Now that the caves are being used again, they've grown stronger." She bit her bottom lip.

"And?" I was really getting fed up with not being told stuff.

"Tell her." Susan placed a hand on her mother's arm.

"Your mother's sprit has joined them. Eventually, your grandmother will, too." Priscilla smiled. "It will be nice to speak with my sister again."

"Mother is here? How? Why didn't she speak to me?" My stomach flipped. We hadn't been on the greatest of terms after I turned my back on my skill, and there hadn't been enough time to resolve things before she died.

"It's an ancestral thing." Susan put her arm around my shoulders. "Regardless where we move to or where our body is buried, eventually the spirit returns to the homeland, only leaving under special circumstances, like helping with Montgomery and Lorcan. Your grandmother hasn't been gone long enough, but since she was born here, she may return sooner than expected."

"Seriously? So, my spirit will come here, too?"

"Yes."

"But…" My heart felt heavy. I'd hoped to be with Cooper forever, both in life and after.

Susan noticed me fiddling with my engagement ring. "You're thinking you want to share the afterlife with Cooper, aren't you?"

I linked arms with him and nodded, spotting the look she exchanged with Auntie. "What?"

"It may be different with you and Cooper. We don't know yet. Possibly with Drew and Randy, too. But that's far in the future." Priscilla gestured for the ladies to come closer. "We need to find out the solution to our current problem. Now that you're here, the ancestors should tell us where to send Lorcan."

THIRTY-TWO

The partial coven formed a circle around the altar. Priscilla lit all the candles and began. "Ancestors, we seek your advice and wisdom. Marcy has joined us. She's the one you call *the special one.*

I cringed at *special.*

The candle flames flickered, like they did when I performed a séance. A mist formed in the centre of the altar, about two feet tall. The ladies let out a very audible gasp.

"I'm guessing that's new?" I looked around. All eyes were on the mist.

"We normally only hear them." Susan leaned closer and lowered her voice. "Fiona is the first to materialize in here."

More gasps from the peanut gallery.

"It can't be."

"The ancient one?"

"I think I'm…"

"Going to faint."

I snickered at how the twins finished each other's sentences.

"She needs energy. Will you all allow her to take what she needs?" I knew they would.

A mixture of yeses and head nods answered. The mist stayed about the same height, but began to take shape. A mini-version of the apparition I'd seen before, white hair flowing on a breeze we couldn't feel.

Fiona turned to acknowledge each witch. "I have waited a long time to see my coven again, but was not expecting to have to recapture my son."

As before, at the mention of her wayward child, her image turned blue briefly. With a candle, a blue flame simply meant an entity was near, but I felt her sorrow. A blue spirt must indicate sadness.

"I am ashamed at what he has done to my family." She changed to pink, then red. "I am also angry that my coven was careless enough to allow him to escape. It must never happen again."

No one spoke. Gradually, Fiona returned to her original white form. Only then did Priscilla speak.

"We're sorry, Fiona. I'm glad you know that we've reconvened. We tracked down quite a few descendants, but many have moved away."

"Yes, I am aware, and pleased."

I took over. "Fiona, you confirmed that Sorcha correctly translated the Gaelic curse. Can you now explain it? Where exactly is *not on this plane or the other?* I now understand that our world is made up of other planes, but I didn't think we could access them. Do we need to locate a portal?"

"No. A portal only leads to the underworld. The other. You need to send him to… how would you describe it? Another dimension or realm."

"Oh, great. We're going into *The Twilight Zone.* Maybe Rod Serling will pop in and say hello." I mumbled louder than expected, and Fiona heard.

She cocked her head. "I do not understand."

"Not important. How do we find these other realms?"

"It is dangerous, and you will need the entire coven." She gestured to the witches. "Is this all you could gather?"

"No." Priscilla frowned. "The others couldn't come today. Right now, we simply need to know what to do. We won't be attempting anything until after my granddaughter's wedding, just in case we muck it up."

"I understand." She looked at Cooper and smiled. "I am pleased with both betrothals." She turned back to Auntie. "Where are the ring and grimoire?"

"The ring is hidden. Only I know where. The book is in my bag."

"If you wish, we can deal with that now. It will only take a few minutes, but I shall require more of your energy."

Priscilla picked up the tote and removed the box containing the spell book. Bits of crushed brimstone fell to the dirt floor when she lifted it out. The parts of the handprint where the brimstone fell from glowed in the candlelight.

"You have protected it well." Fiona nodded her approval. "Place it on the altar in front of me. Everyone step back, but remain in a circle."

Cooper hesitated, uncertain if he would be included.

Fiona answered the unasked question. "He may join you."

Satisfied we were where she wanted us, she began. Arms raised over her head, she spoke in what I assumed was Gaelic. A strong breeze circled the room, extinguishing the wall torches, but not the candles. They didn't even flicker.

The twins stared, wide-eyed, mouths open. The one who'd commented about Cooper had an odd look on her face. *Jealousy? Maybe. Could she be put out that I had been chosen? Does she not want my family to have their dwindling power restored?*

Anger bubbled inside me. That woman was turning into someone Auntie couldn't allow in the coven. *She's a Grade A witch, with a capital B!*

I refocused on Fiona. She gave me a look that could've turned me to stone. I nodded and cleared my mind.

A low rumble came from nowhere, but sounded everywhere. Under my feet, movement. Barely noticeable at first. The whispers from the witches told me everyone felt it. It grew stronger. Almost simultaneously, we reached out to grab the person beside us. Twin number two fell to her knees.

Fiona didn't stop.

Something moved behind me. We all looked.

"Place the book there." She pointed at the wall.

Before approaching the wall of the alcove, I picked up the grimoire and one of the candles.

Holding up the candle up, I illuminated a small rectangular opening, the right size for the book. Moving the candle around, I searched for a pile of dirt on the floor below.

"How?" Despite no dirt being displaced, a brand new cubby hole had appeared.

"Slide the book in. Hurry! I can't hold it much longer." Fiona's voice wavered.

I slid the grimoire in. When I turned back, Fiona's appearance surprised me. She'd faded almost transparent.

"Take more energy from me." I hurried back to the altar.

"No. It is done. Return after the wedding. I will contact you soon with the information you require to banish my son." The wall rumbled. Fiona vanished.

Priscilla and Susan each took a candle and relit the torches. No sign of any disturbance in the wall remained.

I was puzzled. "How is putting the book in a hole keeping it safe?"

The twins giggled. "Try to dig it out."

A few bits of brimstone had fallen off when I took the book to the wall, so it was easy to find the spot. Reaching out, I scratched the wall. Nothing. Not a single speck of dirt moved. I dug harder. All that accomplished was a broken nail. *Manicure before the wedding.*

Priscilla joined me, carrying the box. She poured some of the brimstone into her hand and rubbed it on the wall. I watched the wall absorb it, completely mesmerized at the magick. *Could I learn how to do that?*

"OK. I guess the book is safe. We still don't know where to send the ring and Lorcan with it."

"She said she'll contact you with the information you need. That should guide you to an entrance to one of the other realms." Susan smiled, but she looked a little worried.

"What are these other dimensions like, and how many are there?" Not certain I really wanted to know.

"No one knows how many there are. Tales say some are wonderful places, whereas others are horrific. As children, we're warned about faerie rings. Both wiccan children and non are told the stories."

I shook my head. "Don't know any of those stories."

Susan explained. "If a ring of mushrooms appeared overnight, it was a sign of otherworldly visitors. If you dared step inside the ring, you will become invisible to the mortal world, unable to escape the ring. Some say you will be transported to a faerie land. The legend varies from country to country. It could be pleasant, or you could become a slave."

"Interesting. I don't want to inflict Lorcan on a bunch of innocent faeries, even if he would be enslaved."

"Enough chatter. Time to head home." Priscilla ushered us to the door of the alcove. "We can do some research while waiting for Fiona to contact you. It will keep Cooper occupied with something other than wedding plans."

Cooper smiled. "More than happy to research for you."

The witch who commented on Cooper being in the cave sneered at me. She didn't look much older than me, but had a similar appearance to Helena. Jet black hair, dark make-up and clothes. *Please don't be like Helena and have turned to dark magick.* "Yes. Wait for Fiona to contact the *special* child."

Cooper took my hand. "Yes, she is special. Let's go."

We exited and piled into Auntie's SUV. The rest stayed behind to explore a bit more.

"What is it with that woman?"

"Kris?" Susan turned to look at me. "She hates not being the centre of attention. Ignore her."

"She's jealous she doesn't have a hot fiancé like you do." Cooper winked at me.

"Naturally, but I don't trust her." Something about her made my spidey-senses tingle.

Auntie P. pulled into a seemingly small gap in traffic, ignoring the blast of a horn. *She must have angels riding shotgun on the hood.*

With Drew's wedding approaching, everyone rushed around, ensuring all details were in place. The night before the big day, Fiona came to me in my dreams. I woke immediately and wrote down everything I remembered, keeping the information to myself. No one needed or wanted the distraction before the wedding.

✳✳✳

I must have fallen back asleep. Auntie pounded on my bedroom door, hollering between raps.

"Marcy! Get up. There's so much to do. Cooper's already making breakfast."

"Coming." *My wedding won't be this complicated.*

Most of the morning we were at the reception venue. Randy's family insisted it be held at De Vere Horsley Estate. Since the wedding today would be mostly non-wiccan, Drew gave her in-laws whatever they wanted. I had to admit, the castle-like building beside the water was gorgeous. It even had a chapel, but they opted for the church the Biddleman family had attended for generations.

After a quick lunch, we assembled at Susan's to change before heading to the church. They'd opted for a mostly traditional wedding for Randy's side of the family, but would have another, but private, wiccan ceremony later.

I changed into the forest green gown Drew commissioned. It fit my body perfectly. The long, pointed sleeve opening made me feel like a wizard. When I came downstairs, Cooper wolf-whistled. My face grew so hot I thought my makeup would melt.

I circled around him. "You don't look too bad yourself." The change from jeans and tee was astounding. He looked like a cover model for a gentleman's magazine. I wolf-whistled right back.

Susan started down the steps. "Are you ready for the bride?" She turned and held out her hand. "I present the future Mrs. Biddleman-Adhamh."

We all gasped when Drew appeared. She stood at the top of the stairs wearing a silk wedding gown, transformed from antique to modern.

Priscilla sniffled. "My mother's gown. It's perfect for Drew. Much nicer than anything we could find new."

Instead of white, the silk and lace were ivory, and had a cowl. A little wiccan touch to the traditional wedding. With Susan holding her hand, she slowly descended the stairs, holding the hem up to avoid tripping. When she stopped at the bottom and let go of the fabric, it nestled around her feet like a cloud. Her sleeves were like mine, only longer, almost touching the floor. She turned, revealing ribbon lacing down the back. The dress fit like it was made for her. Susan's friend must have made many alterations to the original gown. The cowl hood replaced the need for a veil.

"You look absolutely heavenly." I hugged Drew, careful not to rumple her. "The dress is magickal."

Since Drew wanted to keep things simple, instead of arriving in a stretch limo or carriage, she went to the church in Auntie's new SUV. Susan let Cooper and me use her smaller car. Not wanting to risk driving on the wrong side, I tossed the keys to Coop.

The wedding would take place at the church Randy's parents attended, St. Martin's, and would mix traditional with a touch of wiccan. The spire of the church was easily noticeable, although I hadn't paid much attention to it before. Auntie P. mentioned it was one of the tallest in England.

The day before, after rehearsal, Auntie and Randy's mother had given me a quick tour. The Gothic arches in the nave were beautiful, and no church would be complete without stained glass windows. All in all, nice place to be wed, but not for me.

Drew walked in circles inside the room designated for the bride, waiting for her cue to enter and start her walk down the aisle.

"Don't tell me you're nervous?" Drew had always given the appearance of a woman full of confidence. Today, she was a bundle of nerves.

She stopped circling. "What? No, I'm not nervous, exactly. Well, maybe a little. I've lived on my own for several years. Having a roommate will take a bit of adjusting."

"Roommate? I hope Randy will be more than that." I gave her what I hoped was a sly, suggestive look.

She had the good grace to blush. "That's not what I meant. Can you peek and see if they're almost ready to start?"

"Sure." I looked at Susan and Auntie P. "Why aren't either of you reassuring her?"

Susan shrugged.

"Impossible to calm a nervous bride. Besides, it's part of the day. To be expected." Auntie shoulder-bumped her daughter. "Should have seen Susan. Total wreck, of course she was only twenty."

I nodded. "Of course. And Drew is practically an old hag." I ducked out the door before Drew found something to throw at me.

The minister spotted me looking around the doorway and nodded, raising one finger. I nodded back, guessing that meant one minute.

I went back to report. "It's time." I'd left the door open so we could hear when the music began. "Randy seems quite calm. Or maybe he's frozen in fear."

The music started. Mendelssohn's *The Wedding March* echoed through the church.

Randy's father knocked on the open door. "Ready?"

With Drew's father long since out of the picture, she'd asked her future father-in-law to walk her down the aisle.

Susan and Auntie P. led the way, with me following behind. Once we were in place, Drew entered. I watched the guests' reaction to her non-traditional dress. Our side smiled and nodded. Randy's side smiled that polite fake smile. Several whispered to one another. Regardless of what anyone thought of the dress, no one could ever deny she wasn't stunning.

After reading their own vows, Drew's being wiccan, almost spell-like, the reverend read the traditional ones, not minding the mixed ceremony at all. Definitely more open-minded than Randy's family. At least they accepted Drew for who she was, one hundred percent, despite the hyphenated name in what they considered the wrong order.

During the reception dinner, the two families didn't mix much, except for some of the children and teens. Drew and Randy ducked out shortly after dinner. Their flight to New Zealand was early the next morning, and they wouldn't return until after New Year's. Two weeks in the sun, then back to reality and the much smaller witches-only wedding ceremony.

"Best wishes, Drew. You and Randy will be happy together. I can feel it." Hugging her tight, I whispered in her ear. "I'll be back home by the time you return. Wish I could stay for your wiccan wedding." Looking at Randy, I waggled my finger in front of his face. "Treat her right, or I'll be back to send you someplace you'll never return from."

"Not a problem. I know what you're capable of, and I'd never do anything to hurt Drew."

"Good luck with Lorcan." One last hug from Drew and they were off.

Late the next day, the newly formed coven gathered at Auntie's. Time to let them know what needs to be done to banish Lorcan. Fingers crossed, it would be the last time.

Auntie P. did a quick head count. "Everyone's here. No time for chit-chat. We need to locate an opening to another realm or dimension. Marcy received a hint about the location in a dream. We need to figure out the riddle. Marcy, the floor is yours."

"Thanks, Auntie. Those of you who came to the caves with us will remember Fiona said she would let me know how to find the spot. She came to me in a dream last night, like Auntie said, but I didn't want to say anything until after Drew's wedding. This is what she told me." I pulled a piece of paper from my pocket. "Unfortunately, it's another riddle."

My hand shook at the realization of what we were about to do. Looking around at the full coven, any confidence I had flew out the window. *Can I do this? Still a newbie, but it has to be done.*

I took a deep breath, smoothed the page, and began. "Find the land covered in green, the place where coins abound. If you look for the in-between, what you seek will be found."

"Green? Coins? Are we looking for leprechauns?" One of the witches chuckled.

"Ha. That was my first thought, too." I looked at Priscilla. "What do you think, Auntie?"

"Well, the land covered in green could be anything."

I nodded. "Hang on, there's another verse." I started to read the rest. "Tiny creatures…" I blinked several times. "Caves that scowl…"

I stopped. "What the heck?"

The verse faded away, bit by bit.

"Auntie, it's gone."

She reached for my paper. "It has the feel of darkness. Someone spelled it so you can't continue. Whoever did this doesn't want us to send the ring away. They must be nearby in order to cast that type of spell."

We all hurried outside to try to capture the person responsible, but no one lurked about. The streets were quiet. Once off Auntie's property, a spell hit me hard. Not dark magick, exactly. More mischievous. Whoever did this didn't want to cause harm. *Did they not realize by not banishing Lorcan again, it would cause unimaginable harm?*

"I see someone by the water." One of the twins pointed towards the end of Myrtle Road. We all rushed to the bottom of the street.

"Where could they have gone?" I put one foot on the bottom rung of the metal barricade between the road and Pipp Brook and leaned over. "There's no place to run."

"Maybe they went into one of the garages?" The other twin walked down the dirt lane.

"It's too dark to see." Auntie stood with her hands on her hips, looking around. We'll never find the culprit.

I felt another swirl of mischief. The witch casting the spell was near. *Is it one of our own?*

"We need the rest of the verse to figure out the puzzle." My heart raced. "I'll have to try to contact Fiona again. Why didn't I memorize it?" I dropped to my knees. "If I don't get the verse back, we'll lose our powers. Lorcan may find a way to free himself and cause who knows what damage. It's all my fault." I covered my face with my hands and sobbed.

Susan tried to console me, but I shook her off. I got up and raced down the street away from everyone, no destination in mind.

Will this nightmare ever end?

UPCOMING

Thank you for reading Generation Witch: Awakening. Stay tuned for book 3 of the Generation Witch trilogy. If you wish to hear about the progress of this or any of my books, please join my newsletter at:

https://landing.mailerlite.com/webforms/landing/u0q5f2.

Purrfect Press

Reviews are Golden

I would love to hear from you! Please consider leaving a review on your favourite social media platform, Amazon, or Goodreads.

Reviews mean the world to authors. Not only do we enjoy reading how you felt about the book, but they help other readers get a feel for a book in advance, and aid authors in marketing.

Thank you for coming on this adventure with me.

ABOUT THE AUTHOR

Nanci M. Pattenden is a genealogist and a fiction writer, currently working on a collection of detective stories set in Victorian Toronto and an Urban Fantasy trilogy. She also co-authors a funny paranormal series, D.E.M.ON. Tales, with author M.J. Moores.

Nanci has completed the Creative Writing program at both the University of Calgary and the University of Toronto.

She currently resides in Newmarket with her adorable cat Freya.

nanci@nancipattenden.com
www.purrfectpress.com
www.nancipattenden.com
@npattenden

www.ingramcontent.com/pod-product-compliance
Lightning Source LLC
Chambersburg PA
CBHW060429310726
48977CB00001B/107